VĪRION

JAMES R. TEMPLER

Butch + Amie — Thanks for all your support — Hope you enjoy the book.

Black Rose Writing

www.blackrosewriting.com

JR Templer

ISBN: 978-1-61296-020-3

PUBLISHED BY BLACK ROSE WRITING

www.blackrosewriting.com

Printed in the United States of America

Virion is printed in Book Antiqua

Dedicated to the memory of Mom and Dad.

Like people, viruses come in many sizes and shapes. Like people, some viruses are harmless; some are menaces; some are deadly. The root of the word virus means toxin or poison. There are those among us who are pure poison—whose thoughts are as toxic as cyanide. And toxic thoughts at some point poison the soul until it is dead and dried up like the shed skin of a snake. That's when toxic thoughts turn to poisonous acts; that's when the thinkers become destroyers—disciples of Satan some might say. They may be right—after all, a virion is but a disciple of the virus.

1

The white Ford van was parked in the Wal-Mart parking lot in La Marque, Texas, just off of I-45, about fifteen miles southeast of the Houston city limits — or more precisely, Clear Lake City, the home of the NASA's Johnson Space Center. It was late Thursday afternoon, September 14th, and as was the norm for the Texas Gulf coast in September, the temperature was a muggy eighty nine degrees. The dark, tinted windows of the van were up, the engine and air conditioner running. The lone occupant wore a blue jump suit, the kind worn by many of the employees working in one of the petrochemical plants in Texas City, which abuts La Marque to the north and east. The jumpsuit, along with a cap from a local refinery pulled low against the sunshades, would make the driver of the van — should he be seen — indistinguishable from dozens of other locals coming and going from their vehicles in the parking lot. Despite the air conditioner blasting away, rivulets of sweat rolled down the driver's face.

A King James Bible with dog-eared pages and holes worn in the black faux-leather cover lay in his lap. Using the inlaid ribbon bookmark, he flipped the Bible open to the book of Isaiah, verse 45:6-7, which he had highlighted with a yellow marker. He read out loud — but softly — with the cadence of familiarity that comes from memorization: *I am the LORD, and there is none else. I form the light, and create darkness: I make peace, and create evil: I the LORD do all these things.* Closing the Bible, he smiled as if once again reassured...the type of reassurance that breeds a deranged certitude. Looking up with reassured eyes he spots the plump, purple-haired teenage girl — *dressed that way*—unlocking the doors to her Ford Ranger pickup.

"I wonder if her donkey will see the Angel of the Lord," he muttered to his image in the rearview mirror as he pulled in behind the fire-engine red Ranger.

2

As he was standing in the Galveston County morgue looking at the body of the brutally murdered young woman, Richard Alexander was recalling how he first discovered that he possessed an amazing psychic power—by accidently touching the arm of a murder victim on that same table. That's when his hell had begun.

A friend once described Alexander as Harrison Ford wearing a Richard Gere hairpiece. His full head of silver-grey hair was swept back, wavy, and unruly (intellectual dishevelment, a colleague once jokingly labeled it). Standing a little over six feet tall, he had Ford's boyish good looks, even though his fifty-nine years and the Texas Gulf Coast sun added character to his face with a few wrinkles, and a farmer's tan.

Alexander was raised in Southwest Texas in the San Antonio area. He was an exceptionally bright young man and a precocious artist. Just before his seventeenth birthday, he entered the University of Texas in Austin where he earned a Bachelor of Fine Arts degree in drawing and painting, magna cum laude.

Then at the age of twenty one, his parents and friends thought he had completely lost his mind when he joined the army and went to Viet Nam. Two years and a Purple Heart later, he went to work in an uncle's printing shop just outside of Chicago so that he could afford to continue his education. There he earned a Master of Fine Arts degree in drawing and painting from the Chicago School of Art. That would have been enough for Alexander, but at the urging of his uncle who was impressed with his nephew's intellect, he continued on to earn a Ph.D. in the philosophy of visual studies from the University of Illinois in Chicago.

Alexander was a full professor in the fine arts and philosophy departments at the University of Houston at Clear Lake. But because he only taught from September to the middle of May, the summer was his own time to paint and write and pursue other interests.

Dr. Richard Alexander was not a man who was easily confused by what he saw. But that early Sunday afternoon of August 17th as he stood beside the stainless steel autopsy table in the Galveston County morgue, staring down at the mutilated body of a plump, teenage girl with purplish highlights in her blood-clotted hair, his mind refused to make sense of the visual horror. He reached out to touch the girl's arm, just to get a vision of who did this to her, to help bring the bastard to justice…but again he resisted, thinking of the price he might have to pay. Then the door swung open.

"A class of marine biology students from A&M Galveston discovered her body rolled up in a tarp on Snake Island, between Tiki Island and Galveston early this morning," offered Dr. Zeke Zapata, walking into the lab with a slight limp.

Zapata was the Galveston County medical examiner. He spoke with only a hint of a Mexican accent, unlike his parents who were second generation Mexican Americans. Like his father, Zapata was a relatively short man, about five feet, six inches tall, with a stocky build and a head full of curly, salt and pepper hair.

"I say a tarp," Zapata continued, "but it was more like some kind of art work with colored, cloth knots sewn all over it. Very unusual…especially to wrap a body in. I mean, I've seen them in plastic tarps, refrigerator boxes, shower curtains, and even large ice chests, but this is most unusual. Maybe it was the girl's...a craft project or something."

"Possibly," answered Alexander with a wave of familiarity washing over his memory as he mindlessly massaged the scar two inches above his right eyebrow. "I'd love to help you, E.Z., but you know what I've been going through. I've got a lot to lose here."

His friends called him E.Z. (for Ezekiel Zapata), pronounced like "Easy." The nickname aptly described his usually laid-back, easy going personality. Born and raised in Galveston, Zapata was a graduate from the University of Houston and the University of Texas Medical Branch in Galveston, better known as UTMB. His wife, Sandy, also born and raised in Galveston, was an attorney with a small, local firm. Zapata and Alexander were good friends and played in a rhythm and blues band together as a hobby (Zapata played the sax, Alexander the guitar).

Zapata looked up at the ceiling. They had had this conversation before. "I know that, buddy...but not as much as this kid had to lose, goddammit. This is the second female victim to come in here killed in this manner...only this one was wrapped up like a burrito in a very unusual tortilla...and you have the ability to catch this sick bastard. I know what you and Maggie are going through, bro, but I'm sorry, man...God gave you this gift and you have a responsibility to use it."

"It's not a gift, man...it's a goddamned curse!" Alexander shouted back defensively, then immediately felt like an asshole.

Zapata was right. He knew that in the end, using his abilities to serve justice was larger than his own problems...yet, he didn't want to lose Maggie.

"Just throw me a bone here, man...you're an artist...just take a look at the canvas she was wrapped up in. That's all I'm asking."

Alexander stared at his longtime friend for a minute and

then quietly said, "Alright, E.Z., you're right. I need to help. But I don't want to touch the body with my bare hands right now, agreed?"

"Fair enough…the canvas is in my office. The cops want it back, so I had to convince them that I needed more time to analyze the blood stains and whatever the hell else might be on it. We only have it for a few hours. I've actually finished my forensic examination of it…got samples of blood, hair and what appears to be sweat stains. No finger prints, no semen. Now, let's take a quick look at the body."

In the new, state of the art forensic lab that sat within view of Galveston Bay, where I-45 turned into Broadway on Galveston Island, Alexander and Zapata snapped on rubber examination gloves and proceeded to examine the wounds that had been inflicted upon the eighteen year old female's grossly mutilated body.

"See all of these contusions, cuts, and scrapes on her head, face, arms, back, legs…all over her body?" asked Zapata, pointing with the end of his folded glasses. "First observation would lead one to believe that she's been battered and dragged over a very rough surface…most of the wounds are postmortem and there are traces of salt water in all of them. When we tried to get a blood sample, we couldn't find any… she had bled out completely, like Cynthia Fisher, the first young woman. So we inserted a needle into her liver…it was filled with Ibuprofen and warfarin sodium…like the Fisher woman. That's why they both bled out. But that's not what killed them…they drowned first."

"There appears to be grit or sand in most of the wounds," Alexander observed. "Here, above her left eye…there's a fragment in the back of the wound. It looks like…hand me the tweezers."

"No, amigo…I have to do it," said Zapata as he slapped his glasses onto the bridge of his nose, gingerly plucked the object from the gaping wound with a pair of sterilized, stainless steel tweezers, and dropped it with clink into a stainless steel dish.

Alexander understood. He wasn't there in an official capacity — only as an invited observer. In order for the fragment to be considered evidence, the medical examiner or a law enforcement officer would have to bag it and record it as state's evidence. Alexander's presence at crime scenes and autopsies wasn't unusual anymore but was questioned by many in the law enforcement community who were skeptical of the involvement of non-law enforcement types such as reporters and psychics...especially psychics.

Besides, he already knew what the fragment was. He recognized the color, texture, and the crunchy sound made by the tweezers...it was a piece of oyster shell.

Oyster shells are ubiquitous along the Gulf of Mexico shore line and for miles inland. Galveston Bay is rife with oyster reefs. They're often used to pave roads and parking lots. They're the rocks where very few rocks naturally exist. Although the inside of an oyster shell has a smooth, mother-of-pearl surface, the rather ugly outside is extremely rough and jagged with very sharp edges.

"Did you know that three states name the oyster shell as their state shell: Connecticut, Mississippi, and Virginia?" posed Alexander as Zapata peered at the fragment through an X10, tripod mounted magnifying glass.

"No, I didn't know that, but I'm not surprised that you do and I should have known that you already identified the fragment," laughed Zapata.

"I have to record this finding," he said after switching on the microphone that hung over the body.

He spoke into the mic, describing the piece of shell and where on the body it was found. He was amused at the never ending source of trivia that flowed from his friend, Alexander. Mainly, he was amazed and thoroughly puzzled by his friend's special gift—an extrasensory vision that manifested itself through Alexander's artistic talents; a gift ironically brought on by the trauma of a bullet smashing into his brain.

"Ok, buddy," said Zapata, pushing himself up from the lab table and wincing at the ever-present, forty-year old pain in his right thigh—a gift from a Viet Cong mortar, "we've established that the victim was given huge doses of Ibuprofen and warfarin and subjected to cuts and abrasions involving oyster shells. And like the Fisher woman, she has tape residue across her face and rope burns on her arms and legs. Now, let's take a look at that weirdly decorated tarp."

The two Viet Nam vets and Purple Heart recipients walked to the back of the autopsy lab to Zapata's office to inspect the strange tarp in which the purple-haired teenager's body had been wrapped. They both felt that strange sense of anticipation that they shared on these occasions, never knowing for sure if and how Alexander's gift would surface.

In his office, Zapata, donning a new pair of rubber gloves, carefully spread the unusual canvas tarp over a round conference table then sat on the front edge of his desk to rest his aching leg. He leaned back, grabbed a small digital recorder, turned it on and sat it beside him on the desk. Alexander insisted on the recorder since sometimes when the gift—the Muse, as he referred to it—began to take over, he didn't always remember what he had observed or said.

Also wearing a new pair of rubber gloves, Alexander studied the cloth with the anticipation and intensity of an anthropologist who had just unearthed an ancient scroll. He knew he had to eventually touch it with his bare hands to start the Muse working, if it was going to. A minute or two went by before he spoke.

"This isn't just a weirdly decorated tarp," Alexander announced. "You were right, it's a work of art—a painting of sorts. Notice the eyelets along this side...it's meant to be hung, so this must be the top."

Alexander measured the distance between the eyelets with one of Zapata's tape measures—exactly sixty six inches apart—while instructing Zapata to find a couple of nails, something to hammer them with, and a place they could hang the canvas.

"Man, this place is brand new, R.A. If the chief caught me hammering nails in the walls, she'd probably nail my ass to the wall," Zapata laughed, not really all that concerned.

They located the janitor's tool box in a utility closet and found a hammer. While inside the closet, Zapata took two NASCAR calendars off of the wall that the janitors put up and pulled out the small nails on which they were hung. Back in the lab they found a suitable spot on a wall, drove the nails in the freshly painted sheetrock, and hung the canvass by the eyelets.

"The width is seventy two inches, and the height is close to sixty five inches," Alexander reported to Zapata and the recorder. "This looks to be at least twelve ounce cotton duck canvas...maybe a little lighter. The balls appear to be wadded up canvass sewn onto the surface...no, wait a minute," Alexander said, lifting an edge of canvass with the point of his ballpoint pen, "there's something hard inside...it's a ping pong ball...they're ping pong balls covered with canvas and painted orange...Interesting. The paint looks like acrylic. The only place primed with gesso before being painted is that multicolored strip toward the bottom."

"That section looks like a little Jackson Pollock rip off," Zapata observed. "But they look strangely familiar...they look like...no, never mind. Any ideas yet, R.A.?"

Alexander didn't answer. He backed a few steps away from the canvas, squinting at the multicolored strip of squiggly lines about a foot above the bottom of the canvas. "No, not yet," he finally answered, almost whispering. "But I think there's writing in that strip."

"Writing?" asked Zapata, also squinting. "All I see is a

bunch of squiggles."

In fact, the "squiggles" were all rather uniform in thickness — about an eighth of an inch thick with the two outer edges darker than the center, as if outlined with a soft-leaded pencil. The lines were looping over themselves like strands of spaghetti.

"E.Z., you said the squiggles looked familiar", Alexander asked. "What do they look like to you?"

"Oh, that…never mind…it's just a coincidence. It couldn't have anything to do with this," Zapata answered.

"E.Z., you know the first rule of investigation," Alexander began, closely studying the squiggles, "the answer is always in front of your eyes…it's your mind that needs to see it. It might not be a coinci…wait…now I see a couple of letters for sure," Alexander said, excitedly, pointing to the left side of the rectangular strip of squiggles. "Look…right here…it's *VIR*."

"I see it, yes," shouted Z, now equally excited. "And isn't that an *I* and an *O* right here?"

"Yes it is, my astute friend, and to the right of that I see *N,*" added Alexander. "V-I-R-I-O-N…does that make sense to you?"

The word in the rectangle, hidden in the layers of squiggly lines was *VIRION.* Once seen, they stood out to the two observers as if they were sculpted in neon lights — an effect that Alexander would later explain as visual cognitive recognition. Once your mind clicks to what your eyes have seen all along, you will forever more be cognitive of that image. It's the way that after staring at one of those fascinating prints of multicolored splotches, a three dimensional scene finally pops out to your amazement. It was there all along. Your eyes saw it, but your mind didn't until you quit focusing on the individual splotches.

The letters, not uniform in height and only a little less squiggly than the other marks, were almost as tall as the rectangle and stretched the full length of the area. It reminded them both of the passwords you have to decipher and type in when ordering tickets to a concert on the Internet.

"Too weird," Zapata finally said. "The word *VIRION* and those squiggly lines make perfect sense."

3

Richard Alexander's special gift was indeed a mystery. It was both a blessing and a curse. In short, it was the ability to 'visualize' the faces of people who had committed heinous crimes—such as murder or rape—after Alexander had entered the crime scene and touched the victim or something belonging to the victim that was present when the crime occurred—most often the clothing on the victim or something very special to the victim. Usually it worked like this; Alexander would 'see' the perpetrator's portrait or some other valuable clue appear on a sheet of paper, normally a page in his ever-present sketchbook—like a photograph slowly developing—and he would rapidly sketch over the vision with a pencil before it faded away. It only stayed for a couple of minutes. On other occasions, he might blurt out a name or an address while in a trance. At times, he felt compelled to build a three-dimensional object that replicated some obvious landmark or object—much like Richard Dreyfus's character in *Close Encounters of the Third Kind*. But more often it was a drawing.

On one case involving the fatal mugging of a local minister, Alexander drew a blank and could not contribute anything to the investigation—thus raising the level of his detractors' skepticism. However, three weeks after that, a local drug dealer and his wife and daughter were all shot-gunned to death in their public projects apartment in the "Jungle," an area north of Broadway and south of Port Industrial that was home to many of the Island's low income families.

The denigrating term, "Jungle," was coined years earlier by the local cops who had to fight endless drug-related gang wars in the "Projects" and other violent crimes that usually accompany poverty and oppression. In those aspects, the unfortunate label was well earned.

In this particular case, Zapata had invited Alexander to accompany him to the crime scene and two minutes after touching the dead girl's doll, Alexander sat down at the kitchen table and began furiously drawing in his sketchbook. Five minutes later, he had drawn a definitive portrait of a local thug who sure enough turned out to be the executioner. Under the portrait, Alexander scribbled "red conceals the means." He didn't know why he wrote it or what it meant. Alexander's portrait could never be submitted as evidence and most of the law enforcement officers on the scene were tempted to dismiss it—except for the fact that they knew the creep whose face Alexander had drawn; they knew his police record and worse, his reputation.

In light of this knowledge, one of the deputies from the Galveston County Sheriff's department—Gene Vincent— decided to "act on a hunch," stopped the suspect the following day, and found the sawed-off shotgun in a large, red tool kit in the trunk of his car.

For all gifts there is a price...either the giver pays or the recipient pays. There was a huge price to be paid for Alexander's special gift. It didn't take long before the local media found out about Alexander's abilities. They didn't know what to make of it, so they arrived at the same conclusion that some of the cops did—it was some kind of hoax. Alexander must have had some inside knowledge of the crime, they speculated...or maybe he was involved. Consequently, not only was there always a cloud of suspicion hanging over Alexander, he also became a real threat to every criminal who committed a crime in the area.

Eventually, the pressures — the threatening phone calls and letters, Alexander almost losing his job, their son's car being set on fire while he was in class, and finally, the shots fired through their living room window while they were eating dinner — became too much for his wife, Maggie, and she moved out. There was no divorce...yet...but she made it clear that if Alexander didn't stop endangering his family and himself by using his psychic abilities, she would file.

Their twenty-five year old son, Jeffery, was the peace-keeper in their family, but he tended to agree with his mom, insisting that this so-called gift was also threatening his dad's teaching career, and jeopardizing his mental and physical health. Jeffery, a mechanical engineer, had decided to pursue his doctorate and was living and working part time in a northern suburb of Houston while he attended Texas A&M University in College Station. He spent as much time as he could trying to reunite his mom and dad...a task proven so far to be more frustrating than fruitful.

~

When the truth is too far outside our realm of experiences, when it doesn't show up on the radar screen of our comprehension, then it simply doesn't exist. For many of us, the default shape of our logic is a board full of square holes into which we must fit the square pegs of our logical conclusions. Only when by the use of our imagination and faith we try hard to stretch the walls of our logic into flexible receptacles, will we then be receptive to the organic nature of the more mysterious truths in the universe. Therein must lie one of God's most perplexing frustrations with his most gnostic creation.

~

Even a Ph.D. would have a difficult time explaining Alexander's Muse with an explanation that was supported by evidence. Alexander had quit trying…but nonetheless, he did have his theory. He based it on the fantasy movie, *Phenomenon,* written by Gerald Di Pego, in which the protagonist was transformed from an average auto mechanic into an incredible genius with telekinetic abilities by the growth of a brain tumor—an astrocytoma. The tumor had numerous tentacles that, as they spread through his brain, stimulated brain cells that would have otherwise remained dormant.

The premise is based on the disputed theory that the average human uses only ten percent of his or her brain capacity. Regardless of whether that was true, theorized Alexander, it is possible that an intrusion into the brain and a disruption of the normal functions of certain brain cells—especially the receptors in the cortex—can "reassign" those cells and the synapses between them to process different kinds of information that the brain had been receiving but not recognizing.

To explain what new information his altered brain was now recognizing, Alexander relied on the *Zero Point Field Theory,* a fascinating theory that posited a pulsating field of energy between and connecting all molecules in the universe. In fact, according to the theory, molecules are really just areas of concentrated energy—knots in the Field—meaning that as Einstein suspected, energy and matter were one in the same. In other words, humans, other animals, trees, planets, and stars were all concentrated areas of the energy comprised by the Field. But the Field also supposedly carried all knowledge and consciousness in the form of waves. Our brains, then, are tuned in to certain waves, thus receiving certain information that forms our consciousness.

The *Zero Point Field Theory* could legitimize phenomenon such as remote-seeing, future-seeing, mind reading, and telekinesis. If all thought and actions left a memory imprint in the Field and if Alexander's altered brain could now receive the wave frequencies of certain imprints, especially from the past, that could explain his gift. It could also explain—and was beginning to for Alexander—one of the mysterious ways in which God works.

In fact, he was convinced that all this was possible because it had happened to him—it *was happening* to him. A bullet fragment shattered his skull just above his right eyebrow, entered his brain, and blew apart his life...and he now had psychic abilities that he never had before that. What more proof did anyone need? Some people didn't need a bullet in the head to tap into the mystical powers of the Field...but apparently, Alexander did.

4

It all began early one chilly October morning, two years earlier, when Alexander went out to finish a landscape study on the west end of Galveston Island about a mile northeast of the San Luis Pass bridge—the bridge that connects Galveston Island with the mainland just fifteen miles or so east of Freeport, Texas. He had pulled his twenty-foot Baystealth boat up on a sandbar in the West Bay about fifty yards from the shoreline, a location that, as soon as the sun rose enough to burn off the morning mist, would give him a view of the extreme west end of Galveston Island, the San Luis Pass bridge, and the distant coast line of Christmas Bay. He would be facing west with the sun coming up over his shoulders, presenting the soft, yellowish white light of early morning that he so loved in Edward Hopper's paintings.

While most of West Galveston Bay was anywhere from two to six feet deep, San Luis pass was much deeper with a treacherous current that had claimed the lives of many unfortunate swimmers and wade-fishermen. The "Dangerous Current. Keep Close To Shore" signs were perpetually pulled down and used for firewood...an act that was tantamount to manslaughter.

This was the third day that Alexander had been working on the small twelve by eighteen inch landscape study and he had hoped to finish it with this trip so that he could take it back to his studio and from it, paint a larger version that would hopefully fetch a handsome price.

Because he was at the time a professor of art, he didn't have to rely on selling his art to make a living, but nonetheless the extra income was nice; it was also, of course, an affirmation that someone out there appreciated his artwork. As he was setting up his French-style easel to begin painting, he heard a splash in the distance, coming from the direction of the bridge. Peering through the mist, he noticed a light green pickup backed up almost to the shore and blocking some of his view of the bridge.

I didn't even know there was a road out there, he thought, becoming somewhat agitated at the intrusion into the landscape. The pickup was over a hundred yards away but he could make out a man standing behind the tailgate at the edge of the water. He was pulling on a rope, the other end of which was in the water about ten feet in front of him. Alexander surmised that it was a cast net. It was. The man pulled it out of the water, gathered it up, and tossed it through the air as hard as he could. It was obvious that he knew how to throw the net, as it formed a perfect circle before it hit the water. The fisherman waited a few seconds—too long, Alexander thought —for the lead weights to sink the net to the bottom before he gave the rope a firm yank. He yanked on the rope several more times rather violently, but the net had evidently become snagged on something under the water.

That's happened to me more than once, Alexander thought.

Giving in to his curiosity, Alexander walked over to his boat, reached into a back pack on the port side, and pulled out his Nikon camera with a telephoto lens. The sun was up now enough to cast shadows as Alexander focused the lens on the man behind the pickup tugging on the rope. He could see that the net was snagged on something large now floating on top of the water. At that moment, the glare from boat's windshield caught the man's attention and he quickly turned toward

Alexander, obviously startled. He dropped the rope, ran around the truck and disappeared behind some brush.

Alexander shrugged, took a picture of the truck and surrounding area, hung the camera on the side of his easle, and turned his attention to his painting. *Hmmm, maybe the geometry and color of the pickup would provide a nice contrast to the landscape and compliment the geometry of the bridge.*

He quickly sketched it into the painting, not noticing that the man had stealthily returned and was crouched down on the far side of the green pickup. The man came back armed with a scope mounted Remington 30.06. He rested the rifle on the tailgate of the pickup and focused in on Alexander. Because of the distance between them, he didn't think Alexander could have seen much and didn't think that he really needed to shoot him. After all, he appeared unconcerned...he wasn't using a cell phone or in a hurry to leave. Then he saw the Nikon with the telephoto lens hanging off of the easel.

"*Crap*", he thought. "*Now I have no choice*".

He focused the crosshairs in the middle of Alexander's chest, and placed his finger on the trigger. He would take out the damn camera with his second shot. But as he took a deep breath to steady his aim, Alexander stepped behind the easel and started painting. The assassin knew that the special, hollow-point bullets he was using might fragment into a hundred pieces and not take out the painter if he tried to shoot through the easel, so he waited for Alexander to step to the side again.

Then he heard the sound of an outboard motor speedily approaching. The boat with four fishermen aboard pulled up almost parallel to where Alexander was standing on the sandbar, waved to Alexander, cut the motor, and dropped anchor to fish along the shoreline. As is in the case of many fishing trips, the popping of beer can tabs echoed across the bay.

"Fuck!...Fuck the luck," the man said out loud.

Then gathering his composure, he used the scope to make out the registration number and name on the side of Alexander's boat. *In The Eye of The Beerholder* was the name that Alexander's friends had talked him into having painted on his boat. That wouldn't be hard to remember. He wrote down the registration number on his left hand with a ball point pen and then low-crawled through the brush back up to the highway where his pickup was parked on the side of the road.

5

By the second week of February, Alexander had finished the larger version of the landscape painting, which included the light green pickup, and had it on display in a one-man show at the Galveston Art Center on the Strand. His opening took place during the monthly Artwalk, the Saturday night of the month when all of the art galleries in Galveston featured their best artists.

Suffice it to say that it was a shock to the "fisherman" who Alexander observed that October morning behind the green pickup truck when he saw the painting that evening. Furthermore, Franklin Buscanni, the mob-connected businessman who had hired the "fisherman" to assassinate an employee who had threatened to report his illegal toxic waste disposal operation, was extremely concerned.

The assassin had attempted to trace the serial number and name of Alexander's boat, but to his dismay, by the time he had fled the scene and returned to his apartment in Houston, most of the numbers he had scribbled on the palm of his hand were smeared beyond legibility. The name of the boat didn't help either because Alexander hadn't named the boat at the time he registered with the Texas Parks and Wildlife office. The assassin had decided to keep the incident to himself and hope for the best.

The hit-man and his boss, Buscanni—who had only been told that the body didn't wash out and that the retrieval efforts failed — were very much relieved when two days after the scene that Alexander had witnessed, the Galveston County Daily News reported that a fisherman had drowned near the San Luis Pass after apparently stepping off into a deep hole and getting tangled up in his cast net. They also reported that alcohol must have been a factor since several empty whiskey bottles were found in and around the victim's light green pickup. The assassin sweated bullets for the next couple of months waiting to see if the owner of the boat reported what he saw to the police — or worse, submitted incriminating photographs.

He had worried for no reason because Alexander really witnessed nothing suspicious and simply thought that the man he saw casting the net was the ill-fated fisherman who had drowned. He had forgotten all about the incident. Ironically, had Alexander bothered to print the photograph that he had taken that October morning, he would have seen the two tennis shoe clad feet of the victim protruding from the edge of the cast net. But because of his aversion to painting from photographs, he let the image remain an electronic memory in the digital brain of his camera.

Standing in front of Alexander's lush landscape painting of the San Luis Pass area, the very dangerous Franklin Buscanni made two impromptu decisions; he would buy the painting and just to be safe, he would have the artist killed.

6

The following week the assassin was waiting for Alexander to show up at his studio on Post Office street. The night before he had climbed up on top of the old Kress building , directly in front of Alexander's studio, using the pull-down utility stairs in the alley behind the building. He had his 30.06 rifle with a custom silencer and loaded with special hollow point rounds in a leather case beside him. This may not have been the weapon of choice for most assassins, but he trusted its accuracy and its killing power. After all, if it could drop a white tail deer at two hundred yards, it could certainly drop an artist across the street.

There was only one tiny detail that the assassin had not thought about...Mardi Gras. The third week of February was the first weekend of Galveston's Mardi Gras celebration. While most of the Mardi Gras activities took place on the historically famous Strand Street—two blocks north of Post Office Street—revelers parked and walked for blocks in all directions. They were as thick as fire-ants all up and down Post Office Street by ten o'clock that Saturday morning when Alexander strolled up to the wrought iron gate that secured the stairs leading up to his studio. The studio was on the second story above two retail shops—the Post Office Coffee House and the Kelver-Morris Art Gallery.

The assassin, lying prone behind the raised ledge on top of the Kress building had a clear view of the six large windows fronting Alexander's studio. As Alexander climbed the stairs to his studio, opened the door, and sat down at his drawing table in front of the windows, the assassin pulled out his rifle, bolted a shell into the chamber, and positioned himself for the shot. Once Alexander settled down and began drawing, the assassin focused the crosshairs squarely between Alexander's eyes. Piece of cake, he thought as he began to squeeze the trigger.

On the street directly below the studio, a kid threw a handful of Cheetos up in the air, yelling with delight as a flock of squawking seagulls dove to intercept the tasty delights. The assassin pulled the trigger...one of the seagulls exploded in midair...the window in front of Alexander shattered...the fragmented hollow point projectile went in all directions like shotgun pellets. One of the larger fragments hit Alexander above his right eye and he was knocked backwards off of his stool, unconscious. The Cheetos kid on the street below screamed in horror as blood, feathers, and glass rained down on him and his parents.

Almost two weeks later, Alexander woke up in a hospital bed, surrounded by his wife and son. The surgeons had removed the larger fragment from the right quadrant of his frontal lobe. The damage to his brain tissue was miraculously minimal, but the pre-op MRI indicated that at least one tiny splinter of the main fragment had been driven deeper into the cortex. The surgeon determined that the risk of trying to remove the splinter was greater than leaving it since it apparently was causing no hemorrhaging.

Other than a dull pain over his right eyebrow, a two-Advil-a-day headache that lasted about a week, and an exacerbation of the tinnitus that he had developed in Viet Nam, he suffered no significant symptoms from the head wound. He did, however, from that point on, feel a mysterious presence — as if an invisible someone was at all times very close to him. He later came to accept the presence as his Muse and the notched-up tinnitus as her persistent reminder that he had survived to serve a greater purpose.

7

"This is going to blow your mind, R.A.," Zapata exclaimed excitedly. "You do know what a virion is, don't you?"

"Actually, I don't," answered Alexander. "What is a virion?"

"Get this...a virion is a single infective particle of a virus, R.A. The squiggly marks on the canvas look exactly like a filament virus, like the Ebola virus—and I don't mean kind of like it...I mean like out of a text book on virology. Is this frigging weird or not?"

"Wait a minute, E.Z.! It's getting weirder by the minute! Now I remember why the canvas with the orange colored balls all over it looked so familiar...I went to an art show several years ago that was all about AIDS. The artist is a psychiatrist here on the Island and practices at UTMB, or he did at that time. I remember that he had large ball-like sculpture pieces covered with green-painted canvas and they had orange colored knobs all over them. He had several hanging from the ceiling of the gallery. They supposedly looked like the AIDS virus. What was his name...extremely nice guy but very strange...very talented...starts with an A, I'm almost positive. Maybe you know the guy, E.Z."

"Well, there is a shrink from UTMB who works with some of the county prisoners from time to time, using art therapy...I don't know if he's the doc you're thinking about. His name Antoine, Derrick Antoine I think."

"That's him!" shouted Alexander. "Dr. Antoine…a short guy, thin, with an overgrown flat-top, mustache, wears wire-frame glasses?"

"Yep…that's the guy, but I don't think he has a mustache."

"He did back then. I remember he recited a poem at the opening about how his lover died of AIDS. He made it clear that he was gay and that it was pertinent to his work. But I can't remember the details."

"I'll tell you who can" Zapata chimed in. "My old fishing buddy, Doc Milton. He was a research scientist and retired from UTMB several years ago…he knows the scoop on everyone out there and every sordid detail. I can tell you right where he is as we speak…he's fishing on the rock groin in front of 39th street. Let's get the hell out of here for a while, go visit old Doc Milton and get the low-down."

As they were leaving the lab, a Sheriff's deputy was walking down the hall toward them. He had come to retrieve the canvas tarp in which the murder victim's body was wrapped. Zapata fetched the canvas, carefully folded it and stuffed it inside a large plastic bag and gave it to the deputy. It had served its purpose. The two friends walked outside to Zapata's Hummer and drove over to the seawall.

8

It was a typical August afternoon on the Texas Gulf Coast as Zapata and Alexander zipped down 39th street and swung left onto Seawall Boulevard. Galveston can boast that the Gulf side of the boulevard has the longest continuous sidewalk in the country. Galveston's Seawall Boulevard stretches north-east to south-west for ten miles atop of the famous Galveston seawall, a seventeen feet high concrete barrier between the Gulf of Mexico and most of the city, built between 1902 and 1963. It was an amazing response to the deadly 1900 Hurricane, which wiped out Galveston and killed an estimated 8,000 residents. Thanks to that storm and the resulting deaths, Galveston can also boast that it is one of the most haunted cities in the country.

Another amazing response was to raise the grade of the city an average of eleven feet by lifting every building up on stilts and pumping in over sixteen million cubic yards of sand.

Zapata parked in a rare open spot on the beach side across from Gaido's seafood restaurant, a well known Galveston landmark. The temperature was around eighty-nine degrees with random puffs of cream colored cumulous clouds drifting northward over the Island, pushed on shore by the ever present Gulf breeze.

Seagulls were patrolling the skies over the crowded beach, ever cognizant of anything remotely edible. If a rookie tourist threw something up in the air to entice the birds, they would descend on it like a squawking, white whirlwind, fighting each other for the tasty morsel and then often showing their gratitude by pelting their uninitiated feeder with a shower of white bird poop. About fifty yards off shore a pod of nine brown Pelicans flew parallel to the beach, just above the surf.

The surf along the Upper Texas Gulf Coast that day was dirty green with sand and seaweed and crested around four feet high, as was the norm. This was due in part because the Gulf is very shallow there—one has to wade out a good hundred yards before the water is over six feet deep. Also, several major rivers—the Sabine, the Trinity, the Brazos, the Colorado—empty out into the Gulf within a hundred miles either side of Galveston Island, adding to the silt and sand in the surf.

However, none of these factors discouraged the surfers, who were tethered to their surf boards, bobbing up and down with the lazy waves out beyond the surf where the water was a cleaner green, waiting—sometimes all day—for the one wave large enough to ride in to the shore. That's what it was all about and for them and it was worth waiting for.

As Alexander and Zapata exited the Hummer, Zapata pointed toward the end of the rock groin and yelled to Alexander, "Look, there's old Doc out there just like I said he'd be."

"E.Z., what the hell you doing out here? There ain't no happy hour out here you know," the old doc hollered, laughing hoarsely.

Ralph Melton, Ph.D., had been a biochemical researcher and lecturer for U.T.M.B. for fifteen years before retiring in 1999. He was the epitome of the retired, eccentric professor—a salt and pepper beard and thick, curly grey hair. He stood about six feet tall, thin built with a slight beer-belly. His voice was deep and raspy, like an old blues singer. He grew up in the Mississippi Delta, the son of a black minister. The history of his struggle to escape the poverty and oppression of his youth played like a movie in his lucid brown eyes. He relished his reputation as a crotchety old fart, but in reality he was sweet-natured, big-hearted, and brilliant.

Zapata introduced Alexander and told the old doc why they were there...to get the low down on Dr. Derrick Antoine. Zapata and Alexander sat down on one of the large granite rocks as the old man wormed a dead shrimp onto his hook and cast out into the surf.

"Yeah, I know that coon-ass Cajun," offered Doc Milton as he wedged the handle of his fishing rod in a crack between two rocks and took a swig of beer. "Got his degree at LSU. He's gay, you know...not that I hold that against him...to each his own."

"Doc," asked Alexander, "what are facts about the death of his lover?"

"Well, his boyfriend was a promising young researcher in the biohazards lab and was AC/DC, if you know what I mean," Doc began. "I don't recall his full name, but he went by Clint...an East Indian, I believe. Anyways, he was a lot younger than Antoine and quite handsome. What I heard was that he'd screw anything that would bend over. The ironic part was that he caught the HIV virus from a woman—a young graduate student with whom he was evidently researching his sexual preference.

"The story goes that Antoine was insanely furious—not just because his lover was screwing a woman, but because she allegedly knew that she had the virus and failed to tell the man. Rumor has it that Antoine euthanized his lover when he was in the final stages and then murdered the woman."

"Murdered the woman?" Alexander and Zapata asked at the same time.

"Who knows," Doc answered, grabbing his fishing line between his thumb and forefinger. "You know, rumors are just like the tugging on this fishing line...you may have a fish on your hook, you may not. The only way you're gonna know for sure is to reel it all the way in. She just disappeared...and no one bothered to reel it in"

"Why?" asked Alexander, incredulously.

"Antoine is well published and well connected... related to some high-powered muckety-muck on the University of Texas board of regents. He brought in a lot of grant money and is well respected in both his field and the art world. That's not to say he's untouchable, but there just wasn't enough evidence to cause the disruption that pursuing an unsubstantiated rumor would have caused," Doc Melton explained, now taking the fishing rod in hand and giving it a couple of gentle tugs.

"Damn hardheads," Doc Melton exclaimed, referring to the ubiquitous and inedible saltwater catfish that had poison-tipped fins and were notorious for snatching bait before a more desirable fish had a chance to get hooked.

"When did Clint die and the nurse disappear?" Alexander asked, watching the tip of Melton's rod dipping down with the rhythm of a telegraph key.

"Not all that long ago, actually...maybe two years ago around Christmas," the old doc answered, cursing again as he yanked on his rod. "That's another strange part of the story... two years ago not that many people in America were dying of AIDS. They pretty much had that under control. Hell, enough about this shit...you boys grab a beer out of the cooler and learn how to fish. It's therapy for the soul."

9

"Holy crap, R.A., I think we found our numero uno suspect," Zapata declared as the two left the rock groin and walked into Gaido's for an early dinner. "He's an artist who does all kinds of virus depiction shit...ergo Virion...he probably hates women because he blames them for the death of his lover....not to mention they suspect that he killed that one chick.

"Hey, remember that movie about the Boston Strangler with Tony Curtis...the scene when the two cops were in the elevator at the same time the strangler was and they notice Curtis's bandaged hand? They like couldn't breathe for a second because they recognized him from the description of a surviving victim and realized that the Strangler could be right there in the elevator with them. That's how I'm feeling right now."

"E.Z., for one thing, we're not 'in the elevator' with anyone yet. For another, if you were an artist and you murdered someone, would you wrap her body up in one of your own paintings?"

Zapata thought about that a minute as they were being seated. "Look, man, don't screw up a perfectly good theory with logic. Maybe he wants to get caught before he does it again...maybe he was delirious and just not thinking straight... maybe I'll order the blackened snapper and let you frigging geniuses figure it out."

They both had a good laugh, ordered drinks, ate their

dinner, agreed that much more investigation needed to take place before making any substantive conclusions, and silently thought to themselves, "*Antoine has got to be our serial killer.*"

On the way back to the morgue, they both agreed that Dr. Antoine should be investigated, but even though Zapata was a commissioned police officer and Alexander held a private investigator license, neither really had the authority to instigate a formal investigation.

"But I am an artist," offered Alexander, "and he won't be suspicious of another artist. I could call him up and tell him that I'm really interested in his work and would like to see more of it. We could meet in his studio...he'll show me the work in there and I'll ask to see some slides. If he painted our canvas, there will be similar works in his studio and it'll show up in his slides. Trust me, E.Z., we artists are a vain lot and we believe that every work we do is a masterpiece...we *will* capture it on a slide for posterity."

"Well, what if he is the killer, R.A.? Aren't you taking a bit of a risk?"

"Why would I be? If our theory is right, he targets women. If he's the killer, E.Z., I'll know it—I can read it in his face...in his aura. The painting will be our hard evidence. He'll be flattered that another artist admires his work...and actually I do," Alexander exclaimed as he pulled out his cell phone and punched in 411. "Galveston, Texas...Antoine...Derrick Antoine, M.D."

10

Shaneesha Riley pulled the apron over her head and flung it over the hook on the back wall of the Kentucky Fried Chicken on Broadway and 30th. It was midnight and her shift of shoving chicken and biscuits out of the drive-through window was finally over. She said goodnight to the night manager and walked out the employees' exit through the kitchen. Her Ford Probe was parked behind the building next to a white van that she didn't recognize at first.

Odd, there weren't any customers in the restaurant when I left.

It didn't occur to her until she was unlocking the driver's door to her car that a van just like that one had been at the drive-through window an hour earlier. She couldn't really see the driver's face that well because he had a cap pulled down low and was wearing shades, even though it was eleven at night. She noticed that he was a large white man wearing a blue jump suit like a lot of her customers wore...workers at one of the petrochemical plants in Texas City.

Suddenly, the sliding door of the van flung open and Shaneesha turned toward it with a start. Before she could make a sound, a huge hand covered her mouth and the hulk of a man pressed hard into her, crushing her body against the car and knocking the breath out of her. Her head and back hurt so much from the impact that she hardly felt the needle slide into the side of her neck. As her eyes rolled back in their sockets, her legs turned to rubber and her world went black. The whole event took less than thirty seconds.

When Shaneesha finally started emerging from her stupor, she felt deathly ill and strangely numb all over. Slowly, she realized that she was naked...lying on her back in water on some kind of concrete incline, staring up at the underside of a building. The water was warm...almost soothing. She could hear the water lapping against the bulkhead and she wanted to go back to sleep.

Then, to her horror, she became aware that her arms were bound to her sides with a heavy rope and duct tape was wrapped around her head, covering her mouth. Her feet were tied together with the same heavy rope. About five feet in front of her a motor boat was floating and she could see that someone was moving around in it. Suddenly, the boat motor roared to life and the boat began to pull away. As the boat got about twenty feet away, she saw a rope come out of the water. One end was tied to the transom of the boat, and with sheer terror she realized that the other end was tied to her feet.

11

The following Friday afternoon — August 22nd — Alexander met Dr. Derrick Antoine in Antoine's studio, which basically was the downstairs of his home on 14th street, a few blocks from UTMB. The house was a typical old Galveston Victorian home with gingerbread trimming, a front porch and a balcony above that. It was built around 1910 and still had the original cypress siding. The house was a creamy off-white with green shutters and had about three thousand square feet of living space. It was in need of some minor repairs and a good paint job. Nonetheless, it had that old Galveston charm and ample room — a magnet for many of the Island's artists and musicians.

Alexander parked in the driveway and removed the leather holster from inside his waist line that sheathed his model 60 Smith & Wesson .357 pistol that Zapata insisted he carry to the meeting. He stuffed it into the glove compartment and climbed out of his Chevy Tahoe.

"Screw this," he said out loud. "I said I'd wear it over here. I didn't say I'd take inside."

He strolled up the brick sidewalk that was lined with monkey grass. There was a neatly kept flower garden in front of the porch populated with rose bushes and various seasonal flowers. He ascended the four steps up to the porch, grabbed the bronze door knocker, and gave it five hardy bangs.

"Richard?" asked Derrick Antoine as he opened one side of the double front door. "Derrick Antoine…it's a pleasure to see you again."

"Yes, same here," Alexander responded, surprised at the exaggerated firmness of Antoine's grip. Alexander tried to hold the handshake for a second longer to feel any unusual vibes but Antoine pulled his hand away, almost as if he sensed what Alexander was up to.

"I love this house, Derrick. You must have put a ton of work into it."

Alexander noticed that Zapata was correct…Antoine no longer wore a mustache. But he still had the extra-long flattop haircut and the steel-rimmed glasses.

"Oh well, you know how that is, Richard. I'm sure you've been through it as well over there on Avenue O," Antoine replied, shutting the door and twisting the handle to the dead bolt lock.

"Oh yes, these old houses are fabulous, but they are money pits," Alexander answered, now uneasily surprised that Antoine knew where he used to live. "However, I don't live there anymore," he continued, wondering how much about him Antoine knew. "Impending divorce and all that, you know."

"I am sorry to hear that, Richard. Where are you living now…in your studio on Postoffice?"

Jesus, this guy has done his research, Alexander thought. "No, that's a great studio space, but not livable. I rent a small house on Post Office Street, a few blocks east of my studio."

"How convenient," Antoine replied, "Come on, let me give you the tour of my studio. I'm dying to show you my latest work."

Antoine had removed a number of the original interior walls to provide a large open space for his studio. On the ceiling above was a grid of large exposed beams to make up for the load-bearing walls that were removed. The beams, in turn, were held up by two columns spaced apart in the center of the building.

Stepping through the front door, Alexander estimated that the distance from the front door to the back wall that divided the large room from the kitchen and dining area was around fifty feet. Walking up to the house, he had estimated that it was between thirty-five and forty feet wide. To his immediate right was a grand staircase that made a ninety degree turn to the left halfway up to the second floor. Between the staircase and a couple of front windows sat an elegant antique settee and hat tree.

As the two walked through the large room, Antoine pointed out his litho press, drawing table, custom made 4′ x 12′ work table, and several works in progress. Against one wall, was a small series of three cast resin relief sculptures, each in the shape of a woman's torso, sans head and arms, with the shoulders such that suggested their arms were stretched back over their heads. They had various objects suspended in the resin. For some reason, they reminded Alexander of a Dying Niobid theme from early Greek sculpture, based on the myth of Niobe, a woman who crossed the gods and wound up with an arrow in her back—thus her arms stretched back over her head.

Alexander was very impressed with the artwork, the studio space, and the equipment. He thought it odd, however, that in the middle of the room, hanging from a rafter, was a disco ball. *Oh well, like Doc Melton said, to each his own.*

On the walls around the room, Alexander noticed reproductions of Toulouse-Lautrec's portraits of prostitutes, with acidic orange and green faces and distorted expressions. But what was disturbing to Alexander was that Antoine—or someone—had covered some of the women's faces with transparent sheets of plastic with what Alexander had by then grown to recognize as depictions of the AIDS virus painted or printed on them. On one of the prints—the portrait of a young prostitute with cadmium red hair—the transparent sheet had two ping-pong balls cut in half, one placed over each eye, and painted bright, neon green. The surface of each half ping pong ball had been covered with small map-pins—the kind that has a tiny ball for the head of the pin, and the heads were bright orange. Alexander recognized them as miniature versions of the large AIDS virus sculptures that Antoine had hanging from the ceiling at his exhibition. The "eye balls" transformed the already morbidly pretty face of the young prostitute into a monstrously grotesque face.

"Would you like some iced tea, Richard? I'm dying for some," Antoine asked, standing by the kitchen door.

"Yes, thank you." Alexander answered, not taking his eyes off of the poster.

As Antoine disappeared into the kitchen, Alexander's curiosity got the best of him. He noticed that the plastic sheet that covered the prostitute's face was attached to the print only at the top edge of the sheet. He reached up and grabbed the bottom of the plastic sheet and slowly lifted it up. What he saw underneath the ping pong balls almost caused him to gasp out loud. Where the eyes used to be on the portrait there were round holes cut out, the exact size of one half of a ping pong ball. The insides of the holes were painted black and full of black, wavy, plastic worms.

The poster was on the south wall to the left of the kitchen door, and Alexander had his back to the door. He didn't hear Antoine walk up behind him.

"Syphilis," Antoine offered with a laugh, causing Alexander to jump slightly. "Everyone thinks they're worms, but they're blown up 3D images of syphilis bacteria... bacterium Treponema pallidum, to be exact. Isn't that a hoot," he added, obviously amused, handing Alexander a glass of iced tea.

"Shocking," Alexander said, trying to compose himself. "I certainly wasn't expecting this."

"Well who would?" Antoine replied, still laughing. "But when a man screws a whore—and they're all whores—he probably isn't expecting the worse either...the misery...the death that she could possibly be trading him for a few minutes of pleasure."

He wasn't laughing anymore. Alexander tried to study Antoine's eyes.

"Oh, but I feel you're looking for something less offensive," Antoine added after a couple of seconds of awkward silence and turned away.

He walked over to some prints he had stacked on the large work table, once again in a jovial mood. As he spread out a couple of the prints, Alexander looked around at the works that were hanging on the walls or easels or leaning against the walls. He saw nothing really similar to the canvas piece in which the murdered woman's body was wrapped. After viewing the prints, Alexander asked if he could purchase one.

"Well, Richard, I feel like a scoundrel selling my work without involving one of my galleries. But I'll do it for a fellow artist...besides, it wouldn't be much of a commission for the gallery."

"What galleries do you show with, Derrick?"

"My main gallery—the one that handles these prints—is the Watson-Keebler Gallery in New York City."

Alexander asked if he could view some slides. He explained to Antoine that he was looking for something more like he had shown in his AIDS exhibition.

Antoine kept a slide projector set up in a corner of the room and gladly turned it on for Alexander. He loaded the carousel that contained the slides of his AIDS series. It projected a three square-foot image onto the wall. As the projector automatically shuffled to the next slide every twenty seconds, Antoine would give a little history or other explanation of the slide on view.

Then the eighth slide popped up and Alexander almost

gasped out loud for a second time within the hour. It was the exact piece that the body had been wrapped with. The rectangular section toward the bottom wasn't quite the same; the squiggly shapes seemed much greyer and arranged differently. Except for that, this was the same green canvas with the reddish-orange knots attached to it.

"Wait a minute, Derrick," Alexander managed to blurt out, "this is the kind of image I've been looking for. Do you have this piece here in the studio?"

Dead silence...the hum of the slide projector became an unbearable roar.

"No, unfortunately, I don't have this piece anymore, Richard." Antoine finally answered, staring at Alexander with a rather perplexed look on his face. "Of all the pieces you could have picked... this is one of the few from this series that has sold. Its title is *The Face of AIDS II.* I do have a couple of prints similar to this that I did as studies...I'd be happy to pull them out."

"Let me think about it, Derrick. I'm going to have to meet a friend in few minutes. Who's the lucky owner of that piece, may I ask?" Alexander stood, visibly anxious to leave.

"I don't remember off hand, Richard. I'd be happy to look it up and perhaps email you the name. Do you really want the painting that bad?" Antoine asked as they walked to the front door.

"Well, it won't hurt to call the owner and see if he...or she...is interested in selling." Alexander replied, hoping to elicit some kind information from Antoine—to no avail.

They shook hands at the door and Alexander left with the newly purchased print rolled up under his arm. Alexander still did not detect any unusual vibes from the handshake, but he could detect a negative aura around Antoine.

Dr. Derrick Antoine was a delightful man, an extremely talented artist, and a gracious host—although there was something very strange and secretive about him. But the most chilling fact was that the painting in question was Antoine's... and he couldn't convincingly account for it...and he obviously disdained women.

12

"It's him, E.Z." Alexander said into his cell phone as he drove back to his apartment. "He painted the canvas the girl was wrapped up in and he really has a thing against women. But it isn't him...He's the artist, but I don't think he's the killer. I think the killer altered the painting, adding the hidden clues."

"Sabrina Williams," Zapata replied. "The girl's name is Sabrina Williams. We just got confirmation from her parents — they live in Oklahoma. What makes you think this bastard isn't our man, R.A.? The painting ought to wrap it up, man...no pun intended."

"E.Z., if you find a body wrapped up in one of my paintings that I had sold to someone else, does that automatically make me the killer? I just don't feel it with him... not in his touch, his aura, or his eyes. He said he sold that painting, but he couldn't recall who bought it. Hell, man, I can't remember who bought half of my work."

"Well, I hope you remember that the band is playing Sunday night at the Haak Winery, dude. And someone needs to keep an eye on Dr. Antoine. We gotta tell the cops that the canvas wrapping is his painting."

"No, E.Z., that will screw up everything. I'm telling you, Antoine is not the killer. But if he's arrested, it'll be on the news and the real killer will hear about it and if he's the one who bought the painting, he'll split before anyone can make that connection. Believe me, bro, if I thought Antoine was the killer,

I'd take the cops there myself...even though I have little credibility with them."

"Jesus, R.A., you're going to get our asses in all kinds of trouble. We can't keep this quiet forever, hermano. I mean, what if we're just sitting here on our asses and that sicko kills again...that wouldn't just be hard to live with, man, we'd be brought up on charges of interfering with an investigation and maybe even aiding and abetting."

"I realize that, E.Z., but let's at least wait until Antoine emails me the name of his buyer...that could be today or tomorrow. Then we can give that information to the cops and they can bring both of them in."

"Alright, R.A., but tomorrow, email or no email from Antoine, I'm calling the sheriff. Shit, man, I won't even be able to sleep tonight. I don't plan on being some tattooed lifer's bitch in Huntsville."

"Relax sax player, 'We're Gonna Make It'," Alexander replied, trying to hide his own anxiety by quoting the title of the popular rhythm and blues song.

"Hold it, R.A., I'm getting another call. I'll get back to you."

Alexander pulled into the drive of his house and circled around behind the remodeled, light yellow, Victorian house. He managed to unlock the back door, put his newly bought print on the kitchen table, and grab a Michelob out of the fridge before his cell phone rang.

"R.A., we've got another body," Zapata reported solemnly. "Young black female...same indications as we saw on Cynthia Fisher and Sabrina Williams...and guess what—her body was found wrapped in another canvas, much like the one Sabrina was found in...much like our buddy Antoine's work. Amigo, we have a serial killer on the loose...and you and I are in deep shit."

13

As Alexander drove to the county morgue, he was still convinced that Antoine was not the killer…but he had to admit that the art work was awfully complicating. He turned off of Broadway and pulled into the parking lot of the county building. It was 5:45 and Alexander felt relieved that most of the employees would be long gone by then. It was much more difficult for the Muse to work when a lot of people were around.

"E.Z., I ask it again…if you were an artist and murdered someone, would you wrap their body in your own art work and leave it where it would be easily found?" Alexander asked as they stood beside the girl's body on the autopsy table.

"And I repeat R.A., if you're a sick puppy and want to get caught before you kill more…yes, you just might do that." Zapata answered, obviously upset at the turn of events. "We have got to tell the sheriff what we know, Richard."

"O.k., I agree E.Z. But give me a moment with her. Let me see what she tells me. Meanwhile, check out the canvass she was wrapped in…is there a clue hidden on it? Oh, by the way, where did they find this body?"

"The exact same place as Sabrina Williams was found…on Snake Island, just closer to the east end."

As Zapata walked out of the lab to inspect the canvass, Alexander pulled up a chair next to the examining table and gently held the dead Woman's hand. He sat for a full minute, eyes closed, massaging the lifeless hand. Usually he did not come in direct contact with the victim; he received more messages from the clothing or some other possession of the victim. But this time he was mysteriously drawn to the body.

Suddenly, he went into a trance. In his vision, a large man dressed in a blue jump suit wearing shades and a cap pulled down low on his sweat-drenched forehead rushed toward him and smacked him on the side of his face with a tattered bible. Alexander fell out of the chair, still in the trance, as the ominous figure loomed over him.

"Hear me, Seer," the figure growled, leaning closer. "You think you've seen evil...know what evil is? All you've seen are us virions...you have no idea what you are dealing with...what humankind is dealing with. Mark is trying to tell you...fifth chapter, verses eight and nine. See it, Seer...that's your gifting."

14

Zapata was in the process of hanging the canvas on a wall to X-ray it when he heard Alexander hit the floor. He rushed out into the morgue and saw his friend lying on his back on the floor, an arm up in front of his face as if to protect himself from being struck.

"R.A., what the hell happened?" Zapata asked, kneeling down beside Alexander to help him up.

"I saw the killer, E.Z.," Alexander answered excitedly, rubbing the side of his face. "Hand me my sketchbook, E.Z. I want to draw him while he's fresh in my memory."

"O.k., buddy. Are you sure you're alright? Jeez, what happened to your face? It looks like you got smacked," Zapata observed, grabbing the sketchbook from the countertop where Alexander had laid it.

The right side of Alexander's face was red with a couple of superficial scratches just below his cheek bone. His nose was starting to bleed, one of the side effects of using his psychic abilities. "I'll tell you in a minute, E.Z. Let me get to this drawing."

Alexander sat on the floor holding his sketchbook for a couple of minutes, waiting for an image to appear...but nothing appeared on the page. From his memory of the vision, he quickly gestured the hulking figure.

"The Muse isn't helping, E.Z. but this is what I remember seeing," Alexander explained, holding his sketchbook up for

Zapata to see. "I've had vivid visions before, but I've never been attacked by one of them."

"Maybe you just hit your face on the floor." Zapata said, trying to come up with a logical answer.

"Except that I fell on my left side. No, this is where the dude hit me." Alexander explained, pointing to the right side of his face. "This is where Virion hit me, I should say." He added, excitedly. "This is a major breakthrough, E.Z., Virion came to me in a vision and left me a clue...a Bible verse...Mark, fifth verse, chapter, uh, eight, I think. Do you have a Bible here, dude?"

"You got to be kidding, R.A.....a Bible?"

"E.Z., when reality slaps you in the face, you need to sit up and take notice. I need a Bible." Alexander exclaimed, getting to his feet.

"Well, we have the next best thing, buddy...we have the Internet." Zapata answered, walking back to his office.

The wonder of the Internet...limitless information at one's fingertip—albeit, a lot of it worthless. It was sort of like the CB radio, a once useful tool that soon turned into a cacophonous zoo of unintelligible chatter.

Zapata and Alexander huddled around Zapata's desktop PC and Googled Mark:5:8. After exploring a couple of different sites, they found this version: "*For He said unto him 'Come out of the man, unclean spirit!' Then He asked him, what is your name?' And he answered, saying, 'My name is Legion; for we are many.'*"

They both stared at the verse for a minute, then Zapata asked, "What do you think this means, R.A.?"

"I don't know. Maybe it means that our friend has multiple personalities. Maybe it means that there is more than one person involved in these killings. What do you think, E.Z.?"

"Well, when you read the whole chapter, Jesus was confronting one dude who had a lot of demons inside him. I guess that's what we're dealing with here."

"I don't know, E.Z. I'd love to think it's that simple but look at the rest of the chapter…the demons begged Jesus not to destroy them but to put them into a herd of pigs. There were two thousand pigs and they all became possessed and ran off into the sea and drowned…and it doesn't say that the demons died…just the pigs. What happened to the demons?

"I don't know, R.A., but I think you're reading too much into this. I still think it's a story about a man with multiple personalities. I mean, isn't that typical for a serial killer?"

"No, it's not, E.Z. The F.B.I. has a profile on serial killers and it reveals that many of them pretty much seem like the rest of us…family men, church-goers, respected in their communities. What they think serial killers may have in common is a psychopathic personality disorder that manifests in various ways—very controlling, pathological lying, absence of remorse, asocial tendencies, obsessive-compulsive drives. Ted Bundy, for example, didn't have multiple personalities. A number of serial killers reported being possessed by a demon, like the B.T.K. Strangler who killed numerous women in the Wichita area back in the '70s for one. Richard Ramirez, the Night Stalker, was a Satan worshiper. Albert Desalvo, the prime suspect as the Boston Strangler in the 1960's, was portrayed to be a paranoid schizophrenic, but the court didn't buy it."

"Well, there's a huge difference between schizophrenia and multiple personalities," offered Zapata while peering through a magnifying glass at the canvas piece that enveloped the second victim, "so how are we to interpret the verse?"

"I'm working on the demon theory, E.Z. But first, let's take a look at the canvas," Alexander replied.

The painting was not like the first one in that it had no three dimensional balls on it but it was similar…and most disturbing to Alexander, it looked a lot like one of the pieces that he had seen during the slide show in Antoine's studio.

Yet, something wasn't adding up...his eyes were disagreeing with his brain. It was a four by six foot rectangular canvas stained with alizarin crimson and scumbled over with burnt sienna and black patches, creating an eerie dried blood effect. On top of that, numerous circular shapes the size of tennis balls and filled with spaghetti-like marks had been stamped or printed. They were mostly black and white with splotches of cadmium red medium. It would make most medically informed viewers think of some kind of pox infection. This canvass also had a white, gessoed rectangular strip about a foot from the bottom. But instead of being filled with squiggly lines like the painting with the orange balls, this one simply had "350-370 nm" printed in a light reddish-brown paint.

"What do you think that means?" Zapata asked, pointing to the printing.

"It looks like a nanometer value, wouldn't you say?" Alexander answered.

Zapata got on his computer and Googled 350-370 nm. The Wikipedia site confirmed that it was a light-wave length in the ultraviolet light range...better known as black light.

"We have some hand-held black light units in the forensics lab, R.A. I'll grab one," Zapata said, rushing out the door.

Reluctantly, Alexander reached out and took a corner of the canvas in his hand. He was actually relieved that no vision came to him—he had had enough of the Muse for one day. Suddenly the door swung open, startling Alexander. For a fraction of a second he thought the large figure in the blue jump suit was rushing in the room...but it was Zapata with a battery powered black light unit.

Zapata set the black light unit on the front edge of his desk, turned it on, and turned off the lights in his office. They both stood in shock for a minute, staring wide-eyed at the canvas that had been transformed into a totally different image.

Zapata's white lab coat wasn't the only thing glowing in the black light. Diagonally across the canvas, scrawled in two inch letters was the message, **FOR WE ARE MANY!   VIRION**

"Holy crap!" Zapata finally said, "Isn't that in that Bible verse we just saw?"

Alexander nodded his head, the right side of his face still smarting. His brain was also beginning to ache as it tried desperately to pull logic and reason into the scene that seemed more like a nightmare than reality.

"I'm telling you, bro, this creep wants to get caught...that's why he's wrapping his victims in his own artwork," Zapata answered.

"Then why the cryptic messages, E.Z.? The artwork would be enough...in fact, it's too obvious."

"I don't know, man, but I've got to tell the sheriff that these canvases are Antoine's, R.A."

"I know," Alexander replied, the conflict between what he saw about the painting and what logic dictated still waging in his mind, "but I can tell you that Antoine's not the monster in the blue jump suit."

"Jeckle and Hyde, buddy," Zapata answered punching in the phone number for the Galveston County Sheriff's Department. "Antoine may not look like the monster in the blue jump suit, but that's the monster inside of him."

15

The next morning, Saturday, August 23rd, Alexander sat at his kitchen table with a freshly brewed cup of coffee. The modest wood-framed house he rented was small and nestled under several large pecan and oak trees. It had probably been built in the 60's or 70's. There were two bedrooms situated off of the hallway on the east wall with the solitary bathroom between them. The bedroom he didn't sleep in was his office. The house had a nice sized living room and behind that, a surprisingly large kitchen/dining room area. Thankfully, the owners had central air and heat installed several years back. There was a small garage on the west side of the property...too small to accommodate Alexander's Tahoe.

Every room was painted the same color—a neutral tan which would not conflict with his art collection—and every wall space had some kind of artwork hanging on it. The place actually looked like an eclectic little art gallery. Van Gogh and Cezanne prints hung with Janet Fish still-lifes. J.M.W. Turner's violent seascapes hung beside Neil Welliver's methodical landscapes. Interspersed throughout the house were works of various friends which whom he had traded paintings and drawings.

Alexander opened up the Galveston County Daily News that he had just fetched from his neighbor's front lawn. He cursed silently at the teeth marks from his neighbor's Labrador retriever pup, Rambo, a creature so hyperactive that all of the squirrels moved across the street. Alexander figured that the mutt had an IQ just below that of a chicken's.

There it was on the bottom of the front page ...**Second Body Found on Snake Island**. The article described both victims and then went on to say that a local artist as well as a couple of other persons were being questioned. Antoine's name was not mentioned, nor was the fact that he was a UTMB psychiatrist. There was nothing mentioned about the bodies being wrapped in paintings or any other details, thanks to the discretion of the sheriff's department.

The reporter apparently did not connect the first murdered young woman with the two bodies found on Snake Island, but Zapata and Alexander knew there was a connection. The article carefully skirted around the term 'serial killer,' saying instead that the similarities were being investigated.

Alexander's cell phone rang. It was Doc Melton.

"Richard, Ralph Melton here. I got really curious after we talked the other day, so I did a little digging—research, if you will—about Antoine's lover and the woman from whom he supposedly caught AIDS. Can you and E.Z. meet me later today?"

"I can, Doc. I'll call E.Z. Back out on the rock groin?"

"Oh, hell no. Even I get sick of fishing. How about the Postoffice Street Coffee House, say in two hours?"

Alexander called Zapata, who was babysitting his two grandkids. "Yeah, I wouldn't miss it. Sandy will be home in about an hour. I'll meet you guys over there...and don't forget, R.A., we practice this afternoon for tomorrow's gig at the Haak Winery."

By ten-thirty, the three men were sitting outside of the quaint coffee shop on Postoffice Street, under a bright green awning. Alexander's studio was above the coffee shop on the second floor. The temperature was already in the low eighties, headed for the low nineties. Patches of clouds were drifting northward, their shadows crawling across the oaks and crepe-myrtles in front of the shop, creating a few seconds of relief from the muggy heat.

"O.k., here's the scoop," Doc Melton started, blowing on his steaming cup of coffee, "Antoine's lover was named Ali Westwood, but he used the name Clint...you know, as in Clint Eastwood...Westwood...I guess he thought that was cute. His mother was Iranian and his father was American...worked for some oil company and was all over the Middle East in the 70's and 80's...scuttlebutt has it he was also a CIA spook, but who wasn't back then.

"The graduate student who allegedly gave Westwood AIDS was named Leann Muñoz, from down in the Valley...a real looker, evidently. Leann was also a licensed vocational nurse and worked part time at different facilities, often caring for AIDS patients."

"That could be how she contracted AIDS," offered Zapata.

Melton waited to answer until a trolley went clanking past the coffee shop. "Right...that or the more common cause, spreadus-leggus-apartus," retorted Melton sarcastically. "But here's the real clincher...our boy Clint didn't die of AIDS complications. Thanks to some info from an old doc I golf with, I checked the medical archives...he died of a sudden onset of a rare staph infection. He was HIV positive, but he really wasn't symptomatic at the time of his death. Most staph infections of this nature are nosocomial...contracted during treatment in a hospital. But Clint wasn't hospitalized until he was already eaten up with the staph. None of his projects involved staph infections either."

"Didn't that seem suspicious to anyone?" asked Alexander.

"Evidently not," Answered Melton, "those docs had seen so many unpredictable complications with HIV and AIDS that while it may have seemed unusual, it didn't raise any red flags...but it probably should have for two reasons. First, while advanced AIDS patients often died of staph infections, Westwood wasn't even symptomatic, much less advanced. Second, that strain of antibiotic-resistant staph had never been identified around here before."

"So what does that mean to you?" Alexander asked.

"Well, if it looks like a rat, scurries like a rat, and squeaks like a rat, it probably is a rat," Melton answered, squirming, obviously uncomfortable sitting in the small, wrought-iron chair.

"Meaning...?" Zapata asked, gesturing with his hands to emphasize his impatience with his old friend's habit of being oblique.

"Well, it depends on which rat you think you're watching, E.Z.," Melton answered with his slow Mississippi drawl. "One rat in this story could be a case of professional carelessness for not following up on the unusual aspects of Westwood's case... maybe due to inexperience, too much experience, being under staffed, indifference, incompetence, homophobia...who knows.

"But if that's the only rat you're watching, you're going to miss the first rat that was in the room."

"In other words," interjected Alexander after a brief silence, "you suspect that our boy Clint was purposefully exposed to the staph."

"I'm just a research scientist with a Ph.D., boys...not a frigging swami with a crystal ball...it's just a theory."

"Let's assume your theory is solid, Doc," said Alexander, "who do you think did it...and why?"

"Well, Antoine comes to mind, of course...you know, jealous lover and all that. But I'm not convinced that he has the 'pelotas' or the resources to pull that off."

"But you said you thought he killed both Westwood and Leann Muñoz the other day," Zapata interjected.

"I don't think that crap, E.Z....I said that was the rumor. I don't work on rumors...I work on proof. Even if Antoine pulled the plug on his lover doesn't mean he was responsible for his fatal infection. Like I said, it's just a theory...in case you two are interested."

Alexander spoke up quickly. "No, you're right, Doc, we are interested...and we hope that you'll help us figure it out."

Old Doc Melton grunted and nodded while he unwrapped a cigar.

"Speaking of theories, R.A.," said Zapata just to break the uneasy silence that followed, "you said your Muse has given you a vision—a theory—about how that Bible verse fits in to the killings...'My name is Legion, for we are many'"

"Oh, I don't want to bore Doc with that stuff, E.Z.," Alexander answered, glaring at Zapata with a look that said they shouldn't be discussing those details with other people right now.

Zapata instantly interpreted the look, but before he could change the subject, Doc Melton blurted out, "Ah yes, the demons and the swine...I love that story. Do you think the killer has a bunch of demons in him, Richard...or do you suspect some pig farmer?" Melton gave a hearty laugh as he clipped the end off of the cigar and fired it up.

Alexander felt somewhat awkward revealing details to Melton, but he trusted him for some reason—even though he didn't know him that well—and to be honest, he did want to verbalize his theory to critical ears. As he was thinking about how to begin, Melton reached across the table and laid his hand on Alexander's arm.

"By the way, Richard," Melton said in an uncharacteristically quiet voice, "I did a little extra research and I am aware of your special talents...your shooting and your 'Muse,' I believe you call it...and I am fascinated by it. So don't feel awkward...I know how to keep my mouth shut. Have you been the subject of any research? Does medical science know about your psychic abilities?"

"No, and that's the way I'm going to keep it," Alexander said sternly. "Otherwise, they'll have me turned into a lab monkey with probes wired into my skull. No, thanks...and just to set the record straight, this thing is as much a curse as it is a blessing...if not more so." He quickly glanced at Zapata, anticipating the characteristic rolling of his eyes.

"It's like God handed me this amazing ability as compensation for being shot in the head and then said, 'by the way, here's the bill.' That bill—so far—has included my wife moving out, my son staying pissed off at me, me and my family being threatened constantly, being on the cops' top ten weirdo list, getting shot at again, being put on notice at the university, and last but not least, raging headaches every time the Muse visits—not to mention nose bleeds and black-out seizures. So you guys will understand if—just occasionally—the 'Why the hell me?' question pops up."

"Hey, seems to me that you're in divine company, buddy," Melton responded, denying Alexander's diatribe a pause of significance. "Don't you figure Noah, Job, or Moses might have asked that same question at one time or another? So, what's this theory of yours?"

Alexander sat in silence, clinching his teeth and taking turns glaring at Melton, then Zapata. Finally Zapata burst out laughing and before long, they were all three laughing.

Alexander finally told Doc Melton about his vision of the large man in the blue jumpsuit who struck him on the side of the face with a Bible, and the Bible verse that the vision referenced. Zapata told him he had heard Alexander hit the floor and saw the abrasions on his face—and the nose bleed. Then he told him about the black light message on the second canvas and how it supported the Bible verse.

"Holy crap, guys...this is Twilight Zone stuff," Melton replied, still trying to keep his voice down. What did you tell the cops?"

"Nothing about that," Zapata replied, "but we told them about the clues we found on the canvasses...so they know about the Virion part. We had to give them Antoine because of the paintings...otherwise, it could be our asses on the line, given what we know...anyway, I think the bastard's our killer, even though R.A. doesn't."

"And why don't you think he's the killer, Richard?" Melton asked.

"Because the Muse doesn't think so, Doc," Alexander answered.

"No wonder the cops don't know what to think about you, Richard," Melton added. "So you guys have information that the cops don't have...what are you going to do with it?"

"We're going to do our research, Doc, just like you would," answered Alexander. "We're going to catch Virion and we need your help."

"How do you know that Virion is the name the killer uses?" Melton asked. "It's just a viral particle. Maybe he—let's assume the killer is a he for the time being—thinks that his victims are infectious viral particles and that's why he kills them."

"Interesting theory, Doc, but he signed the canvases like an artist would...VIRION," Alexander countered. "The man in my vision referred to virions...he said 'you think you've seen evil...all you've seen are *us* virions.' He wasn't referring to the victims...he was referring to the bad guys. Then he gave me the Bible verse and challenged me to understand its significance."

"By all means," Melton responded, "share with us what Mark was really telling us."

Alexander waited until a couple of mounted city police clip-clopped past them on their horses. He could have sworn that they were staring at the three of them. *Great, now I'm feeling paranoid...but just because you're paranoid doesn't mean they're not after you.*

"O.k., first you have to understand that my visions always lead me to the truth...eventually. So, the man in the vision—who I am calling Virion—tells us that we haven't seen evil, just its virions. Taken at face value, that would mean that the evil people who we see doing evil deeds are only parts of a greater whole...in other words, *evilness* is the virus and all the bad people are but particles—that is, virions—of the virus. Now, let's move on to Mark. Jesus encounters the man, Legion, who lives in a cemetery and is possessed by demons. What does a cemetery symbolize?"

"Death?" offered Zapata.

"Eternity," countered Melton.

"Both," Alexander continued, "But it also symbolizes life... the life cycle that is, which ends in death, which is eternal whether you believe that death is the end of being or whether you believe in life after death, which Jesus promised...both last for eternity.

"The demon that Jesus called out of the man said 'my name is Legion, for we are many.' The man symbolizes mankind since the beginning of the human life cycle until the end of mankind. Mark said that the man could not be shackled or tamed because he was possessed by the demons. In other words, humankind cannot obey the laws of God—or the laws of society—as long as evilness controls our flesh."

Alexander waved at his friends who ran the art gallery below his studio and continued.

"The demons begged Jesus to not just remove them from the man—that is, mankind—but to let them enter a herd of swine.

"Now back to Virion...if evilness is a virus, it has to invade a host in order to live and to replicate. Therefore, the demons had to temporarily possess the pigs or perish. We don't know how many demons possessed the 'man' but we do know that there were about two thousand pigs in the herd and they all became afflicted, ran down to the sea and drowned...the pigs drowned, not the demons. And what is a sea, if not an abundant source of temporary hosts."

"So, why didn't Jesus just destroy the demons — evilness — when he had the chance?" asked Melton, flicking his cigar ash into the street.

"That's what I asked a preacher friend of mine and he gave me this," answered Alexander, pulling a small Bible out of his hip pocket. He turned to Isaiah, 45:6-7 and read out loud, "*I am the LORD, and there is none else. I form the light, and create darkness: I make peace, and create evil: I the LORD do all these things.*

"Jesus didn't have the option of destroying evil...evil was created by God as he created 'peace'...and what is peace... Jesus, the 'Prince of Peace'. So God created Jesus and evil — Satan, if you prefer — at the same time. It's the original evil twin story. Why? Because all of creation is based on contrasts...the tension of opposites...the laws of physics. All matter is just a mass of vibrating particles...but there could be no vibration without an opposite force to push against."

"But the man called Legion was cured...saved, I suppose," remarked Melton. "In other words, using your theory, Jesus can't destroy evil, but he can save mankind from being dominated by evil...right?"

"Exactly," answered Alexander.

"This gives me the perfect opportunity to play the devil's advocate," Melton replied, chuckling. "How do you explain this to people who do not accept Jesus as the savior of mankind...or don't even believe in God?"

"Even if you reject the soteriological nature of Jesus or even if you're an atheist, the theory still holds, Doc. If evil had no hosts in which to propagate...no virions to spread its toxic effects...it would simply lie dormant and mankind would live a life of peace. But we know that can't happen...without evilness there would be no opposite called goodness. We can count on the weaknesses—the fallibility—of humankind to keep evilness alive and well...one of the lessons in Genesis. All we can hope for is that evilness doesn't become the dominate force."

"O.k., R.A., even if all of this is true, what good is it...how does it help us catch the bad guys or stop evil acts...there ain't no cure for viruses," Zapata interjected sarcastically. "And in this case, I think we all know who the killer is."

"Easy E.Z.," Alexander answered with one of his favorite comebacks to an impatient Zapata, "My theory is about how Virion thinks...not how to save the world...at least not yet. Virion not only believes that he is a part of a greater entity, but that the entity—a human-scale virus—is a purposeful entity...it has a mission. He takes no responsibility for his actions because he is only obeying the virus's genetic code...destroy the host or create another virion to survive. Now that's valuable information."

Doc flicked some ashes out into the street. "Do you think all evil people are aware of this interconnectedness, Richard?"

"Highly unlikely...though some killers believe they have a demon in them."

Zapata's cell phone rang. "Dr. Zapata here...Really? When? Where is he now? Ok, thanks, buddy.

"The Sheriff's department arrested Antoine this morning after seeing the artwork in his studio. He made bail, though... he's not in the slammer, where he ought to be."

Then Alexander's cell phone rang. It was Maggie.

16

Alexander didn't return Maggie's call until he returned to his house. He didn't want to get into an argument in front of the other guys...and even if there wasn't an argument, he wanted to talk to Maggie in privacy. He punched number two on his cell phone and Maggie's phone rang...by the fourth ring he was almost hoping that she wouldn't answer.

"Hey, Rich, what are you doing...are you busy?" Maggie's voice was calm...almost too calm. Was she overdoing the Xanax again, Alexander wondered?

"Hey Maggie, no, I'm not busy...how are you doing?"

"I'm ok...thought I'd go up to Baybrook Mall and just wondered if you needed me...needed me to pick up anything for you."

Alexander carefully pondered his response..."Well, Maggie, I do need you...but I don't need anything from the mall. Are you coming by later? We can go to Di Bella's for dinner."

"Sure. You want to go to the mall with me?"

"Can't do it, Mag, the band is practicing in a little while."

"Oh yeah, the band. I'll be there around seven...ok?" There was a hint of resentment in her voice. Alexander knew what he was in for.

"I'll see you then."

By five-thirty, Alexander had finished with band practice, gone home, and taken a shower. He was excited about seeing

Maggie and hoped that they would get along…and that maybe she would spend the night with him…and that maybe she would move back and they could resume their marriage. They did still love each other. But what about the Muse…?

Around seven that evening, Maggie came by the house and they went out for dinner. Maggie was in good spirits but seemed tired and a little sedated. She had become dependent on anti-anxiety drugs after all of the problems began and both she and Richard had begun drinking too much. She moved into her own place—a condo—to "save their marriage and preserve her sanity." Both of them had stopped drinking excessively, but Maggie was still struggling with what Richard thought was an addiction to Xanax.

They had made reservations at one of their favorite restaurants—Di Bella's, a family owned Italian restaurant on the Island.

"I'll have a rum and coke and just a small plate of spaghetti, Nora," Maggie told the waitress. She fumbled around in her purse and pulled out a small prescription bottle.

Richard bit his tongue…they could fight this battle later. "I'll have a Peroni and the ziti." Looking across the table at Maggie, he almost wanted to cry. He always thought she was a beautiful woman…she reminded him of Ashley Judd in a way. He really missed her. She had always been very considerate and very loving—passionate even—but also very preoccupied with her real estate business.

He couldn't complain about that, though…no one is more preoccupied and consumed with their work than an artist…not to mention a Ph.D. who was constantly researching and writing. In a sense, their preoccupations had given each other space to pursue their careers and interest…but too much space has a way of diminishing intimacy and interdependency…it just doesn't work.

To be perfectly honest, he didn't know how Jeffery—raised

by two workaholic parents—had grown up to be such a great kid.

"How's the real estate business going, Maggie?" Richard asked, munching on a bread stick.

"It's going great, especially on the west end of the Island... every millionaire in Houston—and there's a million of them—wants a million dollar beach house," Maggie answered, laughing. He loved to hear her laugh. Her laugh was a sedative that he had long since been addicted to.

"I guess if you have that much money, you're not worried about hurricanes," Richard quipped.

"Oh, Rich, they don't give a shit about that. They'll just rebuild. Anyway, we don't talk about hurricanes in the real estate business...that's something that happens somewhere else...not on Galveston Island. So, Rich, how's your work going?"

He knew what she meant by "work." "I haven't been painting much lately...or anything else...just mainly doing some research."

"About what? She asked pleasantly enough but with that pry-bar edge to her voice. He didn't want to lie to Maggie, but he wanted to avoid the inevitable argument that would ensue the whole truth and nothing but the truth.

"About the appearance and behavior of certain viruses... something I might use later in a paper." That wasn't really a lie...not really.

Anyway, he was saved by the bell...Maggie's cell phone rang. It was Jeffery just checking in with his mom. He was delighted that his parents were together for the evening. She passed the phone to Richard and he talked with his son a minute.

Their meals came and they ate, laughed, talked about Jeffery, had a few more drinks. It was almost like it had been before the Muse entered their lives.

"Maggie, why don't you stay over tonight? You can come hear the band play tomorrow at the winery."

"O.k. Rich, I was hoping we could get together...I miss you. But I don't know about the band...I have to show a couple of houses tomorrow afternoon."

"That's cool, Maggie," Richard answered, trying desperately to reach across that ever-widening space. "We're not doing any new stuff tomorrow anyway."

After dinner, they drove back to Richard's house. On the drive back, Maggie popped another pill and Richard once again bit his tongue...he wanted desperately for the evening to work out. They got to the house, they got undressed, they got into bed, they kissed passionately, and Maggie immediately fell asleep...more like passed out...a not unfamiliar scenario.

17

The next morning Alexander got up around seven. Maggie was still groggy, but reached over and grabbed his arm.

"I'm sorry honey. Come back to bed after you put the coffee on and I'll make it up to you," she said with a sleepy smile.

"That's the best offer I've had in a while," he answered, smiling back. "I'll be back in a jiffy."

He had the coffee brewing as he walked across two of his neighbor's lawns to fetch his Sunday morning paper. He wouldn't have to take it out of the plastic wrapper, because the Lab pup already did that. Across the street a couple of squirrels were laughing at him from the top of an oak tree, probably telling him that he ought to move like they did.

Back in his kitchen, Alexander wiped the pup's saliva off of the paper with a napkin, unrolled the paper to expose the front page, and almost dropped the whole thing on his coffee cup when he saw the headlines — **Local Psychiatrist Arrested for Murder. Medical Examiner and Psychic Accused of Withholding Evidence.**

"Rich, where did you go?" asked Maggie, walking into the kitchen with a towel wrapped around her. "I thought you were running away or something." She saw Richard standing on the porch talking on his cell phone...she saw the paper laying on the table...she saw the headlines...she read the story, which included Dr. Richard Alexander's psychic abilities and how in the past they have assisted in the arrests of fugitives. The morning quickly went to hell in a hand-basket.

"You lied to me, Richard! You're right back in the middle of this shit and this time you could get arrested and lose your job and have yet another fucking psycho come after all of us!"

"I did not lie to you, Maggie. What I told you was the truth...just not the whole truth. I just wanted us to be together and enjoy each other's company...is that so damn wrong?"

"You damn right that's wrong. You obviously don't give a damn about us or you would stop using that freaky-assed thing of yours!" Maggie screamed as she was throwing on her clothes.

"That freaky-assed thing uses me, goddammit...I can't control it anymore than you can stay off of those fucking drugs!" Richard shouted back. Who's the liar here, Maggie? You tell me every week that you have it under control."

The slamming of the front door ended the argument. As Maggie peeled out in her car, Alexander's cell phone rang. It was Jeffery.

"Hey dad, how are you and mom doing? Did you guys have a good time?"

Alexander was standing on the front porch in his pajamas watching Maggie's car get smaller as it raced down the street. "Well, yes and no, son...yes and no."

The two squirrels in the oak tree across the street were staring silently at Alexander...he sensed their disapproval. Rambo was busily shredding the plastic newspaper wrapper all over the front yard.

18

Later that afternoon Alexander and Zapata met the other guys in their band at Haak Winery in Santa Fe, just west of Texas City. The band, which they named The Third Coast Ghost Band, played there about four times a year as well as in various clubs and private parties. The band had six members...drums, two guitars, a bass, a saxophone, and a lead singer. They played blues, old rock-n-roll, rhythm and blues, and some Cajun music. Besides Alexander, there was Zapata, a chiropractor, a videographer, a retired engineer and an administrator in higher education, his good friend Lanis—a genuine Coon-Ass who also played the harmonica and the Zydeco-style squeeze box. They tried to play about once a month. It was great fun...it was cathartic.

They were playing the last song of the gig—*Stormy Monday*—when Alexander glanced out into the audience and totally screwed up his solo...there sat Dr. Derrick Antoine alone at an outside table. He did not appear to be enjoying the music. When they were through playing, he waived Alexander and Zapata over.

"Those are not my paintings that the bodies were wrapped up in," Antoine began in a desperate whisper, looking around like Dr. Richard Kimble in *The Fugitive*. "They're crude imitations...and my life could be ruined because of them. I am not a murderer!"

"In the first place, how did you know we were out here?"

Zapata asked.

"I called your home and asked for you. Your wife said you were playing in a band out here. No big mystery. We're not enemies, Dr. Zapata...Dr. Alexander...I'm not who you're looking for. It looks like you're in trouble, too. Maybe I can help you, though—not to mention clear my own name. I don't remember selling the paintings that were copied by the killer. In fact, I remember now that I did not sell the one with the orange balls all over it...it just disappeared a few years back.

"I work in series...a lot of the pieces in a series look very similar and I've shown them all over the country. The sheriff's deputies confiscated what few files I kept in my studio yesterday, but my secretary, Rose, has the complete files at her house...it's my Lead Pencil Club version of a back-up. She's going to bring them to me later tonight. If you'd like, we can meet tomorrow morning at my place and try to find out who bought what."

"That's very gracious of you, Derrick," Alexander responded. "I can meet you there...E.Z.?"

"I'll have to check. I may have an autopsy to perform," Zapata answered, being intentionally evasive.

"And you, Richard, my dear fellow artist," added Antoine, "I thought you truly admired my work...yet you were just snooping. How deceitful...I'm very disappointed." Tears were welling up in his eyes. He was being sincere.

"Yeah, well take a number and get in line. The truth is, Derrick, I do admire your work and have the print I bought hanging in my home. But yes, I was snooping. You have to admit...the evidence is very compelling. If it's any consolation at all, I came away thoroughly convinced that you are not the killer. That's why we didn't turn you in immediately."

"And that's why we're in shit up to our necks," Zapata interjected, drawing an imaginary line across his throat with a quick gesture of his hand. "Dr. Alexander operates on a very different plane than the rest of us with his psychic abilities and all, so you'll understand if I'm still a tad skeptical."

"But of course," Antoine answered, rising to his feet. "After all, I am a psychiatrist...I know how people think. I'll be waiting for you tomorrow morning at nine o'clock if you're interested in pursuing the truth." Antoine walked away toward the parking lot.

"E.Z, we need to be there," Alexander said sternly.

"I'll be there," Zapata answered. "I'll pick you up at a quarter to."

Alexander's cell phone rang...it was Maggie.

19

At four the next morning, Alexander was awakened first by the sudden silence of the cicadas, whose late summer chirpings provided a convenient and peaceful white noise for his tinnitus. Then, just as he fell asleep again, he was awakened by the incessant barking of Rambo, the idiot Lab pup that lived next door. At first, it didn't really register through the heavy veil of deep sleep that the barking was unusually close. Then, when it dawned on him, he bolted straight up in bed...the mutt was running back and forth between his bedroom window and the back door.

"How the hell did he get into my back yard?" Alexander muttered to himself as he sat up on the side of his bed in the dark. "If he dug under my fence, I'm going to kill that damn dog."

Resisting the temptation to run out of the back door with a golf club and beat the little asshole to death, Alexander decided to call his neighbor next door to come get his goddamn mutt... after all, turnabout is fair play. Then he heard the pup yelp a painful cry, followed by silence. He figured that his neighbor must have come through the gate, swatted the dog, and carried him off. But he kept the back yard gate locked...how could his neighbor have gotten in...surely, the dog didn't dig that big a hole under the fence.

Just as he decided to lie back down, a noise at the back door sent chills up Alexander's spine. It was the creaking and cracking that extreme pressure against wood makes...like a crowbar wedged in between the door and the doorframe. Quickly, Alexander opened the drawer to his night stand and fumbled around to find the handle of the model 60 Smith and Wesson .357 magnum revolver. He reached over and turned on the lamp.

Stomping over toward the door, he shouted, "Who is it?... you need to know that I have a .357 magnum pointed at the door and I will Dirty Harry your ass in a heartbeat."

He actually had the pistol loaded with .38 special hollow-points. No point in blowing down a wall and killing your neighbors to boot...but the .357 magnum sounded more intimidating.

Silence...then the creaking of a step...then heavy footsteps running around the corner, through the gate, toward the front of the house. Alexander ran to the kitchen and threw back the curtains. He could see no one moving through the twelve foot corridor between the houses.

He ran to the front door, flung it open, and ran out onto the front porch. It was unusually dark outside. No one was in the yard, no one was on the sidewalk, no one was in the street, telling Alexander that the intruder was still somewhere in his or his neighbor's yard.

That's when he noticed that his neighbor's irritating faux gas lamp at the end of the walk was not on...it was always on. There was no unusual vehicle in sight. He thought he heard footsteps in the grass toward the back of the house when a couple of alley cats ran across his neighbor's yard. Had they been spooked by the intruder?

He took a step off of his porch when common sense finally caught up with his adrenaline rush. All he had on his body were his boxer shorts and his pistol—he had no shoes and worse, no flashlight, and he was breaking the cardinal rule of engagement...*Know thine enemy.* Was the intruder still in his back yard? He decided not to go look. Slowly backing up onto the porch, then inside the foyer, Alexander closed and locked the front door.

As he turned around to pick up his phone to call the police he was blinded by a bright light shining in his face. He could barely make out the silhouette of a man standing in front of him...but it was the monster in the blue jumpsuit, he could swear. In a blind panic he raised his pistol toward the figure when the man screamed out and fell to the floor.

"Jesus, Richard, it's me! Your neighbor, Jack! Don't shoot me!"

"Goddammit, Jack!" Alexander screamed back, dropping to his knees and laying the pistol on the floor. "You were a half second away from dead! What the fuck are you doing?"

"I'm sorry, man....I heard Rambo barking and crying and you hollering. I got up to see what was wrong. Someone tore up my light out front. Your gate was busted open and your back door is almost off of its hinges. What the hell is going on?"

By four-thirty, he and Jack were sitting at the kitchen table drinking coffee. Both of them were still shaking. Alexander didn't especially like his neighbor, but he sure as hell didn't want to shoot him...Rambo maybe, but not Jack. In fact, he would have probably received some kind of neighborhood award for shooting Rambo.

"How is Rambo?" Alexander asked.

"I don't know. I couldn't find him. He'll turn up. I know he's a pain in the ass, but he's a really sweet dog," Jack answered, clearly concerned about his Lab pup.

Alexander went over the events that woke him up and Jack did the same. Suddenly something came crashing through the busted back door and both men almost hit the ceiling, spilling coffee all over the table. It was Rambo carrying Alexander's newspaper in his mouth. Before their hearts had a chance to settle down, Alexander's doorbell rang, causing more coffee to be spilled. It was the police.

By the time the police officers made out their report and Jack and Rambo went home, it was six o'clock. Alexander managed to get his back door to shut and lock. He took his shower, but instead of going over the attempted break-in, he thought about Maggie's phone call last evening.

She had apologized for her emotional reaction Sunday morning but not for her stand on things. She loved him, but she was not going to deal with all of the crap that accompanied his exercising his psychic abilities...and she was not going to stand for Jeffery being put into danger.

"My god," thought Alexander, "what if Maggie had been here with me last night...she would already be filing divorce papers." Needless to say, he was not going to share the events of the morning with her...but he was going to get to the truth of it...was it just a routine break-in attempt or is someone after him—again?

20

At eight forty-five sharp, Zapata pulled up to the curb in his Hummer H2 and honked. Alexander slid onto the plush leather seat and they drove off to meet Antoine. Alexander had already called Zapata and told him about the events of the morning.

Zapata was excited. "I think we're on to something here, buddy... we're too close for somebody's comfort...and I think we're about to talk to that somebody," he said, alluding to Antoine. "You got your piece strapped on?"

"Yeah, I got it," answered Alexander, feeling very uncomfortable with carrying his pistol, even though he had a license to carry it. "We're not the cops, E.Z. We need to be careful."

"That's where you're wrong, R.A., technically I am authorized to investigate crime scenes for the county and to carry a weapon, and if you recall, you have a private investigator's license. Antoine invited us to his house to search for evidence...so we are one-hundred percent legal."

As the Hummer turned right off of Postoffice street onto 14th street, Alexander and Zapata were surprised to see the block lined with a parade of police cars and ambulances. Red and blue flashing lights made the whole neighborhood seem surreal. They couldn't find a parking spot in front of Antoine's house, so they parked in front of the Mosquito Café and walked back to Antoine's.

Walking up to Antoine's, they still couldn't determine

where all of the commotion was centered…police and sheriff's deputies were on every other porch talking to residents. When they walked up to Antoine's house, the mystery ended…the front door was open and a couple of investigator's from the sheriff's department walked out.

"Hey, Gene, what's going on?" Zapata asked Sheriff's Investigator, Gene Vincent.

Vincent was tall and thin with one of those gaunt, mean faces that indicated he was always disgruntled and probably constipated. What hair he had behind his receding hairline looked like it had been chopped into a flat-top with a weed-eater. Regardless of the weather, Vincent always wore an expensive sport coat over his tailored slacks. That and his gaudy Rolex and gold chains caused Alexander to wonder how well Galveston County paid these guys.

"E.Z, I was just fixing to call you," Vincent answered, not bothering to acknowledge Alexander. He raised his walkie-talkie to his face, squeezed the button, and said, "Never mind, Zapata and his swami are here.

"Looks like your little shrink buddy got his," Gene quipped, gesturing inside Antoine's house with his thumb. "If you two hadn't sat on the evidence, this probably could have been avoided." He then put his hand on Alexander's chest and told him he'd have to wait outside.

Zapata squared off in front of Gene, got right up in his face (on his tip-toes), and said in a quiet, calm voice, "Quit trying to out-asshole all of your buddies, Gene…Dr. Alexander, my friend who you are disrespecting, saved your sorry ass with that shotgun murder in the Jungle a while back…he showed you who the killer was and you went out and got all the glory when you captured him. So, show a little respect to the man who got you your inspector's shield…we are both going in there, fuck you very much."

Vincent gave them both his meanest look and stepped out

the way. "Have it your way, Zapata…it's your ass on the line…but I want to see a license for the piece your buddy's packing under his Caribbean shirt there."

Alexander pulled out his P.I. license and flashed it in front of Gene, trying hard not to lose his cool. "Like the man said, Gene…fuck you very much."

Zapata and Alexander walked into the large studio and stopped in their tracks. If the neighborhood outside looked surreal, the inside looked like a scene from a Wes Craven movie.

The disco ball that Alexander had noticed during his previous visit was illuminated by a red spot light and was rotating in the middle of the room, sending bizarre, blood-red flashes around the room. All over the room, in every corner and on every surface, candles were burning.

At the far end of the room, beside the large work table, hanging by his neck from a rope thrown over a rafter and tied off onto the printing press, was the very dead body of Derrick Antoine. A small, fold-up ladder was lying on its side on the floor just behind Antoine's body.

As they walked closer, Alexander saw the hand-printed note pinned to the front of Antoine's blood-splattered pajama top…the only thing he was wearing. The note read:

Forgive me my demons
Sometimes the swine must be sacrificed
I'm sorry

Alexander and Zapata looked at each other. "Straight from the Bible verse," Zapata whispered.

On the 4 x 12 foot work table, was the nude body of a young man partially wrapped in what appeared to be one of Antoine's paintings. He had been severely beaten and his throat was cut. Over each eye, was taped a round cut out with the plastic worms glued to them, representing syphilis bacteria, that Antoine had placed over the eyes on the La Trec portraits of prostitutes. They made the whole scene seem even more Cravenesque.

The floor under the table was a pond of blood in which laid a bloody kitchen knife. In the corner where Antoine's bookcases stood, a weeping, middle-aged Hispanic woman was being interviewed by a detective.

Standing toward the foot of the table on the left side and in front of Antoine's body, Alexander and Zapata stared at the scene in silence.

"Jesus, R.A.," Zapata spoke, breaking their silence, "I hate to throw the old 'I told you so' at you...but, mí hermano, I told you so...Antoine was Virion...there swings our serial killer."

Alexander stood silently for a few more seconds, absorbing every detail with his eyes, then whispered to Zapata, "I don't want to risk going into a trance in front of all these people. Can you make sure that the scene stays intact until you and I are the last ones in here?"

Just then, a lieutenant from the CSI division walked up to Zapata. "Sorry, Doc, but you two need to step aside and let us take the body down. We're not through with our examination of the crime scene and you two are polluting it."

"I understand, Lieutenant," answered Zapata, glancing at Alexander. "Just make damn sure that these bodies are in my morgue within the hour, son...and just as they are."

"Yes sir, I'll do my best," the lieutenant responded briskly.

"Goddammit," Alexander muttered under his breath. "The Muse is all over this place, E.Z. I can discover something here... and there are a lot of things wrong with this scene."

"Patience, buddy. This is the best we can do at the moment. Let's go talk to the lady over there...I'll bet it's his secretary, Rose."

Her name was Rose de la Rosa. She was an attractive

Hispanic woman in her fifties, wearing a colorful floor length dress, her hair held up in a bun with a turquoise comb. She wore reading glasses perched on the end of her nose. She was visibly upset. They waited until the detective was finished, walked over to her and introduced themselves.

"Oh, mother of God," she cried, "how could this be? I don't understand any of it." She spoke with a fairly thick Mexican accent. Zapata put his hand on her shoulder and spoke some words of comfort in Spanish.

"Rose," he continued in English, "Dr. Antoine asked Dr. Alexander and me to meet him here this morning to go over some sales records with him. He told us that you would bring them to him last night. Did you do that?"

"Sí, I brought to him the files he wants around eight last night."

"Did you notice anything unusual...was Dr. Antoine upset?" asked Alexander.

"No. He didn't ask me in like usual, but I saw his young friend walking out of the kitchen. He seemed ok. He was happy and laughing."

"Young friend?" asked Zapata. "¿Quién es?...is that his young friend on the table?"

"Sí, el pobre," she answered, tearfully. "But, his young friend was...completamente desnudo."

"Naked?" Asked Zapata.

"Sí, he had no clothes on."

They talked with Rose for about thirty minutes and discovered that Antoine occasionally had "men-friends" over but usually not as young as the victim. They showed Rose a picture of the two canvasses in which the young women victims were wrapped and asked her if they were painted by Antoine. She confirmed that the first one—the one with the orange balls on it—was definitely Antoine's...the second one she didn't recognize.

When Alexander mentioned that Antoine could not remember who had bought the painting with the orange balls, Rose started crying again.

"That's because Dr. Antoine did not sell that painting. His special friend, Dr. Westwood—I called him Dr. Clint—gave it to someone who he said was a mutual friend of theirs. He said it was to be a surprise and that I was not to say anything to Dr. Antoine...he said if I did, he would see that I got sent back to Mexico. But I don't think the man was a mutual friend...he was Dr. Clint's friend more than Dr. Antoine's, if you know what I mean."

They knew what she meant. Zapata asked her if she know who the friend was.

"I don't remember his name, but I have it written down somewhere...he is also a doctor here at UTMB, I think. He is a very large man...a Gringo," she said, stretching her hand as far above her head as she could to demonstrate his height. "But I have something that will help."

"Rose," said Alexander gently, "it is really important that we know who had that painting."

She said that she had kept a copy of an email that Westwood had sent to his friend from Antoine's computer about three years earlier...just in case.

Most of Antoine's files had been confiscated the day before by the Sheriff's department and what were left had been ransacked. Rose said that the sales records she had brought over the night before were missing. But the copy of the email wasn't in Antoine's files—Rose had stuffed it in a copy of Gabriel García Márquez's *One Hundred Years of Solitude*, a book that Antoine had figured would take one hundred years to finish and put it up...so she knew that he would not pick up the book again and find the email. She walked over to one of the bookshelves, squatted down, and plucked the book from the bottom shelf.

"If a book is on the bottom shelf, it will not be read again," she pronounced. "Many secrets can be found on the bottom shelf if you know which book they're in."

Rose pulled the folded sheet of paper from the book and handed it to Alexander. The email message was very revealing, but it gave no name for the recipient. Because Westwood had sent it from Antoine's computer, it read as if Antoine had sent it to a <u>mnilm59@eblast.com</u>.

It read, "Lover, I found the painting that you have been wanting. It's titled *The Face of Aids II*. He has it in storage, so it will not be missed anytime soon. I am expecting a special reward, of course."

Obviously, Westwood had deleted it from Antoine's computer, but he did not realize that Rose could monitor Antoine's business email on her Blackberry. She may have come off like an illiterate immigrant, but she was far from it... Rose was a sharp cookie. The longer she spoke, the less they could detect her obviously feigned strong accent.

"Why did you plant the copy of the email in one of Antoine's books instead of keeping it at your place?" Alexander asked.

"Because, if something happened to me...or I got sent back to Mexico...I have made arrangements that would have let Dr. Antoine know to look in the book for the message. He had a right to know," Rose answered, still sobbing. "If I remember where I wrote the name of Dr. Clint's friend, I promise I will give it to you."

Alexander and Zapata tried to out-wait the police and CSI investigators by visiting with Rose, but eventually the CSI lieutenant approached them and announced that the bodies were on route to the morgue and that everyone had to vacate the premises. Zapata chose not to argue as he watched his partner's face turn red with anger.

Alexander, however, took the cue and protested not...he

knew that they could get back into the house later because when he had visited Antoine on August 22nd and was waiting for Antoine to answer the door, he noticed the head of a key barely protruding over the edge of the transom. Galvestonians often would stick a spare house key up there in spite of the fact that every burglar on the island knew that.

"We need to get back inside that house, E.Z.," Alexander said as they walked back to the Hummer. "That place is rife with clues."

"That's going to be pretty difficult, R.A. They will post a guard or two out here, you know."

"We'll see about that...but here's what I observed. Antoine's feet were almost exactly twenty-six inches off of the floor and his house shoes were on the floor directly under his body."

"So? And how do you know they were exactly twenty-six inches off the floor?" asked Zapata.

"So, first, it's a known fact that when a person hangs himself by standing on a stool and kicking it out from under him, his neck doesn't usually break, he chokes to death and his legs thrash around violently searching for solid ground. Antoine's neck wasn't broken...his face was blue, his tongue was swollen and protruding out of his mouth, indicating asphyxiation. His house shoes would have been kicked a good distance from his body.

Secondly, I know his feet were twenty-six inches off of the floor because while you were talking to the lieutenant, I took out my trusty little tape measure and measured the distance," Alexander answered, pulling a small tape measure from his pocket.

"Thirdly, the little fold-out ladder that he supposedly stood on has a top rung of twenty-seven inches. I know that because I have the exact same ladder and it has the dimensions on the label. Chalmer's Hardware had them on sale last year."

"And what does all this mean, pray tell?"

"Assuming he stood on the top rung, his feet would be twenty-seven inches off of the floor. He was hung with a hemp rope tied in a hangman's noose, which if there was no slack at all in the rope, would have tightened up lowering the body at least six inches and stretched under his weight at least four to six more inches, leaving his feet only fifteen to seventeen inches from the floor...not twenty-six inches.

"And fourthly, there were very light brown skid marks on the floor, the same color as the soles of his house shoes, indicating that he was hoisted up from the floor. My guess is that you'll find a mild sedative in his blood...and probably in his young friend as well.

"What all this means, amigo, is that he didn't hang himself by jumping off of that ladder...I think he was murdered and the killer set it up to look like a murder-suicide. And by the way, I believe Rose is right about the second painting... something about it caught my eye, but I was distracted by the murder. Now I realize what my eyes were telling my brain...I don't think Antoine painted it...it wasn't his touch."

"Wasn't his touch...you know, R.A., we could just walk away and let this case close neatly," Zapata said with an edge of frustration. "The cops will be satisfied, the victims' families will be satisfied, the news media and the community will be satisfied, you and Maggie can get back together, you can get back to your painting...everybody's happy, amigo."

As the words were coming out of his mouth, Zapata knew they were falling on deaf ears...hell, he didn't believe them either—he had witnessed too much working with Alexander to really doubt his friend's intuition, observations, and visions.

"Right...let's go to the morgue and see what Dr. Antoine and his young friend have to say about all this," Zapata sighed as they climbed into the Hummer. "You're always trying to screw up my theories with facts."

21

On the way to the morgue, Zapata suggested that they stop at the El Napalito restaurant and pick up a couple of breakfast burritos to go. Alexander protested, saying that he didn't like eating in the morgue.

"Hey, you eat in your office...what's wrong with my office?" Zapata countered.

"I don't have dead bodies lined up outside my office...and dead bodies have a habit of talking to me, remember? Not very appetizing conversation, I might add," Alexander answered, smiling but not joking.

They agreed to eat in the restaurant and give the EMT guys plenty of time to get the bodies to the morgue. The little Mexican restaurant was a local favorite, patronized by as many gringos as Hispanics...but only in the daytime, for it sat several blocks north of Broadway in the heart of the "jungle," not a place most gringos cared to be after dark.

Everything in the restaurant came from Mexico, from the plastic-laminated tables to the rather garish velvet paintings depicting Mayan-like warriors and half nude Indian women dancing in front of Aztecan edifices and pyramids...artistic license has the authority to mesh cultures and historic periods with myths and legends and set them against surreal airbrushed skies of cobalt blue.

While they were eating and discussing the murder scene and arguing theories, a television in one corner of the room, facing Alexander, had the weather channel on. The meteorologist was pointing to a swirling mass of clouds in the eastern Atlantic, south of the Cape Verde Islands. Alexander found himself trying to divide his attention between the conversation he and Zapata were having and what the meteorologist was so excited about, "...already a tropical depression, could be a tropical storm later today...the thirteenth named storm of this very active hruuicane season... *Michael.*"

If it went into the Caribbean and followed the most likely scenario, it would turn northwest, intensify, fight the upper level westerlies across the Caribbean, get ripped apart by mountains, crawl its way over the Yucatan Peninsula or the western tip of Cuba, and if still intact, try to make its way into the hot waters of the Gulf of Mexico. There it could breathe... there it could grow to its logical conclusion and become everything it could be...a meteorological monster.

Alexander palmed his cup of coffee in response to a sudden chill. *Survival on this planet is a struggle*, he thought, even for a hurricane.

To everything there is a season, a time for every purpose under heaven...that's what the author of Ecclesiastes tells us. That means that there is a purpose on this earth even for monsters—whether of nature or of humankind. There is something to be learned from both, for the wise man loves council while the fool hates instruction.

He was pretty sure that was from the Bible, too...probably Proverbs, but he couldn't remember for sure. Alexander sat as in a stupor, moving his juevos a la Mexicana and refried beans around in a counterclockwise fashion with his fork, listening to Zapata swear once again that Antoine had to have been Virion, when he was suddenly jolted upright by the roof of the restaurant being ripped off above their heads. He was being pelted by shingles, debris, and driving rain...the roar of the wind was deafening.

He looked up at Zapata who along with the other patrons were staring at him as if he had stood up on the table and taken off his clothes.

"R.A., what the hell is the matter with you?" Zapata finally asked in a loud whisper.

"My God, E.Z, I had a terrifying vision...I'll tell you about it later," Alexander finally answered, trying to shake off his trance.

As he raised his coffee cup to his lips, he noticed that the coffee was swirling rapidly in a counterclockwise direction as if it had just been stirred violently.

"I'm afraid this place is in for a really bad time," he added quietly, pushing his plate away and staring up at the TV as the meteorologist was pointing out that the projected path of the storm would place it into the Caribbean in a few days.

22

By eleven thirty that morning, Alexander and Zapata were in the morgue, preparing to examine the bodies of Antoine and his young friend. Blood tests confirmed what Alexander suspected about sedatives. Both sodium pentothal and high levels of alcohol were confirmed.

Alexander sat on a stool out of the way, sketching the bodies and waiting impatiently for Zapata's assistant to make all of the preparations for the autopsies and leave. Finally the assistant finished, asked Dr. Zapata if he needed his assistance during the autopsies, and left the lab when told he would not be needed for the rest of the day.

Alexander hopped off of the stool and walked over by Antoine's body. He lifted up Antoine's left hand and noticed the colored stains of paint or printing ink under his nails. He stood there for a minute or two and then moved over to the next table where the young man's body was laying. The young man's nails were long, elegant, and painted with a clear polish. There was blood under all of them—the results of grabbing his throat after it was slit—but underneath two of the nails on his right hand there appeared to be some type of solid material, greenish colored. Zapata later confirmed that it was a cosmetic material and some skin cells. A thorough examination of both bodies revealed that neither had any such makeup or superficial scratches on them.

"R.A., are you getting anything from these guys?" Zapata

asked.

"Nothing so far," Alexander answered. "The Muse isn't here right now," he added, knowing full well where he could find her, but not about to mention it to Zapata again.

Later that afternoon, after the lab results showed that the substance under the younger man's nails was some kind makeup, Zapata had to admit that a third person may have been involved. They also identified the younger victim as Doug Millsome, twenty eight years old, from Houston. He tended bar at various gay bars. His latest place of employment was a bar in the medical district of Houston called the Rusty Scalpel.

"He could have gotten that makeup under his nails anywhere, R.A.," explained Zapata. "So, it doesn't conclusively prove that someone else was at Antoine's last night...but granted, it was pretty fresh, so we have to keep that possibility open. But come on, amigo, do you really think a woman could have slit the kid's throat and hung Antoine?"

"Who said anything about a woman?" Alexander countered. "You ever hear about metrosexuals...and don't forget, these guys were gay and gay men sometimes wear makeup. Didn't you ever see *The Bird Cage*? Nathan Lane played a drag queen who was always wearing makeup...yes, it was a movie, but it was based on a real lifestyle. Anyway, the makeup under Millsome's nails was dark green...that's more like camouflage paint.

"And that suicide note...it had no punctuation, so it could be read two ways...as Antoine asking us to forgive him for the demons that possessed him — *forgive me my demons* — or as the killer apologizing to his demons because he couldn't pass them on to the 'swine' who he had to sacrifice — *forgive me, my demons.* I'm telling you, E.Z., someone else was there last night and killed them both...and that someone was wearing makeup...and that someone was Virion."

Zapata started putting on his apron and gloves to perform

the autopsies. "R.A., I know you have an inside track to these mysteries, but until you have more conclusive evidence, you can't close your mind to the possibility—the distinct possibility, I might add—that Antoine was Virion, killed his younger lover, then hung himself." The edge to his voice was getting sharper.

"I know that, E.Z., but bear with me a little longer. Did you notice when we walked up to Antoine's house that he had just re-sodded and mulched the flower bed in front of his porch?

"No, not really."

"Well, he had…and the garden gloves and trowel were in a box on the porch, leading me to believe that he did the work himself. He had also lined the bed with mums…fall perennials…they are usually replaced with spring flowers. My point is, that's not the behavior of a suicidal person…that's working for the future. Add to that the fact that he has a new antique table in the foyer and at least three art projects in progress on the easels. He wasn't ready to check out.

"And another thing…did you see one Bible…anywhere? I scanned his book shelves carefully…not a Bible in sight. And Antoine told me that he was not a religious person."

"What's the Bible got to do with it, R.A.? You can find Bible verses on the Internet. He could have had one in his bedroom."

"Hey, you're right…let's go check it out."

"Maybe I can get permission from the CSI guys for us to enter the house tomorrow, but right now they told us it's off limits. Besides, I still think you're blowing the Bible thing out of proportion."

"Perhaps, but the vision I had when Virion slapped me with a worn leather-covered Bible and the red welts it left on my face were the Muse's way of telling me that Virion is a religious man…someone who believes that the Bible is a form of authority…a man who would own a Bible…keep it close to him. Antoine's studio was his sanctuary…he would have kept it there. Don't you see, E.Z.? Virion believes he gets his authority to do evil acts from the Bible."

Zapata snapped his second rubber glove on and picked up a saw. "Look, Bro, draw me a picture of the killer and if it isn't Antoine, we'll go find him...but I'm having a hard time following your theories...at least not to the point of acting on them."

"In time, my friend, you'll get your conclusive evidence," Alexander answered as he left the lab. He knew what he had to do...besides that, he couldn't stomach autopsies.

23

At three o'clock that afternoon, Maggie Alexander was driving her deep-water blue Lexus GX west on state highway 3005, better known as Seawall Boulevard, to Jamaica Beach to show a house to a prospective client who identified himself as Dr. Mark Legion from Houston. Maggie's boss had warned the female agents not to show houses to males by themselves, but all of the other agents were out showing houses or picking up kids from school. So Maggie left a message with Phil, a fellow agent who was also showing a house in Jamaica Beach just a block from the house she was showing. She knew that she should have waited until Phil was finished, but Legion was interested in a $500,000 canal house and sounded rather impatient…and commission on the sale of a house in that range was quite handsome.

The west end of Galveston Island, less than a mile across at some points, used to be ranch land covered with shrub-brush, cactus, cattle and horses, and an oil well here and there. Now it was heavily developed with beach houses, canal houses, resort centers, palm trees, and multi-million dollar ranchettes all the way out to San Luis pass, the far west tip of the Island…mostly playland for the Houston wealthy. The threat of hurricanes seemed to be a myth as million dollar beach homes sprang up like crawdad mounds in a Louisiana rice field.

Maggie cruised past Pirates Beach and the Texas State Park, and arrived in Jamaica Beach, turning right on Bob Smith Road.

To her left and on the west side of a barbed wire fence (so typical of Texas) were undeveloped wetlands, a beautiful bird sanctuary that the Jamaica Beach residents prayed would never be developed. Prayer is powerful...but so is the promise of profit. *Beaches and wetlands are here for a purpose*, Maggie thought— *the renewal of life cycles including that of humans.* As odd as it might seem for a real estate agent to be against development, Maggie knew that there was a line that humans shouldn't cross, less it becomes self-destructive...push nature too far and she will push back ten-fold.

Turning right on Pelican Drive, Maggie spotted the three-story canal house on the main canal that she was to show. Parked in front of the house was a dark blue Ford van. Maggie noticed that it was a rental.

"Dr. Legion?" Maggie asked as the large man stepped out of the van. He was wearing a Hawaiian shirt over light khaki trousers and sandals. A pair of dark shades hid his eyes and a straw fedora covered his head. Maggie, exercising the special training that all of the agents in her company had to go through to memorize not just the names, but also the physical details and faces of prospective clients, noted that Dr. Legion was between six-four and six-six, and weighed around two hundred and eighty pounds.

"Mrs. Alexander, I presume," he answered smiling broadly and taking off his hat to expose a balding head with obviously died black hair flowing back on both sides of his head. For a man of his size, Maggie thought that his voice was somewhat effeminate...maybe something only a woman would notice. His face seemed rather long because of his bare forehead that was beaded with sweat and the jet-black mustache made his pale skin look pasty. He held a handkerchief in one hand with which he repeatedly mopped his face and forehead.

"Please, call me Mag...," she started to reply as she held out her hand.

"What a magnificent place," he blurted out, interrupting her introduction as he started walking toward the front door, pretending that he didn't notice her attempt to shake hands. "I must say, I didn't realize it was this large…hard to tell from the pictures," he continued. "I live alone, you know, so I'm probably dreaming way past my needs."

"Well, as the ad says, it's only thirty-two hundred square feet, Dr. Legion. I think the oversized lot and the two-car garage makes it seem a lot larger," Maggie replied, deciding that it wasn't rudeness but excitement that caused him to ignore her outstretched hand.

"Let's walk around and let me show you the exterior," Maggie suggested, stalling a bit to give Phil a chance to get there. "The back deck is fab…"

"Can we see the inside now?" Legion interrupted once again. "I have to be in Houston shortly."

"Certainly, Dr. Legion," Maggie answered.

All of these precautions are silly anyway, she thought. *Phil will get here shortly.*

She briefly entertained the notion of pulling her cell phone from her purse and giving Phil a call, but then didn't want to risk insulting her client…he seemed harmless enough. She unlocked the lockbox and the front door and entered the foyer in front of Legion.

As they walked in, Legion reached back under his shirt and unzipped a small leather bag that was in his back pocket. While Maggie was walking through the living room toward the kitchen and pointing out all of the features, Legion quickly pulled a syringe from the bag and hid it in the palm of his right hand, which he slid inside of his front trousers pocket.

"That's odd," Maggie said suddenly, walking over to a window in the breakfast area that looked out onto the deck. "This window has been forced open…the screen is all bent up. Kids, I guess. Let's make sure there's been no vandalism as we walk around."

"Absolutely," Legion responded. "Perhaps we should call the police."

"No, everything looks ok down here. I'll report it when I get back to the office," Maggie said.

"Whatever you think is best. Tell me, Maggie, is there a powder room or a full sized bathroom down here?" Legion asked. "I can't abide those small, cramped powder rooms."

"Then you'll be glad to know that there is a full sized bathroom right down the hallway here." Maggie walked over to the bathroom door and opened it.

"What in the world is this?" She asked, half laughing.

Lying in the middle of the floor was a large, black plastic bag, about six feet long and two feet wide. It had a zipper all the way down the middle. It was unzipped. As she stood there trying to figure it out, she was suddenly aware that Legion was standing directly behind her.

Legion had the syringe out of his pocket, flicked off the plastic needle cover with his thumb and focused on Maggie's neck where her carotid artery would be. As he reached out to cover her mouth with his left hand and raised the needle toward her neck, the front door opened. He quickly stepped back and jammed his hand back into his pocket as Phil yelled out.

"Hello...Maggie. Don't sell this gorgeous place...I want it for myself."

"Phil, come here and look at this," Maggie hollered.

Phil walked briskly over to Legion, his hand outstretched, and boisterously introduced himself. "Phil Neederman, West End Realty."

Legion's right hand was in his pocket, cradling the syringe. He backed up a step and covered a fake cough with his left hand. "Sorry, don't mean to be rude...seems I may have a little bug. Occupational hazard, I'm afraid."

"Really?" Phil snapped back. "What do you do, Mr....?"

"Doctor...Doctor Mark Legion. I'm, uh, an epidemiologist...I work with all kinds of bugs," Legion answered evasively. "Listen, I have to leave. I'm afraid I'm not interested in this place, Mrs. Alexander...too many weird things going on here...anyway, it's far too big for me." He walked hurriedly toward the front door.

"So, Dr. Legion," Phil asked loudly, "Are you with UTMB? I have a smaller canal home just a block away. Be glad to call you...or Maggie can."

Legion muttered, "No, I work in Houston," as he exited the house.

"That's one weird duck, Maggie," Phil said, laughing as the front door slammed shut.

"Phil, look at this...what is this?" Maggie asked, pointing to the large plastic bag.

Phil stepped over to the bathroom door and peered in. "My God, Maggie...that's a body bag. What the hell is that doing here? And look...on the mirror!"

24

The man who identified himself as Dr. Mark Legion turned left off of Bob Smith Road onto highway 3005 and drove his rented Ford van back toward Galveston. He was sweating so profusely that the fake mustache began sliding off of his upper lip, so he yanked it off of his face and stuffed it in his shirt pocket. He slammed his huge fists down on the steering wheel repeatedly as he furiously talked to himself.

"Goddammit, goddammit, goddammit! You fucked it up, Lee. Hey, I couldn't have known that asshole was going to show up. You didn't plan ahead for that contingency. I planned everything to a T...I broke in the patio window early this morning and planted the body bag. I was going to knock her out with a shot of sodium pentothal, zip her up in the body bag, roll that up in the foyer carpet and carry her out to the van. I left a message on the mirror. But why bother...everyone thinks Antoine was Virion. No...not everyone...not Alexander with that fucking gift of his...he knows...I have to get rid of him...she was going to be the bait...he'd come after her and I'd kill them both. You should have killed him last night after you dispatched Antoine and that little whore...you were right there at his back door, but you botched that up, too. Now you've let us all down...the brotherhood...they can trace everything to you. Hell no they can't. Yes they can! Maggie can identify you. She met a Dr. Legion who has long black hair and a black mustache, she doesn't know what I look like. Right, the town is full of six foot six, two hundred and eighty pound men. They'll find out about us...what we are...how to destroy us! No they won't...they can't connect me with any of this...not the body bag, not Clint, not Antoine...nothing! Nothing except for a small, goddamn little Mexican problem...Rose! Rose is nothing more than a mosquito...she will get swatted tonight! But you had to go and leave all those clues like some fucking amateur... the Bible verses for God's sake! Not clues! Not clues! They are my authority! They are clues to Alexander you moron! He will figure it out...he already has. No, he may have me figured out, but he doesn't know what he is dealing with...what humankind is dealing with...they've never known and they never will. Even Jesus knew he couldn't deal with us because God the Father sent us. God the Father calls us Satan and is getting ready to cast us all into the lake of fire, you ignorant bastard! Yes! But until then, we have work to do. God created evil as he created good...we have a purpose here...we are the virions of evil. Why do you think God created viruses with no brains, no hearts, no will? We just replicate and destroy! That's what we do! We do what we're programmed to do! I've killed many, but they don't know that...they only know of the last three because I've let them know because they need to know they need to know they need to know...they...I...need for them to know...I am the left hand of God...I am...we are His sword. Evilness is His sword...evilness is his...virus. God wants them to know. Otherwise, why would he have us do this? Why?

25

While Alexander waited impatiently for darkness to fall, he got on the internet to find the owner of the email address Rose had given them...mnilm59@eblast.com. It was no longer a valid email address according to the several sources he checked. When he tried to send an email to that address, it bounced back. Then he thought how foolish that would have been to give Virion his email address.

Around 10:30, he hopped in his Chevy Tahoe and drove the few blocks over to the Mosquito Café. He parked in the back and started walking down 14th street toward Antoine's house. As he walked, he pulled a Houston Astros cap down low over his forehead, hoping that would adequately disguise him from any law enforcement types that might still be hanging around...especially that thug, Vincent.

The house was dark and there were no vehicles parked directly in front. As he passed in front of Antoine's house, Alexander carefully surveyed the cars parked on the other side of the street...no one was inside any of them. The crime scene tape was still wrapped around the front porch and the porch light was off.

He casually walked to the end of the block, turned right and walked to the alley that ran behind Antoine's house, figuring that the odds of being spotted were a lot less if he entered through the back. He spotted a white Ford van parked on the side street but paid it no mind because it had some kind of commercial plumbing sign on the door. Walking down the dark alley, Alexander counted off the houses and stopped behind the third one—Antoine's.

He was pleasantly surprised that the back gate was not only unlocked, but jarred open. This alleviated his concern that he would have to climb over the fence and possibly make a lot of noise...or worse, break a frigging bone. The gate creaked as it opened and the neighbor's dog barked a couple of times. It was dark as hell and Alexander crept slowly toward the back porch.

Suddenly, out of the corner of his right eye, he thought he saw someone standing in the yard. "Crap," he said beneath his breath as his foot hit a landscape timber and he fell to the ground, landing on his hands and knees. He could smell the fresh mulch...some kind of garden. He pulled a small metal flashlight from his back pocket and pointed it toward the figure. To his great relief, it was some kind of statue. He quickly shut off the light, got to his feet, and cautiously moved forward, feeling like some Chevy Chase character.

Finally, he arrived at the back steps and walked up to the screen door, every wooden step protesting with a creak beneath his feet. The neighbor's dog barked again. He reached inside a rear pants pocket and pulled out an Italian switchblade that he had ordered from some macho mercenary magazine years earlier to use as a fishing knife. Figuring that he would have to cut the screen and pry up the door latch, he punched the button and the blade sprang open with a solid 'clack'. He grabbed the door handle. Another surprise...the screen door was unlocked...the screen was already torn open. Folding the stiletto blade back into the handle, he walked over to the back door of the house and grabbed the door knob. "Shit!" he uttered beneath his breath. After all this, the door was locked. Remembering the key that he saw above the front door, he reach up and felt along the transom. Pay dirt! He grabbed the key, jabbed it into the deadbolt lock after a couple of tries, and flicked it open.

Once inside the cave-dark house, he fetched the small flashlight from his pocket and discovered that he was in the kitchen. He instantly felt the presence of the muse.

I knew she was waiting here for me, he thought as he cautiously crept through the kitchen, keeping the beam of the flashlight low.

Reaching the island, he placed his hand on the counter top while he surveyed a path into the large studio room. Feeling some metal objects, he shined the light on them to reveal a set of keys. An oval tag attached to the chain had the name ROSE etched into it. "That's odd," he thought, "Rose must have left her keys here this morning...wonder how she got home."

Still trying to keep the light down to the bare minimum, Alexander spotted the door, turned off the flashlight, and felt his way over. The door between the kitchen and the studio was a double swinging door like a lot of restaurants had. There was a stainless steel plate on both sides that one pushed against instead of door handles and a glass panel on each door. The plate seemed uncharacteristically cold to his touch compared to the tepid temperature in the kitchen and it sent a chill up his spine...it was trying to warn him. He quietly pushed his way into the studio.

The large studio was not quite as dark as the kitchen because of ample windows that let in the ambient light from outside. Antoine's etching press was to his right and the long work table on which Doug Millsome's body was laying was to his left.

A prickly chill ran up his spine again as he thought he heard the floor creaking somewhere...maybe upstairs...maybe the stairway...maybe the front porch. He froze in his tracks for a good sixty seconds listening, his eyes fixed on the oval glass window toward the top of the front door. Nothing...no more creaking...no one on the porch.

He began feeling very vulnerable and wished that he had worn some kind of black ninja outfit and had dark camouflage makeup on his face like the commandos in movies. Actually, he wished the hell he hadn't come there...but he knew he had to. Alexander ever so slowly crept toward the work table.

Whap! Something slapped him in the face. He almost fell backwards and barely managed to keep from yelling. Reaching up, he felt the noose on which Antoine had been hanging and grabbed hold of it to break his fall.

"Crap," he muttered while trying to catch his breath.

The Muse began working on him as he held onto the noose. The spiritual energy was so violent he felt like he was being electrocuted. Releasing the noose, he staggered over and leaned against the work table. The evil energy kept jolting his body as violent visions of the large man—the monster in the blue jump suit—Virion—kept firing off through his brain cells. Virion was slitting the younger man's throat and hoisting a sedated Antoine up with the noose around his neck.

Then suddenly, as if a breaker blew, the visions and the violent energy stopped, leaving Alexander leaning against the table, exhausted and in a calm trance. He reached behind his back and extracted a small sketchbook that he had wedged in the waistband of his trousers and took his mechanical pencil out of his shirt pocket. Holding the small flashlight in his mouth, he opened the sketchbook to a blank page and began reading the white surface as if it was a page out of a novel.

Gradually, a dark shape would appear, and then another and another until Alexander could see the blurry details of a face emerging on the paper...not all at once, but a shadow here and a shadow there. The dark patches would come and go, fading out only to reappear a few seconds later so that he could never see an entire face until he finished drawing it on the page. The panic he always felt during this process was the fear that a shape would fade away before he could draw it and never reappear.

As he began quickly hatching over the shadows, he realized that he was drawing a furiously furrowed brow over the most evil eye he had ever seen. As often happened during these trances, a song began playing in his mind, as if he had a set of headphones over his ears—this time it was the Rolling Stones' *Sympathy for the Devil*. It, too, should have been a warning.

Lurking in the shadows of the foyer between the staircase and the front door was the man who had earlier told Maggie Alexander his name was Dr. Mark Legion—the man whose intention it had been to sedate and abduct Maggie in order to get his hands on Richard Alexander. He was watching Alexander in the dim reflection of the oval front door window. His hands were sweating inside the latex gloves and he could not believe his good fortune.

Lord, you've delivered him to me.

Please allow me to introduce myself, I'm a man of wealth and taste.

He ever so slowly took a step toward the center of the room where he could see Alexander and the floor board creaked again.

I've been around for a long, long year, Stole many a man's soul and faith.

Freezing in his tracks and keeping his eyes on Alexander, the dim light outlining his distorted face, he resembled Rodin's statue of Balzac.

And I was around when Jesus Christ had his moment of doubt and pain.

Alexander had his back toward the front door and Legion, working at the end of the long table. But he did not look up...in his trance, as he hurriedly drew in his sketchbook, he was oblivious to Legion's presence.

Made damn sure that Pilate washed his hands and sealed his fate.

Legion took another step and as he released his weight off of the creaking board, it creaked even louder. No reaction from Alexander. Legion kneeled down and untied his tennis shoes and quietly slipped out of them. Sliding his feet along the slick oak floor, his thick athletic socks made only a slight hissing sound—barely audible to him and not registering with Alexander at all.

When about three feet behind Alexander, Legion lunged and wrapped his huge, sweaty right arm around Alexander's neck in a classic sleeper hold and lifted him off of the floor.

Pleased to meet you, Hope you guess my name!

Alexander came out of his trance kicking and squirming. He was in serious trouble. The blood was being shut off from his brain and his ears began buzzing. He couldn't breathe. In desperation, he grabbed his mechanical pencil with his left hand like an ice pick and plunged the tip of it deep into Legion's right triceps. Legion grunted and barely loosened the hold around Alexander's neck. With Legion sweating profusely, that was enough for Alexander to slip out of the death grip.

As Alexander's feet hit the floor, he whirled around just in time to catch a massive fist square on his forehead. His feet flew out from under him and he landed on his rear, sliding back until he hit the kitchen wall.

Dazed and fighting desperately to keep his consciousness, Alexander realized that his flashlight was still on and laying on the floor about a foot to his left. He snatched up the light and pointed it at the figure looming over him, wishing to God that he it was his pistol instead...the pistol he was licensed to carry...the pistol that he hated to carry and that was tucked safely away in his bed stand...the pistol that could have guaranteed he would survive this ordeal.

For a second, he thought he was having another vision...it was *him*...the monster in the blue jumpsuit...it was *Virion*! But Virion *was* wearing dark green camouflage paint on his face with a cap pulled down low over his forehead and Alexander couldn't make out any details, especially given his blunt-force-trauma-induced blurred vision. But this wasn't a vision... because visions don't continue to kick the crap out of you... they tend to fade away, and Virion wasn't going anywhere — that was pretty clear by now — until he was through with Alexander.

Virion pulled the pencil out of his right arm and threw it at Alexander, who dodged as it hit the wall beside his head with such a force that it flew into several pieces. Then Virion unsnapped a holster on his belt and pulled out a large folding knife. He slung it open with a flick of his wrist. By then, he was standing almost over Alexander's feet and reaching down to grab Alexander by the hair.

Alexander, still dizzy from the blow, came to his senses enough to dive under the work table, out of Virion's reach. He knew that the table's metal legs were bolted to the floor for stability, so it couldn't easily be moved. As he made his move, Virion made a lunge at him with the knife and sliced into Alexander's right shoulder, causing him to scream in pain.

Once under the table, Alexander remembered he had his switchblade in his back pocket. He thought to himself that he would be a fool to get into a knife fight with a giant maniac, but what the hell did he have to lose...it could buy him a little time. Alexander kept the light on Virion's legs to determine where he was...which was right at the side of the table, trying to kick the shit out of him. Alexander grabbed the switchblade and flicked it open. As Virion kicked at him again, Alexander sliced across his shinbone, causing Virion to curse and stumble back a ways.

For a second, all was quiet. Alexander felt the blood running down his arm and soaking his shirt, but didn't dare turn his attention to it...he knew there were no major veins or arteries involved...but it hurt like hell.

Alexander thought that it was almost comical that the two haven't even said anything to each other. But both of them knew why what was happening was happening. Dialog just didn't seem apropos. Alexander felt panic well up in his chest as he shined the light around but couldn't locate Virion. He did see fresh blood on the floor, so he knew he did some damage.

There! he thought...someone moved past the window in the front of the room!

Just as he was wondering if Virion was about to exit the front door, he heard heavy footsteps running toward the table and a guttural growl. Virion grabbed the edge of the table and lifted it up, ripping the bolts out of the floor. He threw the table over on its side, leaving Alexander exposed. Alexander instinctively struck out with his knife, but Virion kicked his hand so violently that the knife went flying. He grabbed Alexander by his hair and raised his knife to plunge it into his neck when the front door was flung open and a beam of light shown on both of them.

"Drop it!" shouted Zapata, pointing his flashlight and his Glock at Virion. "Step back and put your hands in the air!"

Virion let go of Alexander, turned to face Zapata, then with surprising speed flung his knife at Zapata. Before Zapata could react, the knife struck his flashlight, knocking it out of his hand and shattering the lens. Startled, Zapata also dropped his pistol and dove down to the floor to retrieve it. When he got back up, Alexander was still sitting on the floor, frantically shining his light around the room to locate Virion.

"E.Z., turn on the light by the front door!" Alexander hollered hoarsely. "Hurry...this bastard is quick!"

Zapata found the light switch and slapped at it. The room filled with light, but the disco ball with the red spotlight on it also came on, the circling blood-red dots creating a house of horrors effect. Zapata noticed that he had slapped up all three switches, turning on the main lights in the room, the disco ball, and the porch light. He turned everything off but the main room lights.

Virion was nowhere to be seen. The dog next door was barking steadily now, indicating to Alexander that Virion had left out of the back door and was probably halfway down the alley...at least he hoped so. He knew that he was in no shape to go running after him or to confront him again.

Back in possession of his pistol, Zapata ran to the kitchen door only to see that the back door was wide open. Hurrying over to the back door, he noticed a couple of light switches and slapped them up. Along with the kitchen light, a series of outside lights that looked like Japanese lanterns came on. No one was in the yard and the back gate was jarred open. There was a third switch beneath the others and he flicked it on, only so see colored lights come on in a round, concrete fountain. In the center of the fountain was the statue of a male figure, much like a Greek Kouros figure. Water began streaming out from its plaster penis. Zapata quickly shut off the fountain, shaking his head in disbelief.

26

"He's long gone. Just a statue pissing in the back yard," Zapata said as he rushed over to his friend who was trying to stagger to his feet. "Here, let me help you...you ok, buddy?"

"No, I'm not ok...that big asshole beat the crap out of me and sliced my arm open...almost broke my neck...I probably have a concussion," he complained, feeling the goose egg that was now swelling up on his forehead.

"Are you cut anywhere else...did he stick you?"

"No, I don't think so...but I stuck him and cut him good. He'll think twice before he picks a knife fight with me again," Alexander said, trying to laugh, but now feeling the kicks he took to his ribs and hip.

"You must have...there's a pretty good trail of blood leading out to the back porch. Who do you think that was?" Zapata asked, tearing Alexander's shirt open to inspect the cut...fortunately, it wasn't very deep.

"We both know who that was, bro...it was Virion...the asshole in the blue jumpsuit who slapped me around in a vision damned near killed me in here tonight."

"You're the asshole, R.A. You had no business coming in here...but I just knew that you would...and lucky for you, when I couldn't find you at the house, I knew immediately where you were."

"Well, so did Virion," Alexander retorted, limping into the kitchen and sitting down at Antoine's café-style breakfast table covered with a red checkered tablecloth. He grabbed a cup towel hanging on the back of the chair and wrapped it around his arm.

"That wasn't Virion...Antoine was Virion and he's dead," Zapata snapped back, clearly irritated with his friend. "The lab confirmed his prints were all over the knife that he used to kill Doug Millsome."

"I know who the hell that was, E.Z...he's the devil straight out of my vision who calls himself Virion...and he was wearing dark green camouflage paint on his face!"

"I don't give a shit if it was Elvis in drag...if you hadn't been in here, he wouldn't have attacked you, and the crime scene in there would not be totally fucked up! Our buddy, Gene, will be only too happy to arrest your ass! Maybe they'll let you paint in prison!"

"Listen," Alexander protested as he slammed his hand down on the table. He looked at his hand...it was wet with warm, pink colored water...and the middle of the tablecloth was soaking wet. Then he noticed rose-colored drops from the ceiling beginning to hit the tablecloth in a steady stream.

"What the hell is this?"

"It's coming from upstairs," Zapata answered with a puzzled look on his face. "Come on, 'Mack the Knife,' let's check this out."

As irritated as he was getting with him, Alexander had to smile at the jab and managed to limp up the stairs behind Zapata. As soon as they reached the landing, they could hear water running in the bathroom down the hall. Zapata reached the door first and turned on the bathroom light.

"Holy Jesus!" Exclaimed Zapata. "Is that who I think it is?"

"It's Rose, isn't it?" Alexander hollered, still hobbling up to the door.

A woman was lying fully clothed in the old-fashioned, claw-footed tub with only the top of her head above the blood-red water. The hot water was running, about half open. Zapata reached into a rear pants pocket, pulled out a pair of latex gloves, slid them over his hands making the characteristic slapping sounds, and turned off the water. Placing his hands on both sides of the woman's head, he pulled her up so that her face was out of the water.

It certainly looked like Rose de la Rosa, but she had been badly beaten. Her eyes were half open, her lips were blue, and there was a nasty knife wound on the right side of her throat that Zapata figured severed her jugulars and the right carotid artery.

"Don't touch anything, R.A.," Zapata said firmly as Alexander walked over to the tub. "How did you know it was Rose…dammit, R.A., you're going to be a primary suspect in this if we don't start thinking on our feet here."

"I saw her keys on the kitchen island when I first came in. I thought she had left them this morning. She told us that she lived within walking distance of here. Besides, E.Z., you saw the killer attacking me."

"I saw someone attacking you…we can't prove that he killed Rose."

"His knife…didn't he throw it at you? There's our proof," Alexander replied.

"Do you mean this knife?" Gene Vincent, the inspector from the sheriff's office asked, standing in the doorway and scaring the life out of Zapata and Alexander. He was holding up Alexander's switchblade in an evidence bag.

"Jesus, Gene!" Zapata shouted. "Sneaking around like that is a good way to get your ass shot."

"Sneaking around a restricted crime scene is another good way to get shot Zapata.

"My, my…what do we have here?" Vincent asked, spotting the body in the tub. "This place is a regular slaughter house … bodies popping up all over the place. I got an anonymous phone tip ten minutes ago from a guy who said he witnessed Alexander arguing with Ms. De la Rosa in Antoine's house… said that Alexander paid him to shut her up, but he chickened out and left. I'm afraid that the good Dr. Alexander is under arrest."

"That's a crock of shit, Vincent. Alexander was with me," Zapata lied. "We came here together after Rose called me at the house saying that she wanted to show us some evidence that would exonerate Antoine. I stopped by and picked up Dr. Alexander because she wanted to show both of us. Do you see another car out there?"

Inspector Vincent's face was screwed up into snarl of doubt. "And then what, Zapata…the lady proceeded to tear the place up downstairs, stab herself in the throat, drop the knife, run up here and jump into a tub of water before you and your buddy could stop her?"

"Don't be a fucking jerk, Gene," Zapata answered. "Rose was dead by the time we got here. We came in the front door and saw the kitchen light on where Rose told us to meet her. We went to the kitchen, saw the water leaking from the ceiling…I ran up to check it out and while I was up there, the murderer, who was hiding downstairs, attacked Richard and almost killed him before I got back down and scared him off. That's why the place is torn up. Look at him, he got sliced up himself," Zapata insisted, pointing at Alexander, who did look like someone who just took on a gang of Hell's Angels.

"So, this is the knife that the alleged murder cut you with?" Vincent asked, once again hold up Alexander's switchblade.

"No…that's my knife," Alexander answered, "it's a, uh, fishing knife. Fortunately, I had left it in these pants."

Now Alexander was lying and he wasn't very good at it.

"At least I had something to defend myself with. You'll find the killer's blood on the blade because I cut his leg."

"Right," Vincent retorted sarcastically, "or maybe Ms. De la

Rosa's blood. "

"Gene," Zapata interrupted, "the killer had his own knife. He threw it at me and I blocked it with my flashlight. It ought to be downstairs by the front door somewhere. He left his tennis shoes there, too."

"You don't say?" Vincent replied, maintaining a constant level of sarcasm. He grabbed the two-way radio that was clipped to his belt and told the deputies downstairs to find the knife and shoes.

"No knife, no shoes down here, boss," came the answer across Vincent's radio after a minute. "Just a busted up flashlight on the floor."

"So, I catch you trespassing in a crime scene, with a dead body, and an illegal weapon, and a witness who said you hired him to 'shut Rose up' and who saw you and her arguing, and that ain't enough to haul your ass in?" Vincent asked Alexander, almost smiling.

"Gene...hello...I told you he was with me and I told you what went down," Zapata said loudly, losing his patience. "The freaking phone caller is the freaking killer. Why don't you try to find out where the call came from?"

"Don't worry about it, buddy, we're working on it...and I'll also be looking into the call you got from Rose, here. Now the both of you get the hell out of my crime scene and stay the hell out...and stay where I can reach you, Alexander. You and I aren't done. Get the fuck out of my sight!"

Alexander and Zapata left the bathroom and walked back toward the stairs as the crime scene crew was coming up. When they reached the bottom of the stairs, Zapata reached for the front door but Alexander walked briskly over to the where the work table was laying on its side.

"R.A.!" Zapata whispered loudly. "What the hell are you doing?"

"My sketchbook!" Alexander whispered back, searching

the area around the table, but not seeing it.

Reaching Antoine's small office area, he noticed that the file cabinet had been totally ransacked since the morning. Glancing around the floor, he saw that his sketchbook had slid all the way over against one of the bookcases. He kneeled down to pick it up and something caught his eye.

Directly above his sketchbook, on the bottom shelf of the book case where Rose had hidden her information earlier, was a book, the title of which almost glowed with a neon brashness. He snatched it off the shelf, and stuffed it under his shirt.

27

"You lied for me back there, amigo. I've never known you to lie, except when we play golf," Alexander said as they drove away from Antoine's house in Zapata's Hummer. "I owe you big time for that and for scaring off Virion before I wound up like Rose."

"Well, I wasn't lying about Rose calling me. She called around 10:20 tonight."

"Well, when were you going to tell me that?" asked Alexander grimacing from the pain in his arm.

"Just as soon as I got through chewing your ass out for being in that house on your own. She called to tell me to come in through the back door and she would meet me in the kitchen."

"What...what the hell are you talking about?"

"My words exactly...she thought that I had called her earlier asking her for more information about who Westwood had given Antoine's painting to. I told her I hadn't called and she said well, maybe it was you...she sounded very confused and upset. She said if we met her at Antoine's she would give us the information. I told her to stay put and not go to Antoine's, but she said she was already there...then her phone went dead. That's when I went to pick you up...I called you about six times."

"Crap! I didn't have my cell phone with me," Alexander said. "My car is parked at the Mosquito Café, by the way."

"Uh uh...someone is tailing us. We're going straight to your place just as if I had picked you up, like I told Vincent."

Alexander violently leafed through his sketchbook and suddenly cursed out loud. "Goddammit! It's gone...torn out! He came back in there, E.Z. while we were upstairs!

"What are you talking about?"

"I was drawing a sketch of the killer...the Muse was showing me...I was drawing when that asshole grabbed me. Now it's gone...he came back in the house and tore the drawing out of my sketchbook. That's why the cops didn't find his knife or shoes...he took them."

"Sonofabitch!" declared Zapata. "That sucker has some balls!"

"That sucker has some balls," repeated Alexander, "and he is a very smart and a very dangerous animal."

"Well, amigo, they'll take her body to the morgue. Maybe you can do a drawing of the killer there."

The black Hummer pulled into Alexander's driveway and Zapata immediately turned the headlights off so that someone driving by could not tell if Alexander's car was also in the driveway. Five seconds later a dark-grey Ford Crown Victoria slowly passed by.

"One of Vincent's deputies," said Zapata, peering into the rearview mirror. "I recognize the car."

28

Inside Alexander's kitchen, he laid the book that he took from Antoine's bookcase on the table. They opened a couple of cold beers and sat down. It was now 1:00 A.M. on Tuesday, August 26th, but both men were too keyed up to be tired. They stared at the book. It was Umberto Eco's *The Name of the Rose*.

"So tell me amigo, why did you take this book?" asked Zapata.

"It told me to."

"Oh...silly me," Zapata replied, sarcastically, "I should have known.

"Plus, the name...it's a dead give-away...The Name of the Rose...Rose. It just made perfect sense to me."

Alexander picked it up, held it by its binding with the front of the pages toward the table and gently drew his fingers across the pages, separating them as if he expected something to fall out. Nothing fell out.

"Brilliant author, brilliant story...very tedious reading...the details clog one's mind, like Eco is want to do," Alexander recited, like a bored reviewer as he kept watching for something to fall out.

Still nothing. Laying the book on its back, he flipped through the pages and found what he was looking for almost at the very end of the book. Rose had scotch-taped four folded sheets of paper to the top left margin of page 476, cut to the exact size of the book pages. The pages were type-written on both sides. Alexander carefully removed the sheets.

The letter was addressed to "whom it concerns" and was dated January 15, 2007. Rose had written a full account of what happened to Leann Muñoz, Antoine's role in Leann's disappearance, and her own role in the cover-up. The letter explained that Antoine had confessed the details to her. According to Doc Melton's account, January of 2007 would have been about a month after Clint Westwood died and Leann Muñoz disappeared.

Alexander read the letter out loud. Leann Muñoz had been a beautiful young Hispanic woman—a licensed vocational nurse who had worked in an AIDS clinic and also as a lab assistant for Dr. Ali "Clint" Westwood. Muñoz had contracted the HIV virus by being careless with needles while injecting AIDS patients. Apparently, she failed to share this information with Westwood, fearing that she would lose him and her job as his lab assistant. Westwood was gay, but like a saloon door, he swung both ways. He always had an eye out for attractive young women and Muñoz hoped that the cure for his homosexuality lay between her thighs.

Westwood and Antoine had been lovers for several years and Antoine did not know about the heterosexual affairs of his partner…that is until Westwood discovered that he was infected with the HIV virus and confessed all to Antoine.

Antoine was furious with Westwood and fearful that he might have been infected, too. If he was, Rose never knew it. But what she did know was that unbeknownst to Antoine, Westwood also had another male lover. That's who Westwood gave Antoine's painting to.

Around the first of December in 2006, Westwood fell out with what appeared to be a hemorrhagic fever. The autopsy later proved that the infection was due to an unknown strain of staphylococcus that did not respond to any antibiotic. He suffered from horrendous pain and constantly threw up blood.

He was hospitalized and put into the AIDS wing, even though the doctors were baffled by the fact that Westwood did not actually have full-blown AIDS. The prognosis gave him less than a month.

On Christmas Eve, Westwood died of what turned out to be an inexplicable overdose of morphine...just thirty minutes after Antoine had visited. Because of the holiday, there was a skeleton staff on duty and no one really saw anything suspicious.

On the night of December 26th, Leann Muñoz called Antoine and asked him if he'd come to her house to talk to her about Westwood. She was very upset and crying. Antoine decided he would pay her a visit...just to make certain that she understood she was responsible for Westwood's death and to tell her that he was going to report her to the hospital, the health district, and to the police. Something told him to leave his car at the house and walk the few blocks. When he got to her house—a small, wood-framed house on 12th street, a couple of blocks from UTMB—her front door was ajar. He found her dead body sprawled out on her bed, naked. Her arms and legs were tied to the bed and she had been stabbed once in the chest. Several candles were burning on her dresser and night stands.

Antoine gagged and ran to the bathroom. When he returned to the bedroom, he noticed that Muñoz had also been strangled with a necktie...a very colorful necktie...a very familiar looking necktie... in fact, it was one of his favorite neckties, wrapped tightly around her neck and tied in a knot. Then he noticed that the rope securing Muñoz's ankles and wrists was the red, white, and blue rope that he had special ordered to use in some of his sculptures.

Antoine panicked. He had, in a moment of blind anger when Westwood was admitted into the hospital, threatened to kill Muñoz. Several nurses and doctors in the emergency room heard him. The police could surely find her phone call to him that evening in her call log. And his tie...what the hell was his tie doing there?

Obviously, someone else hated Muñoz more so than he did...obviously, he was being set up...but by whom? In the kitchen, he almost slipped down in a puddle of blood. He wiped it up with paper towels. He ran out into the garage and spotted a wheelbarrow and a shovel. He noticed that the garage floor was a dirt floor...lucky break. Muñoz's car was in the driveway and the garage door was down...another lucky break.

He rolled the wheelbarrow inside the house, cut the body loose and tried to untie his necktie, but couldn't. Grabbing a pair of scissors from the kitchen, he attempted to cut the tie... but it was twisted so tightly around her neck that the scissors cut into her flesh. He kept at it, almost throwing up again, until the tie was cut. He threw the tie and pieces of rope into a canvas shopping bag.

Antoine wrapped the body in the bloody bed sheets and then in a large, plastic tablecloth, taped it all around with duck tape, loaded it into the wheelbarrow, and wheeled it out into the garage. Fearing to turn the light on inside the garage, he brought out a couple of the candles and worked by the flickering, yellow flames — much, he thought, as his favorite artist, Goya must have done...only painting, not burying bodies.

As he was digging the grave to conceal the body, it hit the very intelligent Dr. Antoine in the back of his head like a baseball bat...he had been snared in a love triangle. Westwood must have had another lover who hated Muñoz and him...who wanted Muñoz dead and wanted Antoine to take the fall.

Sweating inside the garage, he could feel that hatred hanging in the humid, musty air. He could feel that hatred watching him and it burned the back of his neck as the candles cast ghost-like shadows shimmying against the wooden walls.

But he could not panic or get in a hurry...he had to be thorough, methodical. He felt dirty — guilty of a heinous crime — but he kept telling himself that he was only buying some time...he'd tell the police when he could figure things out. He patted the final shovelful of dirt down, raked drier dirt, leaves, and shells over the grave area, stacked a couple of bags of weed and feed on top of the freshly dug grave, and swept around the area with a broom to cover up any remaining shovel marks. He figured that he had dug the grave deep enough that no odors would escape...at least for some time.

Another lover, Antoine thought as he hurried back into Leann Muñoz's bedroom to look for any clues that he or the killer may had left behind. *And I think I know who.*

Noticing a small purse on the dresser, he opened it and riffled through it, looking for her cell phone. It wasn't there, but he found a Southwest Airlines ticket to San Antonio for December 28th...in two days.

"Crap!" he said out loud. *Her absence would surely be noticed even sooner.*

He was about to get ill again, when he looked out the window and saw a police car pulling up.

"Shit!" he said this time, "I really am being set up."

He threw the purse in the canvas bag and ran through the kitchen to the back door. Looking back, he spotted Leann's cell phone on the kitchen counter and ran back in and grabbed it as he heard the police walking up the front sidewalk. As quickly and quietly as he could, he ran across the back yard and out the gate into the alley.

As Antoine was nervously walking back home, a brilliant idea popped into his head. He would get Rose to use Leann's credit card and driver's license and take the flight posing as Leann. They were about the same size and if Rose put on a lot of makeup and wore a black wig, no one would notice the difference. She would then check into a hotel as Leann, change clothes, go back to the airport and catch the flight that would be reserved in her name back to Houston Hobby airport.

As far as the world was concerned, Leann Muñoz flew to San Antonio, checked into a hotel, and disappeared. Stranger things have happened. It would shift all suspicions to San Antonio and away from Galveston and Antoine. Only the killer would know that events didn't unfold as expected.

Rose reluctantly agreed to do it, and Antoine threw in an extra thousand dollars to calm her nerves.

Antoine's plan was flawless...except for one small detail. Leann was evidently supposed to have visited her sister in San Antonio because her sister was waiting to pick her up at the airport. Rose walked right by her. In fact, Leann's sister stood up and was about to hug Rose as she approached her before she realized that it wasn't Leann. She apologized to Rose, telling her that she looked a lot like her sister, Leann.

Rose was horrified. Leann, of course, never appeared and luckily for Rose, the sister never made the connection with the woman who looked so much like Leann and the airline's insistence that Leann was on that plane. The police, in spite of the sister's protests, simply assumed that the two sisters missed each other and Leann, for whatever reason, went on to the hotel.

29

"Holy Mother of Mary!" Zapata exclaimed when Alexander finished reading Rose's letter. "That is one bizarre story. We need to get a forensics team out to Muñoz's house and find her body and then contact her family."

"That sculpture in Antoine's studio," Alexander blurted out, "the one leaning against the north wall that was sort of shaped like a woman's figure...it had pieces of red, white, and blue rope and pieces of a bright yellow tie in it."

Zapata looked at him like he losing it. "What?"

"I felt there was something unusual about that piece," Alexander continued. "He must have done it as some kind of secret memorial to Leann Muñoz. No wonder it reminded me of the *Dying Niobid.*"

"The dying what?" Zapata asked, incredulously.

"Greek mythology...this woman Niobe, offended Apollo's mother...never mind...she pissed off the gods and wound up with an arrow in her back. My point is, when Antoine saw Leann, she had her arms stretched out above her head — tied to the bedpost — and it must have reminded him of that sculpture."

"Whatever, dude. My money says Antoine killed Leann Munoz just like he killed those other women."

"E.Z., look at the bottom of Rose's letter. I think she's telling us who the real killer is, even if she didn't know she was."

Rose had written in her letter that Antoine told her he suspected Westwood's lover was "Lee."

"Let's face it, E.Z., Antoine didn't have the painting that the body was wrapped up in...this Lee character did! The defunct email address that Rose showed us yesterday morning must have been his."

"I have to admit, R.A., you do have a strong point. But you saw a different version of that painting in Antoine's slides... who knows how many versions he may have painted."

"Rose knew. She kept up with his inventory, sales, etc....she would have mentioned that he had painted more than one version."

"Maybe so, maybe no, amigo. But I agree that this adds another person to the possibility list."

"That also makes this Lee a prime suspect for the Leann Munoz murder," Alexander added.

As Zapata was phoning the forensics lab to send a team out to Munoz's house, Alexander remembered that he had left his phone in the bedroom. When he picked it up, he saw that he had five missed calls...all from Maggie.

30

The voice mails Maggie had left weren't very pleasant. She was hysterical and she was angry. And she was drunk. Alexander would wait until late morning to call her back.

It was 10:00 A.M., Tuesday, August 26th, and Alexander had only gotten a couple of hours sleep. Every inch of his body hurt from the beating he took and when he reluctantly looked into the mirror, two black eyes and a goose-egg in the middle of his forehead stared back at him. The cut on his arm throbbed and was still oozing blood. He cleaned it off, smeared some antibiotic cream on it, and wrapped a clean piece of gauze around it.

Maggie answered her phone after several rings. She was surprisingly calm—the mother of all icebergs—but calm. She agreed to meet Alexander for a brief lunch at the Spot on the seawall where they could sit outside under a covered patio and talk more privately.

It was a hot day, but thankfully the sea breeze kept things a little cooler and a summer thunderstorm was building up toward the east to help block the sun. The beach was crowded as usual and throngs of people were walking, biking, and skating up and down the Seawall. The water was a little sandy but turning a pretty emerald green not far out due to the wave action being minimal…the kind of day when the surfers spent far more time laying on the tops of their boards waiting for a wave large enough to ride than they did surfing. Seagulls were everywhere with the occasional frenzied flock being fed by the uninitiated. Between the gulls and the grackles mooching food on the deck, it was sometimes hard to eat outside in peace.

But Alexander thanked God every day for seagulls...had it not been for one of them, his brains would have been etched into his studio wall. Maggie was already sitting at a table next to the railing, eating a sandwich.

"My God, Richard, what on earth happened to you?" Maggie asked when Alexander sat down at the table with a hotdog.

"I don't want to talk about it right now, Maggie. Let's just say I had a collision and leave it at that. Let's talk about your messages...you've filed for a divorce?"

"I told you this was coming, Rich, if you continued putting your son and me in danger by playing the mystic detective," Maggie answered, still calm, but clearly on the edge of losing it. Finally, she lost it, throwing her half-eaten wedge of a club sandwich at Alexander, which hit him in the chest and bounced off onto the deck. A grackle immediately flew off of the railing and pounced on one of the tidbits.

"Goddammit, Rich, why can't you just be satisfied teaching and doing your art? What makes you think this freaking ability of yours gives you the right to...to...get messed up with cops and murderers and put us all in harm's way...to destroy your family?"

Alexander sat silent for a second, noticing that everyone on the deck had now stopped eating and were staring at the two of them. "Maggie, it doesn't give me that right...but it does give me an obligation to use it. God would not have given me this..."

"God has nothing to do with it, Rich!" Maggie interrupted, none too quietly. "If anything other than a freak occurrence, it's the devil! It's Satan himself! He rode that bullet right into your head and right into our family...and you can't tell the difference!

"Do you know what was waiting for me yesterday at a house I was showing in Jamaica Beach? A fucking body bag and a message on the mirror that said 'I have Maggie and Jeffery is next. If you want to see them alive again, wait for my call!'

"I cannot…I will not deal with this another second Richard. I called Jeff and I am moving in with him…tonight."

"Maggie, wait a minute. Did you call the cops?" Alexander asked, not know what else to say.

"Of course I called the cops, Richard," Maggie answered curtly as she stood up and walked away.

As Alexander started to go after her, a man who was sitting a couple of tables away stood and walked over to him. "Richard Alexander?" he asked, smiling.

"Yes," Alexander answered, still watching Maggie.

"Here you go, sir," the man said, handing him an envelope, "You've been served…and these gawking waiters are my witnesses. You have a good day now."

Alexander opened the envelope. It was a notice to appear in divorce court. Maggie must have filed for a divorce a month earlier for it to be this far along, he thought. He turned around in time to see a seagull swoop down and steal his hotdog off of the platter. "Help yourself, buddy…you earned it," he said to the bird as he picked up a wedge of Maggie's club sandwich and stuffed it in his mouth on his way out.

Glancing up at a flat-screen television on one of the walls of the dining room, Alexander noticed that the weather channel was on and one of the meteorologists was excitedly pointing to a swirling mass of clouds a few hundred miles east of the Virgin Islands. Michael had become a hurricane and it was moving west, northwest. "Great," Alexander said sarcastically as he exited the building, thinking about the vision he had in the Mexican restaurant…thinking about the storm that was now blowing their marriage apart…thinking about how Jeffery would take it.

31

Alexander called Jeffery, but Jeffery wasn't in a talkative mood. He wasn't rude to his dad, but he was brief. He said they would talk later after his mom got settled into his apartment and calmed down. Alexander could tell that Jeffery was angry with him, but ever the peace-maker, Jeffery tried not to show it.

Meanwhile, Alexander drove over to the county morgue and waited for Zapata to finish an autopsy so he could tell him about Maggie's experience in Jamaica Beach.

"Jesus, man, I am dead beat after last night," Zapata said as he met Alexander in his office. "And you look like warmed over death."

"Well, thanks, but I don't feel *that* good," Alexander answered, trying to hold on to a semblance of humor. He told Zapata about Maggie filing for a divorce—which didn't surprise Zapata—and about her ordeal in Jamaica Beach.

"Oh, dude...no wonder Maggie is so upset. That's some serious shit. Did she call the cops?"

"Yes...and I thought you could pull some strings and get a copy of her report. Who would have known that she was going to show that house but the guy she showed it to? We need to find out who that was."

"Someone in her real estate company could have known... that Phil guy, maybe."

"Phil evidently came onto the scene and prevented the abduction. This has Virion written all over it...who else would be after me at this point in time?" Alexander added, caressing the goose-egg on his forehead. "Do you think you can get your hands on a copy of that report?"

"No sweat," Zapata answered, picking up the phone. "My cousin, Manny, works in the records department of the police department...and legally, I have a right to see it if I think it's connected to one of my cases."

"Great, amigo. Say, was that Rose's body you did the autopsy on?"

"No...she's still in the cooler. We can't find any relatives to sign off on the autopsy. I have to wait a period of time, then I can do it without any permission. Do you want to see her...see if you can pick up any clues?"

"If I thought I could save my marriage, I'd say hell no...but I've got to do it. Yes, I do want to see if I can get Virion's portrait from her, but later. I'm really not up to the stress of the Muse right now. I'll give it a shot later when my head stops throbbing."

About thirty minutes later, Zapata's cousin emailed a scanned copy of Maggie's report and Zapata printed a couple of copies.

"What did I tell you, E.Z.?" Alexander said. "Look at her description of this guy...around six-six, two hundred and eighty pounds...heavy. That's him, amigo."

"We don't know that for sure, R.A. A lot of guys could fit that description...but I admit, it's got my attention."

"Yeah, well check out the name that he gave...Dr. Mark Legion," Alexander said excitedly as he pointed to the page.

"So...?"

"Mark Legion, E.Z....the Bible verse...my name is Legion... that is in the book of Mark. Now that's a bit much to call a coincidence... Holy cow...wait a minute!" Alexander declared as he flipped through his sketchbook to where he had written the email address that Rose gave them.

"Check this out...Westwood sent the email to *mnilm59*... *my name is legion, Mark 5:9*. If Antoine was right, Westwood gave the painting to the mysterious Lee...and our Mr. Lee is none other than Virion."

"Mother of Mary!" Zapata exclaimed. "This is starting to make sense. He had it all set up to take Maggie out in the body bag and lure you into a trap. And if Rose was the only person alive who knew Westwood had given him that painting..."

"It's right there in her letter. He suckered her over to Antoine's to shut her up...and he did just that. And when I showed up, it must have really made his day...all the trouble he had gone to to get to me, and there I was."

"Ok, Bro, so assuming that Mark Legion and the guy who killed Rose and attacked you are one in the same, that doesn't prove that the 'Lee' Antoine was referring to is the same guy."

It's hard to argue with geometry, though...the third side of the triangle."

"What the hell are you talking about?"

"The love triangle that Antoine was in, E.Z. It was a scalene triangle and Antoine got the short side. Westwood was the second side, and his lover—to whom he gave Antoine's painting—is the third side...our mysterious 'Lee'. Remember, Rose referred to him as a very big man."

"As far as we know, Westwood could have had numerous lovers."

"He probably did, but he gave that painting to only one of them, whose email address points to Virion. Rose knew who he was and when Antoine told her he thought Westwood's lover was 'Lee,' she didn't register any contradiction. It's as good a place to start as any...actually, it's the best place to start. I don't mind acting on a 'what if'...what if Lee, Mark Legion, and Virion are one in the same?"

"I know what your 'what ifs' lead to, R.A. We need to keep our butts out of it and turn all this over to Vincent, since he's in charge of the investigation. We're probably already in trouble for withholding evidence."

"E.Z., I'm already a suspect with him...he isn't going to give any credibility to anything we say until we have dead-on proof. He benefited from one of my sketches before. Even if he doesn't trust me, he just might trust another sketch...especially when we throw in Rose's letter, Westwood's email, the painting, and Maggie's description. If this Lee character is Virion, I'll know it the second I meet him. Then maybe we can paint a picture of this thing that even Vincent can't deny."

"If he is Virion, he could go off the deep end and do something violent, or follow you out to the parking garage. And anyway, we have to find him first. There could be a lot of 'Lees' at UTMB...if he really even works there."

"You're absolutely right, E.Z., but UTMB is our best place to start. Rose was sure that he worked there."

"I hate to keep playing the devil's advocate..."

"No you don't...you love it."

"...as I was saying before I was so rudely interrupted, the devil's advocate would simply point out that Lee can be either a sir name or a given name. In fact, Rose probably spelled it phonetically...L-e-e. That's how I've been thinking about it all along. But it could be spelled L-e-i-g-h or L-e-a, or L-e-a-h, or L-i."

"You're right again, buddy. We just have to search all of those possibilities."

"Not we...you. You might have noticed that I have a job here, while unemployed, about-to-be-single art professors have plenty of time on their hands to do research of this sort," Zapata said, smiling.

"You're right for the third consecutive time, my friend...a record indeed," Alexander answered limping toward the door. "I'll be back in the morning with my trusty sketchbook and see what I can pick up from Rose or some of her belongings. Oh, and when I meet Virion, he isn't going to recognize me. I can play the same game he plays."

Zapata's phone rang and he told Alexander to hold on a second while he answered it.

"There's no body in the garage where Leann Munoz used to live," Zapata announced walking out of his office.

"What...no body?"

"That's what the CSI team reported, amigo...no body."

"So, who was the liar, E.Z....Antoine or Rose?"

32

Early that evening Alexander sat at his computer and researched every 'Lee' that worked at the University of Texas Medical Branch in Galveston. For 'Lee,' he found fourteen first names and three last names; for 'Leigh,' he found six first names and three last names; for 'Lea,' he found three last names; for 'Leah,' he found one last name, and for 'Li,' nineteen last names.

The online directory was not consistent with middle initials, but he found three male employees whose middle initials were 'L.' His intuition kept telling him to focus on the men with the first name of Lee...it just seemed more logical that Antoine would use his first name. If that didn't pan out, he would look up the last names and then the middle initials.

Luckily enough, ten 'Lees' could be eliminated because they showed up as students, support staff, or nurses. Rose had made it clear that Westwood's lover was another doctor...but was he a M.D. or a Ph.D.? Of the remaining four 'Lees', three were Ph.D.s and one was a surgeon with the last name of Nguen. He would concentrate on the Ph.D.s. They were Lee Forester in the Medical Humanities department, Lee Adams in Epidemiology, and Lee LeGuin in Virology.

Alexander remembered that Maggie's report said that her client, Mark Legion, told them he was in Epidemiology. But Virion being a virologist also made a lot of sense. Nonetheless, Adams would be the starting point.

But how to start? Then it occurred to Alexander to call Doc Melton. He might know some, if not all of the players.

"Hello, Doc...Richard Alexander here," Alexander said, sitting at his kitchen table. "Do you like twenty-one year old Glenlivet well enough to come over here and help me find Virion?"

Twenty minutes later Doc Melton was ringing Alexander's doorbell and cursing at Rambo who was barking incessantly at him.

"Goddamed mutt," Doc said as Alexander let him in. "If he lived next door to me, I'd make tamales out of him."

"I know, but he did let me know that an intruder was at my back door the other night. Neat or on the rocks?"

They sat at the kitchen table sipping the single malt scotch and going over the list of names that Alexander had come up with.

"Lee Forester is as old as I am. He's been with the Institute since Baby Moses was floating down the Nile," Melton said with his old blues singer voice, unwrapping a cigar.

"By the way, if you don't want me smoking, don't invite me to your house. I can't drink good scotch without a good cigar."

"Not a problem, Doc," Alexander answered, dreading the idea, but knowing he needed to be flexible in order to get Doc's help. He opened the back door and set up a fan to blow most of the smoke out.

"But don't come to my house thinking you're going to smoke a cigar and not offer me one."

They both sat sipping scotch, smoking, and going over the names...even the names that Alexander had eliminated. Doc knew a number of them but most were new.

"This Lee Adams in Epidemiology...I don't know him, but one of my golfing buddies told me the other day that a co-worker has filed a sexual harassment charge against him...if it's the same fellow. LeGuin, I think I know…big fellow, weird as hell."

"Big, you say? How big?"

"Huge…maybe six-six…but that's how my buddy described Adams, too. He said he was as big as Shaq."

"So, we can't rule either of them out," Alexander said, struggling to keep the fifty-two-ring-sized Churchill cigar lit that Doc gave him. "Later this week, I'll go over to UTMB and see if I can recognize either of them."

"How the hell you going to do that? If one of them is Virion, won't he recognize you?"

"You sound like Zapata. He won't recognize me…trust me."

"Tell you what I'll do. To show you how much I appreciate twenty-one year old single-malt scotch, I'll go with you to UTMB. Since I'm a professor emeritus, I can ask to talk to those guys without raising any suspicions. I'll make up some bullshit story about recruiting them for a golf benefit I'm trying to organize. But how do we fix it so that you can see them?"

"I'm going to take a trip to Pasadena to a little costume shop I found on the internet called 'Face to Fakes.' They sell all kinds of disguises, mainly for theaters. I can buy a traditional doctor's white frock, a fake beard or whatever, and just follow behind you. I just need to get a glimpse of them…the Muse will help me."

"O.k. , but it's your butt if you get busted for impersonating a doctor…I'll swear to Zeus that I've never seen your white ass…I'm just jiving you…no one will even notice you as long as you don't stop and talk to anyone. Just hang around in the background and get the hell out of there as soon as you've seen them."

"My plans exactly, Doc," Alexander answered, puffing vigorously on the huge cigar, "my plans exactly. I'll be like the Invisible Man or the Shadow." *God knows I don't want to get busted in front of Virion.*

They made plans to meet at UTMB later that week when Alexander was ready with his disguise.

33

Wednesday morning, August 26, Alexander was still reeling from his encounter with Virion and from Maggie filing for divorce...and maybe one too many glasses of scotch. But he refused to succumb to the guilt and sadness that squatted on his soul like an eight-hundred pound gorilla. And he had made up his mind that he was not going to stop using his unique psychic abilities. He thought of the story of Lot, who was willing to give up his daughters to the mob to protect the angels who had come to help him. *Maggie thinks my Muse is the devil...I don't. She could be my angel.*

The cut on his arm was sore as hell, his eyes were still black, the goose-egg on this forehead had gone down somewhat, and his ribs still ached. But he felt well enough to go to the morgue and dance with the Muse. He wanted desperately to get a drawing of Virion as a point of comparison when he saw the two Lees at UTMB. After his third cup of coffee and perusing his Rambo-challenged newspaper, he hopped into his Tahoe and backed out of his driveway.

As he drove to the county morgue, a weather update on hurricane Michael was on the radio. The storm was already a category three hurricane and trucking west at sixteen miles per hour. If it stayed on this course, it should strike Cuba in about a week as possibly a category four or five storm. All of the computer models indicated that it would eventually find its way into the Gulf of Mexico.

"Hola, amigo," Alexander said, greeting his friend, Zapata, who was working on his computer. "I am here to wrestle my angel and hopefully get a good portrait of Virion."

"Good morning, R.A. I see you're feeling better, if not looking better. Let me pull Rose out of the cooler. All of her effects are in that red bag. I'll set up the recorder on the slab next to Rose and you can just do your thing," Zapata answered, if not cheerfully, at least encouragingly.

"Believe it or not, E.Z., Doc Melton and I have narrowed the suspects down to two guys named Lee at UTMB...going on the premise, of course, that Antoine was referring to a man with the first name of Lee. It's a start, anyway. If I can just get a definitive portrait this morning, I'll at least have a point of comparison."

"A point of comparison to what?" Zapata asked as he opened the cooler door and slid Rose's body out as far as the slab would extend. He sat the recorder on the slab by Rose's side.

Alexander explained his plan to meet Doc Melton at UTMB to create an opportunity to see the two men named Lee.

"Not a bad plan, amigo...mainly because it doesn't involve me and it doesn't involve you having to confront Virion."

"Well, that is just part A of the plan. If one of them happens to closely resemble Virion, we'll have to get a closer look...we'll have to talk to him."

"What the hell do you mean by 'we'?"

"Well, part B...that's where you come in, my friend. I'll explain all that later. Right now, if you'll kindly leave Rose and me alone..."

"I knew you'd drag me deeper into this," Zapata said, closing his office door, not too gently.

Alexander opened the red bag containing Rose's belongings and pulled up a chair next to her body. He laid his sketchbook on his lap, opened it to a blank page, and rolled the

Ebony pencil between his thumb and forefinger in anticipation. As he pulled her clothes out of the bag, he began to get that familiar dizzy feeling that accompanied the Muse when she floated into his mind.

Dark patches began appearing on the blank page of his sketchbook. Alexander quickly hatched in the dark shapes and a familiar sight began to take shape. It was the same evil looking eyes that he had seen forming on the page when he was in Antoine's house...just before Virion attacked him.

His head began pounding, as if a giant claw was suddenly squeezing his brain. Slowly, the portrait began taking form... bags under the eyes...bald forehead...prominent chin...very wide face...a menacing face...an evil face. He stared at the face in awe, frightened by it. His head felt like it would explode any second. A drop of blood fell from his nose onto the page at the bottom of the drawing and formed the shape of a rose.

All of the sudden the Rolling Stones were blasting through his mind again as if someone had turned the stereo on with the volume all the way up. *Please to meet you, hope you guess my name! For what's puzzling you is the nature of my game!*

"Stop it!" Alexander screamed, jumping to his feet and throwing the sketchbook against the wall. "I rebuke you, Satan! In the name of Jesus Christ, I rebuke you! Get out of my mind and out of my life...you may not come into my life. You will not interfere with my purpose or my family! In the name of Jesus Christ be gone!"

Zapata flung his door open and ran out of his office. "Good God, R.A, are you alright?"

Alexander fell back onto the chair and lowered his head between his knees. He was babbling...as if speaking in tongues, but much quieter now. His headache was completely gone and a huge calm enveloped him. Zapata stood behind him with his hand on Alexander's shoulder. A couple of staff members came running into the morgue to see what the uproar was about.

"It's ok, guys. Thanks…it's ok," Zapata assured them and they left.

"R.A., are you alright?"

"I am now," Alexander finally answered. "I'm good…I feel great, even though I have a nose-bleed. Look at the sketchbook, E.Z.…there is your killer…there is Virion."

Alexander pulled a handkerchief out of a back pocket and blotted his nose. It had stopped bleeding.

Zapata picked up the sketchbook and stared at the portrait that Alexander had drawn. "My God…may I never run into this demon in a dark alley."

"You already have, my friend. You already have…and so have I," Alexander answered, now resting his head in his hands, elbows on his knees.

"And now we're going to find this demon and stop him. But let me warn you…he is only a soldier in a massive, evil army. When we go after him, his general will come after us."

"What are you talking about, R.A., your theory about evil?"

"It's no longer a theory, my friend…I have just been shown the terrible, dark truth."

34

Wednesday afternoon after Alexander had left the county morgue, he drove up I-45 to the Sam Houston toll-way and east to Pasadena to the theatrical supply shop. There he purchased a white doctor's smock, an ID badge, brown hair dye that could be shampooed out, and a fake beard. He was prepared to meet Doc Melton at UTMB and not be recognized by anyone.

UTMB sits on the east end of Galveston Island, with the Galveston ship channel just a couple of blocks to its north. It is an impressive campus with a mix of old and new buildings, the oldest being "Old Red," finished in 1891. At that time it housed the entire medical school.

The university now comprised over fifty-four buildings, including six hospitals, a nursing school, a graduate school of biomedical sciences, an institute of medical humanities, and allied health sciences, in addition to the medical school. The grounds were beautifully landscaped with a large rose garden next to the library building, which housed one of Alexander's favorite collections, the Truman G. Blocker History of Medicine Collections. He loved to peruse the anatomical atlases, some printed in the 1500s.

When Alexander met Doc Melton in the epidemiology department at UTMB on Thursday morning, Melton walked right past him.

'Excuse me, Dr. Melton," Alexander said in a terrible fake German accent, "I believe I have an appointment with you."

Doc Melton stopped and turned around to look at the brown haired, bearded, bespectacled doctor wearing a white smock and carrying the ubiquitous doctor's clipboard.

"My Lord, man...I didn't recognize you. You look... invisible. Good to see you again, Dr....Melvin Alexander from the University of Texas Medical Center in Houston," Melton replied, staring at the fake name badge that looked just like all the name badges worn by UTMB employees. "Ok, I'll ask to see Dr. Adams and ask him if he cares to play in a benefit golf tournament that, of course, will never occur. Why don't you stand over there contemplating your clipboard and see if you recognize him?"

Alexander backed against the wall of the hallway while Doc Melton approached the counter and asked to see Dr. Adams. Physicians, researchers, staff, and patients filed past Alexander and never gave him a first look, much less a second look. He began to think that he *was* invisible. Melton was arguing with the receptionist at the counter. Finally, she disappeared through a door behind the counter. In a few minutes she reappeared and totally ignored Melton, who was still standing in front of the counter.

Then Alexander noticed a very large man in a white doctor's smock walking down the hallway focused on Melton. He walked up to Melton and said in a loud voice, "I'm Dr. Adams. What is it you needed with me?"

"Hello. My name is Melton...Dr. Ralph Melton. You were recommended to me as a possible player in a benefit golf tournament that we are trying to organize," Melton explained holding out his hand.

Adams looked at his watch and ignored Melton's offer to shake hands. "Who the hell told you that? I don't play golf...I find it a moronic waste of time. Now if you don't mind, I have to get back to my lab."

"Not at all. Anyway, we have our quota of assholes. Have a

good day," Doc Melton responded, smiling broadly. Adams grunted, turned and walked away.

"Doc," Alexander said as they walked down the hall toward the virology department, "you could have saved us both a lot of time and grief if you had told me that Adams is a black man. Rose described the Lee we're looking for as a large 'Gringo'."

"I told you he looked like Shaq."

"No, you said that he was as big as Shaq."

"How many white men do you know that are as big as Shaq? And, I might add, you never told me if your Virion was white, black or orange."

After walking through a labyrinth of hallways and taking a couple of elevators and crosswalks, they found themselves outside in a courtyard. About twenty yards in front of them was a new building that, except for a couple of ominous looking entry doors, looked like most of the other buildings on campus. An armed guard stood at the door and nodded to them as they approached. The heavy doors parted with a hiss and closed behind them, leaving them in a very cold air-lock for a few seconds before the interior glass doors hissed open.

Finally, they arrived at the reception center of UTMB's level four facility, the National Laboratory, where scientists studied various deadly organisms—especially those that could be used by terrorists. It was clear from the guards and ID-controlled elevators that they would get no further than the reception center...which was perfectly fine with Alexander. A guard directed them to sign in at the reception desk.

"Ok," Melton said, "same game plan. You stand over there and act invisible and I'll ask to see Dr. LeGuin."

Alexander stood against a wall and pretended to study his clipboard while Melton walked over to a receptionist's desk to ask for LeGuin. Suddenly, Alexander was aware of someone standing in front of him. It was a doctor in a white smock. He had white hair, steel-rimmed glasses perched on the end of his nose, and looked very much in charge.

"Excuse me, I haven't seen you around here before. I don't believe you're a member of the Laboratory, are you?" the man asked, extending his hand.

"No, I'm not. I'm Dr. Alexander. I'm a visitor," Alexander replied, using his best—but still terrible—Hollywood German officer accent.

"I see," the man answered, staring at Alexander's ID badge. "And what is your specialty, Dr. Alexander?" It was obvious that he was having trouble reconciling the name Alexander with the German accent.

"Actually, I'm a researcher in visual studies...part of the Medical Humanities, you know," Alexander answered, sort of telling the truth.

"I see," the doctor answered again, with a good deal of skepticism in his voice. "I wasn't aware that they had a Medical Humanities department in that facility. I worked there for quite a while. And as a visitor, why would you be wearing your doctor's coat? Forgive my questions, but you can surely understand our caution in this facility."

Just then a very large man wearing a white lab coat, with close-cropped grey hair that had receded back off of his forehead to the top of his head, walked up to Melton in front of the desk and shook his hand. He then signed the book, acknowledging that he had two guests. Alexander estimated that he was about six-six. He was walking with a noticeable limp.

Could it be because he had his shin sliced up?

Alexander flipped up the first page on the clipboard and looked at the portrait of Virion that he had drawn in the morgue. He held his breath...the drawing on his clipboard was a dead-on portrait of LeGuin.

"Absolutely I understand," Alexander answered quickly.

"If you'll excuse me, I'm here to speak with Dr. LeGuin." Wanting desperately to end this interview, Alexander rushed over to Melton and LeGuin and reached out his had to LeGuin.

"Dr. LeGuin, I'm Melvin Alexander. I'm here with Dr. Melton and we certainly hope that you will agree to play in our most worthwhile golf tournament," Alexander blurted out loud enough in his fake German accent for the nosy doctor behind him to hear. Doc Melton was staring at him incredulously, mouth opened.

Le Guin glared at Alexander a moment then heartily shook his hand. A bolt of electricity shot up Alexander's arm and he knew that he was in the presence of evil.

"Very nice to meet you, Dr. Alexander. I was just about to tell Dr. Melton that I'd be honored to play in the tournament. I will, of course, have to check my calendar and confirm it with you later...if I could have a card," LeGuin asked, wiping beads of sweat from his balding forehead. LeGuin couldn't have been more charming. Melton whipped out a business card, grabbed Alexander by the arm and started dragging him away.

"Thank you so much, Dr. LeGuin. I'll be looking forward to your call," Melton said, cheerfully while squeezing Alexander's arm with every ounce of strength he had. Suddenly, Alexander bolted away from Melton's grip and ran back to LeGuin.

"Excuse me, Dr. LeGuin," Alexander hollered with his goofy German accent as LeGuin was walking back to his lab. "May we have one of your business cards...in case we need to change dates for the tournament?"

LeGuin stopped and turned around, looking somewhat perplexed. "Of course...but I'm afraid it's rather dated. The phone number is good, though." He fumbled in his wallet a second and retrieved a card and handed it to Alexander, staring intensely at his face.

Alexander stared back, not seeing any sign of the camouflage makeup but noticing two faint scratch marks on Le

Guin's left cheek. *Put there by the young murder victim in Antoine's studio?*

Alexander thanked him, turned and walked past the inquisitive doctor back to Melton, who resumed his death grip on Alexander's arm. The two exited the building as if a contamination alert had gone off.

"What the hell were you thinking? Melton asked in a hoarse voice, still ahold of Alexander's arm as they walked briskly toward the parking garage. "What if he had recognized you? And that Dutch accent...what the hell was that about?"

"It was German, thank you...I didn't know what else to do. I was about to get busted by Dr. 'Gatekeeper' so I had to do something. Anyway, Doc, LeGuin is Virion...look at this portrait I drew earlier in the morgue. And check out his business card."

"Jesus, that does look remarkably like LeGuin. But alas, Richard, your drawing is not hard evidence. It won't be accepted in a court of law. It's from intuition...or some supernatural source that has no empirical weight...it's circumstantial. So, what about his card?"

Le Guin's card, which he admitted was outdated, contained all of his relevant UTMB contact information. While it did not have his home address on it, it did have an old personal email address...mnilm59@eblast.com...the email address of Westwood's lover...the email address that referred to the Bible verse that Alexander believed tied Westwood's lover to Virion...the email address that now tied Dr. Lee LeGuin to Virion.

This and the likeness of the portrait, added to his size and profuse sweating, which correlated with Maggie's description of Mark Legion, his limp, and the evil force exuding from his handshake cinched it for Alexander...LeGuin was Mark Legion and LeGuin was Virion. He explained this to Doc Melton.

"Well, the email address definitely identifies LeGuin as

Westwood's lover, and apparently the recipient of the painting, but there is no hard evidence that those initials stand for anything in particular, nor does it prove that he's Virion. We have to operate on hard evidence, Richard.

"I will admit, though, the incredible alignment of the initials with the Bible verse is pretty damned hard to ignore and the likeness of the portrait is intriguing. And the fact that LeGuin was in possession of the painting certainly implicates him...unless, of course, he sold it or gave it away."

"That, my friend, is what Zapata and I have to find out... somehow," Alexander answered as they reached the parking garage. "And Doc, we're not working on a quantitative thesis here...we're working on a qualitative thesis, like with the bulk of crime investigations. We have to look at the preponderance of evidence...the aggregate. Intuition and gut feelings cannot be scientifically proven—but they cannot be ignored. That's often the way God speaks to us. We don't just see the truth through the mind's eye...we must also take instruction through the eye's mind.

"When I add up all of the information that has come to me both empirically and supernaturally, I can arrive at only one conclusion...LeGuin is Virion. And he isn't going to stop killing just because he thinks he's framed Antoine...he'll just change his M.O. He has a huge agenda, and in his warped mind, it's Biblically mandated."

"Don't lecture this old agnostic, Richard, about God speaking to us or about gut feelings, supernatural cognition, or scriptural decrees. I have been a scientist all of my adult life and I have dealt only with empirical evidence. If God exists, he is one cryptic dude." Doc paused to fire up a cigar.

"But having said that, a true agnostic has an open mind. If you're that convinced about LeGuin, then I take it very seriously, too...and I'm prepared to pursue it with you.

"Oh, by the way, I almost forgot...you and Le Guin have

something in common. I found out that his first undergraduate degree was in art."

35

That evening, Alexander drove over to Zapata's house for a barbeque dinner with the other band members. Zapata and his wife, Sandy, lived on the west end of Galveston Island on Ostermeyer Road. Their property backed up to the wetlands of a cove off of West Galveston Bay and was bordered on the east side by a canal that was dug years earlier by an oil company that had planned to moor barges there. It was a great fishing spot.

The large field between the house and the road was fenced off…home to a couple of horses that kids and grandkids rode. A lean-to shed for the horses sat on the north-east corner, close to the house.

The Zapatas had their three-story house custom built toward the north end of the ten acre plot so that their back balcony faced the canal. The ground floor was a vast open patio area that had been planned for parties.

The Third Coast Ghost Band practiced at the Zapatas' house every other Thursday night and occasionally—like this evening—met there just for fellowship and planning and a little fishing.

After dinner, while the other guys went down to the canal to fish, Alexander filled Zapata in on his and Doc Melton's morning at UTMB and how he was now convinced that LeGuin was Virion.

"We can't prove that LeGuin ever had that painting,"

Zapata said, taking a long pull off of his beer. "Westwood's email isn't proof that LeGuin actually received the painting and all LeGuin has to do is deny ever getting it."

"That's true," Alexander answered, puffing on a cigar and rocking in a wooden rocking chair. "But what if...just what if he admitted that he had it at one time. That should be enough for a grand jury...or at least for Vincent to bring him in, because it connects him to Westwood, Antoine, and Sabrina Williams."

"I don't know about a grand jury, but it ought to be enough to get him brought in for questioning. But how would we get him to admit it...that's what I'm wondering."

"Call him ask him," Alexander answered, taking another puff.

"Right."

"No, I mean it. Get someone to call him and tell him that they're with the New York art gallery that handles Antoine's work — the Watson-Keebler Gallery — and that they're trying to track down some of Antoine's work to settle his estate. Say that some of Antoine's records identified LeGuin as the owner of the painting titled *The Face of AIDS II* and the gallery was wondering if he still owned it. The call will be recorded. If he admits to owning it or having had possession of it, we've got him."

"That's brilliant, R.A., but I'm not calling him with all that bullshit...he'd never believe I was a New Yorker...you call him...you're the master of disguise."

"Wait a minute," Alexander said, laying his cigar butt in an ashtray, "I know just the person to do it...Midge, the receptionist at the Kelver-Morris Art Gallery, below my studio. She's from New Jersey and has a perfect accent for this."

Alexander's cell phone rang as he was finishing his sentence. It was Doc Melton. Alexander had asked him to find a Dr. Mark Legion in the Galveston-Houston area...he didn't.

No doctor or researcher by that name was working anywhere in Texas.

About that time the bass player, Tony, started yelling something from the bank of the canal. He was holding up a nice sized redfish that he had just caught. It was getting late, so Zapata and Alexander ran down to the canal, fishing poles in hand, to get in on the action before it got too dark to see what they were doing. About all that was biting for the rest of the evening were mosquitoes the size of sparrows.

36

The next morning, Friday, August 29th, Alexander was at his studio bright and early. He fooled around with some sketches, but couldn't really concentrate on making art. He was waiting for the art gallery below his studio to open so that he could ask Midge if she would make the phone call to LeGuin. LeGuin's phone number and address were unlisted. Zapata had asked a cousin of his who worked in the county tax office to look up LeGuin's address, then used a cross-reference phone book to get the phone number.

Around 9:30, Alexander went down to the coffee shop to sit out and wait for Midge to open the gallery. It was a cloudless morning and the sea breezes were very light, as they always were in August. It was already a muggy eighty-five degrees.

Through the shop window, he could see a flat- screen TV on the wall behind the counter. It was showing the image of a hurricane in the Atlantic. It looked like a spinning, white cinnamon roll with a hole in the center, flinging its icing off in a classic pinwheel pattern. It was Hurricane Michael and his 'cone of uncertainty' was centered between the Caicos Islands and the northern edge of Haiti...straight for the southeastern tip of Cuba. It should cross over Cuba by September 1...that would be Monday...two days away.

Sipping on his luke-warm cup of coffee, Alexander wished that he had a personal 'cone of *certainty*' that pointed him in the right direction every day instead of the ever-present cone of *uncertainty* that seemed to be dominating his life. Then a familiar, quite inner voice said, "*You do…use it, dude!*"

The trolley pulled up in front of the coffee shop at 9:50 and Midge got off. She waved at Alexander as she walked up to the gallery door. He got to his feet and followed her into the gallery.

As Midge walked around turning off the alarm system and pulling up shades, Alexander explained the situation—without going into too much detail. All he told her was that LeGuin was a suspect in a serious criminal investigation and that they think he might have stolen the painting in question. He explained his plan to call the Watson-Keebler Gallery and asked Midge if she would mind helping with this investigation.

"Geez, Rich, I just don't frigging know…I'm not very good at lying. On the other hand, if this is as important as you say it is, I ought to help. Geez, I just don't frigging know."

They talked about it a little longer and Alexander went next door to get her one of those frozen coffee drinks while she finished opening up the gallery and thought about the plan. By the time he returned, she had made up her mind to help…but not to make the call.

"Really?" Asked Alexander, puzzled at her response. "Why not?"

"Well geez, Rich, if this guy has an unlisted phone, then you know that he's bound to have Caller ID…we don't frigging know. If I call, he'll know that it's a local call. I don't want the creep knowing that the call came from here, for Christ's sake."

"Good thinking, Midge. I didn't think of those things… obviously. So, how are you going to help?"

"My sister, Dianne, happens to live in Jersey, right outside Newark. She's a great sport and a little nutty and will be happy to make the call for me. The area code won't be a Manhattan area code, but close enough. She can say that she's calling on behalf of the gallery…not from the gallery. He'll never know the difference."

"Midge, you're a genius and an angel," Alexander declared as he handed her the script for the phone call.

"Oh, one more detail, Rich. What is Dianne supposed to say when this guy wants to know how she got his unlisted number?"

Alexander took the script from her and added a note at the bottom...*If asked about unlisted phone, answer, "Geez, I just don't frigging know."*

37

After getting Midge to agree—with the help of her sister in New Jersey—to make the phone call to LeGuin in hopes of getting him to admit that he at one time had possession of Antoine's painting, Alexander went back up to his studio to paint. He was hoping that the smell of the oil paint and the feel of the brush spreading the buttery pigments across the canvas would consume his mind for a while—get it off of Virion and his victims, and Maggie's filing for divorce. He was hoping he could paint over his 'cone of uncertainty.' None of the above was happening.

At around 11:30, Alexander gave it up and decided to eat lunch at his house. He was standing at his kitchen counter making a sandwich when the doorbell rang. He thought it odd that someone would be at his door in the middle of the day, then he felt a tightening in the pit of his stomach... *what if it was Virion coming to finish the job? Should I go get my pistol? Nah...I'm just being paranoid. Even Virion wouldn't show up in broad daylight.*

But just to be safe, he tiptoed to the door and peered through the little viewer. To his relief, it was a woman with a scarf around her head and wearing sunshades. He couldn't recognize her but was beginning to feel foolish standing there like a frightened child.

He opened the door. "Yes, can I help you?"

Suddenly, the knot in the pit of his stomach was replaced

by the cold, steel barrel of a pistol being shoved into his belly button.

"Get inside and don't try anything stupid," the woman said with a familiar Mexican accent. She pulled the scarf off of her head and yanked the sunshades off of her face. To Alexander's shock and awe, it was Rose de la Rosa...the supposedly dead Rose de la Rosa. She kicked the door shut with her foot.

Alexander stepped back with his mouth hanging open, trying to form some words. He wondered if it was another vision from the Muse, but dropped that thought when she poked him in the stomach again with the barrel of her snub-nosed .38 and told him to sit the hell down.

"Sit the hell down and don't make one fucking move I don't tell you to make," she ordered harshly.

He sat down on the sofa and finally managed to form a word. "Ro-Rose?"

"Yes, Rose. What's the matter...you never seen a ghost before?"

"Well, actually, I have...and you're no ghost."

"No, but somebody wanted me to be and instead they killed my cousin, Gabriela. And you and your buddy were the ones who called me to meet you at Dr. Antoine's house that night."

"Now, wait a minute, Rose...neither one of us..."

"Callate!...just shut up and call your buddy Zapata and tell him to get over here if he ever wants to see you alive again! And don't you tell him I'm here!"

"Yeah, like he would believe that."

Rose was clearly upset and as far as Alexander was concerned, unpredictable and capable of pulling that trigger— and her shaking gun hand wasn't making him feel any better. He entertained telling her that his cell phone was on his night stand so that he might have a chance to grab his pistol, but did he really want to have a shoot-out with Rose? Besides, his phone was in clear view on the kitchen table. He told her that and she followed him into the kitchen with her pistol pointed at his back. Alexander called Zapata.

"E.Z., we have a situation here at my house and I really need for you to come over here ASAP."

"What kind of situation, R.A.? I'm kind of rushed here," Zapata answered.

"I can't tell you the details because you wouldn't believe them, but it's a matter of life and death and it definitely involves you."

"Jesus, R.A., is it Virion? If yes, just say 'how long.'"

"It's not. Just hurry."

"Do I need to bring my gun?"

"How long?"

"I'll be right there, buddy."

It was a very long and awkward fifteen minutes before Zapata pulled into the drive. Rose insisted that Alexander not say a word while waiting. Zapata walked cautiously up the front steps to the porch. He knocked loudly and called out. "R.A....?"

"Come on in, Ezekiel," R.A. answered. Using the first names Ezekiel or Richard was a code for them that they were in a dangerous situation. Zapata opened the door slowly and walked in, holding his 9MM automatic down by his side. He saw Alexander sitting on the sofa and a woman pointing a pistol at Alexander's head sitting next to him.

"Whoa...what is this? You can't be..." Zapata started to say, his jaw dropping to his belt.

"Put the gun down on the floor and kick it away or I swear I'll blow his brains out."

Zapata followed her orders, figuring it was too risky to get a shot off. Anyway, he had a pistol strapped to each ankle. "You...you're..."

"Rose...that's right, Zapata. You're not seeing things. I'm not back from the dead. Tell him who you two are responsible for killing, Alexander."

"What?" Zapata yelled. "Who's that lying in my morgue?"

"Rose's cousin, Gabriela, was the person Virion killed in Antoine's house," Richard answered calmly.

"Virion, Smirion...you two are the ones that tried to get me over there. You two were the last ones to see Gabriela alive. I don't know no Virion."

"Rose, we never saw Gabriela alive. She was dead when we found her. A killer who calls himself Virion killed her and almost killed me. What was she doing over there?" Alexander asked calmly, trying to settle her down and get her to talk.

Rose got up and made Zapata sit next to Alexander, then sat in the chair across from them. She looked confused, but not about to believe them at that point. She began to tell her story.

"I asked Gabriela to go over to Dr. Antoine's house to pick up something I had hidden there before you two could find it," she started. "It was something that Dr. Antoine wanted to disclose at a later date. But then I got worried that you would find Gabriela there with it and then I would be in trouble. She was easily intimidated...she would have just handed it over to you and I would be implicated in a horrible crime and sent to prison or back to Mexico and never be allowed to come back."

"What horrible crime are you talking about, Rose?" Zapata asked.

"You don't know what I'm talking about? Well, someone knows what I'm talking about because the book isn't there anymore. You two were the only ones I told about keeping secrets in the bottom shelf of a bookcase."

"Ok, Rose," Alexander spoke up, "I did pick up the book... we thought you were dead and something just told me that you would want us to know some things."

"Well something told you wrong. And how did you know?

How could you know I had something hidden in that book?"

"It's hard to explain...call it a hunch...a lucky guess," Alexander explained, guessing that she wouldn't accept the truth any better.

"Well, I don't think that guess is going to be very lucky for you...for either of you," Rose snapped back, waving her pistol back and forth at both of them.

"Now take it easy, Rose," Zapata said, casually crossing his right foot over the top of his left knee so that the small .32 automatic pistol that was strapped to his ankle was in easy reach. "You don't want to be shooting anyone. You're not in any trouble with the law," he lied. "You were just trying to help Dr. Antoine."

"To hell with Dr. Antoine!" Rose shouted. "I was trying to protect me! He told me what to write...dictated every word of it. I wrote it because it made me look innocent!" She was crying, now, on the verge of hysteria. "He never suspected anything because I played along with him...he never figured it out."

Zapata and Alexander looked at each other, confused as hell.

"Figured out what, Rose?" Alexander finally asked.

"That I killed that diseased whore, Leanne! She killed my lover, so I killed her!"

As Alexander and Zapata both sat with their mouths open, Rose went on to explain that she and Clint Westwood were lovers. During their affair, Westwood repeatedly told Rose that if Antoine ever found out about them, he would be furious and fire her and see that she got sent back to Mexico. On the evening of December 26th, 2007, two days after Westwood died, Rose snuck into Leann Munoz's house and waited for her to get home. When Leann arrived, Rose surprised her and stabbed her in the chest with a butcher knife. Rose didn't know if Leann was dead or not, but dragged her to the bed, stripped her, and tied her up the way Antoine found her. Rose had taken the multicolored rope that Antoine used in his sculptures and his necktie to Leann's house for the express purpose of framing him. She wrapped the tie as tightly as she could around Leann's neck...just to make sure.

"So why frame Antoine?" Zapata asked.

"Because he was bound to find out about Clint and me and he would have had me deported. So I called him from Leann's house pretending to be Leann, waited until I figured he was almost there and called the police to report a loud fight and a woman screaming. The police took their time getting there... giving Dr. Antoine enough time to bury the body and clean up the place. I couldn't believe it. Then I had to go to San Antonio pretending to be Leann so he wouldn't suspect anything."

"But Leann's body wasn't in the garage," Zapata interjected. "The forensics guys said there had been a large hole dug in there, but no body. How do you explain that?"

Rose sat on the edge of the chair, clearly agitated. "I got to worrying after Dr. Antoine said that he would tell the police about it when he felt the time was right...worried that maybe there was some evidence on the body that could be traced back to me...you know, DNA and stuff. So I got Gabriela to come visit and we dug the body up, put it in the back of Leanne's car, and disposed of it elsewhere. Gabriela was scared, but I told she'd better never say anything or she'd go to prison, too."

Alexander and Zapata were still exchanging looks as if both of them were stuck in the same insane nightmare.

"What did you do with her body, Rose?" Alexander asked, making a concerted effort to keep his voice calm.

"That's none of your concern. Let's just say that she's sleeping with the gators instead of the fishes," she answered with such truculence that neither man could believe that it came from the attractive, passionate woman whom they met at Antoine's house.

"And I'll tell you something else...I think I know who murdered Dr. Antoine and his little fag friend. After I took Dr. Antoine's files to him that night, I walked back to my car. Across the street, I saw a white van parked with a man sitting in it. It was a plumber's van, but I recognized the driver and he ain't no plumber. As I started to drive away, he got out of the van and walked over to Dr. Antoine's house. I saw him in my rearview mirror. It was Clint's ex-boyfriend...the very large doctor who Clint gave Dr. Antoine's painting to."

"Rose, I saw that same van with the plumbing sign on the side parked around the corner from Antoine's the night Gabriela was murdered and I was attacked," Alexander said, now more excitedly. "We know who he is...he murdered Gabriela because he thought she was you. It was he who called you...not Zapata or me. He must be worried that you saw him that night! And he knows you know about the painting! You can help us catch the bastard."

Rose looked even more stressed as all of this soaked into her frenzied mind. "To hell with that bastard and to hell with you! I'm not helping anyone but myself. If what you say is true, even more reason for me to go to Mexico. I'm getting the hell out of here." Rose sprang to her feet and pointed the gun at Alexander. "Too bad for you two...you already know too much!"

As Rose cocked the revolver, the front door flew open with a loud thump. Zapata, in his surprised state, hadn't shut the door completely, and Rambo, the idiot dog from next door came charging through the slight opening with somebody's newspaper in his mouth. Rose screamed and turned toward the door. Zapata pulled his pistol from his ankle holster as Alexander tackled Rose. Her pistol went off, striking Rambo near his tail, then it went flying out of her hand as she hit the floor.

With surprising agility and strength, she kicked Alexander

off of her, knocking him into Zapata, who then dropped his gun. Rose sprang to her feet and ran out the front door toward her car, which was parked across the street.

In her blind rage, Rose didn't notice the trolley motoring full steam down Postoffice street. The impact knocked her across the street, head-on into a parked car. She fell back into the street and lay there, blood gushing from every orifice in her head.

Zapata, who had retrieved his pistol, ran over to Rose. The trolley had screeched to a stop and the some of the passengers were yelling and scrambling out to see what had happened. Zapata kneeled down beside Rose and felt her neck for a pulse. Rambo was yelping loudly and trying to get back to his house. The owner of the car, like other near-by neighbors, were out on their porches after hearing the gunshot. He ran out and looked at his car and said, "Shit!" Then he looked at Rose as if she was a dead deer in the road. "Who's going to pay for this?"

"R.A.," Zapata said as Alexander came running toward him. "Rose is dead…again…for sure."

38

Alexander didn't sleep well that night. He kept waking up with every little noise, imagining that Rose was standing over his bed with a gun in one hand and a knife in the other. When he finally dozed off, he would jerk awake, imagining that Virion was standing over him in his blue jumpsuit.

He had cleaned up the blood from poor Rambo while his neighbor took the dog to the vet. Fortunately for Rambo the bullet did little damage, just knocking a chunk out of the top of his tail where it attached to his rear. It missed Alexander's open front door and ended up in the same car that Rose smashed in to when the trolley sent her flying. Alexander now had a new respect for the mutt. What are a few teeth holes in the newspaper compared to a few bullet holes in him? Who would have thought that rambunctious Rambo would turn out to be a hero?

After finally getting a few hours of sleep, Alexander rolled out of bed and turned on the coffee maker. It was Saturday, August 30th. When He walked out in his front yard to pick up the paper, his neighbor, Jack was outside. Alexander inquired about Rambo, who was under observation at the vet's but was doing fine. They chatted a few minutes and Jack was cussing Hurricane Michael, which was scheduled to strike the Turks and Caicos Islands the next day and Cuba by Monday.

"I got a bad feeling about this one," Jack offered, as he did with every storm that formed in the Atlantic basin. But this time Alexander had to agree with him, for he, too, had a bad feeling about this storm every since that morning he and Zapata ate breakfast at the Napolitos Café.

After a quick breakfast of whole grain cereal and a banana, Alexander stepped out onto his front porch to plan the day. Typically, even the mornings were humid and hot on Galveston Island during the month of August. This was a typical August morning...only eerily still, which tended to happen when the barometric pressure was unusually low.

"To heck with it," he said out loud to the chattering squirrels in the large oak tree across the street. "I'm going to walk to the studio this morning, if you guys have no objections."

Even though he realized he would have a really hot walk back, he needed the exercise. He had been reluctant to walk because he felt somewhat paranoid after his experience with Virion, but he decided that he was not going to let fear control his life. He fetched his sketchbook, locked the front door, and strolled out onto the sidewalk. As he fired up a cigar, he looked up into the trees where the squirrels had grown silent.

"I'll take your silence to mean that you guys don't actually give a shit." *Now I'm seeking approval from squirrels.*

Walking west on Postoffice Street, Alexander admired the rows of Victorian houses, most of which were built in the first half of the twentieth century. Some of the houses needed a lot of attention and some had been beautifully restored with pastel colors and green wooden shutters. Almost every yard was shaded by large oaks, sycamores, palms, crepe myrtles, or magnolia trees. The crepe myrtles and hibiscus bushes were still blooming, adding a brighter spectrum of color to the serene landscape. The briny smell of the sea breeze mixed with various breakfast aromas drifting through the neighborhood to lock in his olfactory framework of home and belonging.

Four blocks to his right, out in the Galveston ship channel, a cruise ship let out a low bellow that reverberated through the town, promising the adventures of exotic ports. Tugboats beeped and seagulls screeched. Everything was Galveston-normal. But the uneasy fluttering in Alexander's stomach served as a rude reminder that the world he was walking through was anything but normal.

Ten minutes later, Alexander walked up to the coffee shop beneath his studio. He bought two cups of coffee and strolled next door to the Morris-Kelver art gallery to find out if Midge's sister contacted Le Guin.

"He what?" Alexander asked incredulously, almost sloshing his coffee on the counter.

"That's what he told Dianne, Rich. Careful! Don't spill coffee on those prints...they're reproductions of Leonardo da Vinci's anatomical studies."

"Le Guin told your sister that he still had Antoine's painting?"

"Yes."

"Hanging in his house?"

"Yees!"

"As we speak?"

"Geez, Rich...for God's sake! Isn't that what you were hoping to hear? Doesn't that prove he stole it?"

There was a long pause. "Uh, right," Alexander answered, remembering the story he told Midge. "I just figured that he would have gotten rid of it by now."

He blew the steam away from his cup of coffee and took a sip as he stared out of the showroom window at the people milling around on Postoffice Street. *If Le Guin still has the painting, where did the one that the Williams girl was wrapped in come from? Antoine specifically told me he only painted one like that. I've got to see this for myself.*

"You're welcome, Rich," Midge said, sarcastically.

Coming out of his stupor, Alexander leaned over the

counter and kissed Midge on the cheek. "You're a sweetheart, Midge. Tell Dianne I love her."

He sat his coffee down on the counter and started for the door. "By the way," he added, pointing back at the prints on the counter, "those are not reproductions of Leonardo's work. He was left handed and whoever drew those was a right-hander pretending to be left handed. Check out the way the diagonal hatch marks curve...they're rip-offs."

"Geez, Rich..."

As Alexander ascended the stairs to his studio, it struck him. *Not left handed...neither was Antoine. Yet the paintings found around the two victims...so much for my studio time today. I have to check this out.*

39

Lee Le Guin sat up in the recliner on the deck under his house and laid down the cordless phone on the stainless steel table beside him. He lifted up a frozen daiquiri, took a long drink, and gazed out at the boats coming and going in the canals of Tiki Island.

Luckily, the Watson-Keebler Gallery in New York City was open. Yes, Derrick Antoine was one of their artists but no, they were not even aware of his death and certainly had no one calling around about his work. However, because dead artists were worth a lot more than live ones, their interest was now piqued.

Le Guin snatched up a pack of cigarettes, flipped one up and trapped it between his thin, purplish lips. As he lit it, he bolted up out of the recliner and began pacing back and forth on the deck while talking out loud.

"Who could have known that I have that painting? Rose knew. But I killed the bitch. First, you didn't kill her, you killed her cousin...Rose died yesterday...don't you read the fucking paper? Second, she had plenty of time to tell the whole world that Clint gave that painting to you. No, she didn't tell the whole world...she wanted to protect Clint, even after he was dead. That is so pathetically lame. You should have taken care of her eons ago. Shut up! Shut the fuck up! I know who she told...we know who she told...and you could have gotten rid of him the other night when you had him, but noooo! He hurt your little leg and you backed off. Where were you, asshole? *WE* backed off! He has the powers of the Spirit...he's protected. You have the power of the Spirit! Not the same One! He's powerful...he's covered! *For, lo, thine enemies, O Lord. For, lo, thine enemies shall perish.* He is but a Chihuahua. A little Chihuahua bit you and you went running. That cop came in or I would have cut his friggin' throat. That cop came in...you're a pathetic excuse for a soldier. You make me sick. You have let Him down and you will answer to Him! Yes! Yes I will...but not before Richard Alexander answers to Virion!"

40

Franklin Buscanni braced against the howling wind on the second story balcony of his Grace Bay Beach condo in Providenciales in the Caicos Islands. He watched the large gulls as they seemed to hang in mid-air, motionless against the powerful wind one second, then diving gracefully into the surf after prawns that had been washed up by the storm.

Ever since childhood, he had fantasized about flying like a hawk and silently swooping down on his prey. In his late sixties, Buscanni stood about five-eight and weighed about two hundred and thirty pounds. His mid-section was round like a barrel, but his shoulders and arms were extraordinarily muscular with thick wrists and large, rough hands. His olive-complexioned face was clean-shaven, round and pockmarked by a history of acne and fistfights. Added to that, years of over indulgence rendered his nose bulbous and battered looking. His hair was still jet black with only patches of grey around the temples, and he kept it slicked back. What he lacked in looks he made up for with a ruthless brand of charisma. Franklin Buscanni *was* a ruthless man…indeed, he was an evil man.

Watching the angry surf crashing onto the beach and racing closer and closer to his condo, Buscanni was weighing his reliefs against his regrets. He was relieved that Hurricane Michael had been downgraded to a category two storm; he regretted that it was still forecast to pass between Grand Turk and East Caicos Island the next day, putting Providenciales on the dirty side of the storm.

He was relieved that Provos, as the natives called Providenciales, was on the west side of the Caicos archipelago and somewhat protected from the major storm surge; he regretted sinking two million dollars into this condo only to have it battered by every frigging storm that passed between Haiti and Florida.

He was relieved that when it got through with Provos, Hurricane Michael was going to crash into Cuba; he regretted that it would probably only drown poor coast-bound Cuban peasants and not the communist bastards who had kept some of the most profitable casinos in the world shut down since 1959.

He was relieved that his illegal toxic waste disposal racket and the murder of one of his employee *rats* were never discovered; he regretted that instead of killing Richard Alexander two years ago, they turned him into some kind of *super swami* who could still expose him under the right circumstances.

He was relieved that the drunken asshole hit-man who botched both hits and then tried to blackmail him for a million dollars now laid at the bottom of one of his toxic waste pits; he regretted that it was his sister's idiot husband...but what the hell...you have to take care of *Numero Uno*... and hit-men were a dime-a-dozen.

Buscanni had been told by his late brother-in-law that Alexander's body had been taken out of his studio in a body-bag. Then a week later he was told by a cousin who was a maintenance worker at UTMB that Alexander was alive but in a coma...a vegetable...not to worry...he wouldn't be remembering anything. *Not good enough, but it may have to do for the present,* Buscanni had thought at the time. *I can't afford another botched attempt and I've got business in Provos to tend to.*

Buscanni enjoyed operating out of Provos during the winter months, but sometimes he had to go during the summer to tend to financial matters. He was nervous that the British government had signed an extradition treaty with the U.S. years ago that included the Turks and Caicos Islands. In fact, the U.S. had extradition agreements with almost the whole of the Caribbean, Central, and South America, all centers of international banking. However, big money, property ownership, and a timely show of philanthropic gesture offered a certain web of protection for foreign businessmen.

It wasn't until his Galveston cousin started sending him newspaper articles about Alexander's psychic crime-solving abilities that Buscanni's worries were rekindled. He had waited long enough…too long. The time had come to finish what he had started…to finish Richard Alexander. And he knew just the person for the task. In fact, he had already set the wheels in motion.

Having had enough of the wind, Buscanni stepped off of the balcony into his bedroom, pulled the doors closed, and hit the switch that lowered the metal storm shutters on the balcony. He loved the thrill of riding out storms and found it sexually stimulating. He was relieved to discover that the little blue pill he had taken thirty minutes earlier had performed as designed and had majestically countered his impotence; he was greatly regretting, however, that the beautiful young model who had been lying naked in his bed, waiting for his pharmaceutical resurrection, was no longer there. Frightened by the increasing fury of the approaching storm, she had gathered up her scanty clothes, the five one hundred dollar bills on the dresser that was her reward for staying with him through the storm, and fled to higher ground—a decision for which she would later be very thankful. Mr. Buscanni would be riding out this storm alone—it would be his last regret.

41

After he had told Midge about the fake Leonardo prints, Alexander talked Zapata into borrowing the painting that the Williams woman had been covered with so that they could take it to his house and study it more carefully. Zapata was reluctant to leave the solitude of his West End home to fight the Labor Day Weekend traffic that had already begun clogging Galveston's roadways...that is, until Alexander told him about Le Guin's claim to still possessed the Antoine painting. Fortunately, Zapata's cousin was on duty at the Sheriff's office and he unceremoniously shoved the rolled up canvas out a back door to Zapata.

"I don't think they are even interested in this anymore, Cuz," Zapata's cousin offered as he handed off the painting.

"How so, Bro?" Zapata asked.

"From what I hear around the station, they all think that Antoine dude did the girls, did his gay buddy, and did himself...the painting was marked for disposal. You can keep it as far as I'm concerned."

Zapata laid the painting in the back of his Hummer and headed for Alexander's house.   Inside Alexander's, they unrolled the canvas and spread it out on the living room floor. Alexander shoved push-pins through each corner into the floor to keep it from rolling back up.

"I knew it," Alexander proclaimed after studying the painting for a few seconds. "Whoever painted this is left handed and Antoine was right handed."

"How can you tell, R.A.?" Zapata asked.

"Look at the direction of the larger brush strokes and especially how the gesso was applied before the paint was applied. They move from upper left to bottom right, bowing slightly out toward the right. That's very natural for a left-hander...not that a right-hander can't paint in that direction, but it's not natural and the curve would be in the opposite direction. An artist will usually start a stroke at the highest point on the side of his dominant hand and move down across his body to the lowest point. There will be a natural curve to the line, sort of like with a compass, because the artist's shoulder is the point of the compass—just as with shorter cross-hatching lines, the elbow or the wrist will be the point of the compass. That's how I knew that the so-called copies of Leonardo's anatomical studies in the gallery today were fakes. The cross-hatch marks were in the right direction, but they had the wrong curve for a left-hander."

"And our big buddy, Le Guin...?"

"Left handed. I saw him sign a document when Doc Melton and I were in UTMB...and his wrist watch was on his right wrist, which is pretty normal for a lefty...and his cell phone was on his left side."

"Geez, R.A. Do you notice all of that crap about everyone you see?"

"Not unless I'm looking for it...but I did notice that you have on two different colored brown socks today," Alexander added with a wry smile as he popped the tops off of a couple of Michelobs. "And I might add, Virion was holding the knife in his left hand when he was trying to make sushi out of me."

"But all of this is still circumstantial evidence. We can't swear in court that it was Le Guin who tried to make sushi out of you because we never saw his face. Even if he does have the original Antoine painting, there's no one left to prove that he was the one Westwood gave it to."

"There is the email though...that Westwood sent to mnilm59...he named the painting...and we have Le Guin's business card with that email address on it, so it should at the very least place Le Guin on a list of suspects. You agreed the other night at your place."

"I know, R.A., but it's flimsy. I mean, think about it...if he still has it, he couldn't have wrapped Sabrina Williams' body in it...don't you see? Her body was found in the one lying on the floor in front of us...which leads us right back to Antoine."

"No, E.Z. This one is a forgery. The left-handed Le Guin used the original to make this one in hopes of framing Antoine...and so far it seems to be working pretty well on most everyone."

"But R.A., this begs the question, If Le Guin had Antoine's original painting and wanted to frame him, why didn't he just use the original? Why go to the trouble of forging this one... and the second one that Shaneesha Riley's body was wrapped in?"

Alexander took a long swig of beer and stared down at the painting for several seconds before the answer occurred to him.

"Practice makes perfect, E.Z."

"What...?"

"You hit the proverbial nail on the head. The second painting...to really frame Antoine good, he needed for another victim to be found wrapped up in an Antoine painting...but he didn't have one. So he copied the one he had and made this one," Alexander explained, pointing to the canvas on the floor, "to see if he could pull it off. He thought it was perfect and saw no reason to part with the original, which he covets because it was a gift from his lover, Westwood. Then he had the confidence to make the second one look like an Antoine painting. Talk about diabolical persistence.

"Now, add all this to Maggie's ordeal with the non-existent

'Dr. Mark Legion,' whose description fits Le Guin to a 'T', and there ought to be enough circumstantial evidence even for Vincent. "

Zapata sat down on the sofa, took a sip of beer, and stared at Alexander while he mulled over his friend's theory. "Ok... maybe you're right...but it's still not solid evidence. Are you saying that anyone can pick up some art supplies and make a painting?"

"No, of course not. But here's the kicker, E.Z.... I didn't pay much attention to it until this morning, but when we were at UTMB, Doc Melton mentioned that all he could find out about Le Guin's past was that his first bachelor's degree was in art. Now that's beginning to make a hell of a lot of sense...he knows how to paint. What if the cops found in his house the painting supplies needed to paint the two paintings? Surely... that would be enough to question him...right?"

"Ok...maybe. But I know you and your 'what ifs' buddy. Let me call Vincent and lay it all out for him. Meanwhile, you don't go do anything really stupid like you did when you went into Antoine's house. Deal?"

"Deal," Alexander answered. *But I'll use my definition of stupid.*

42

The next day, Monday, the first of September, was Labor Day. Since Alexander had to start teaching at the University of Houston at Clear Lake City the following day, this was the only day he would have before the next weekend to see if Le Guin really had the Antoine painting. The problem was, UTMB was also closed for Labor Day and Le Guin would not be leaving his house for work. So Alexander got Doc Melton to call Le Guin the day before and invite him out for a round of golf... ostensibly to practice for the upcoming tournament. To both their surprise and relief, Le Guin enthusiastically accepted and agreed to meet Melton at the Galveston golf course at nine Monday morning.

It was 7:00 A.M. as Alexander drove toward the Galveston causeway pulling his boat behind him. Just before reaching the causeway, he took the Teichman Road exit, crossed under the freeway, and drove over to the Causeway Marina, nested at the foot of the causeway. By 7:30, he had launched his boat and was motoring across the Intercostal Canal. The skies were mostly clear with a morning thunderstorm brewing out in the Gulf. About twenty feet above him, a pod of nine brown pelicans paced him for a few minutes before veering off to the west.

Just to his right — eastward — the causeway made its two mile span across Galveston Bay. Beneath the causeway, a tugboat was pushing two large chemical barges filled with God-knows-what through the precariously narrow pass where the Intercostal Canal cut under the causeway. To his west about half a mile, lay Snake Island where the bodies of Virion's victims had been found.

A few other boats were zipping about as Alexander guided his Baystealth into the main canal of Tiki Island. According to the map that he and Doc Melton printed out, Le Guin's house was on the main canal about half way up—1257 Tiki Lane. Alexander throttled down as he entered the "No Wake" zone of the canal and slowly motored a couple of hundred yards in until he spotted the numbers on one of the timbers of the modest three-level canal house. He let the boat drift back toward the Intercostal about thirty or forty yards then dropped anchor and pretended to fish as he waited.

Just before eight o'clock, Lee Le Guin stepped out onto his deck with a cup of coffee. He stretched, took a deep breath and savored the smell of the saltwater and briny breeze. Surveying the scene around his house, he noticed the twenty-one foot boat anchored out in the main canal about forty yards to his west. The lone fisherman was wearing sunshades and had a floppy hat pulled down over his forehead. He was casting a lure and slowly reeling it in.

Amateur, thought Le Guin as he lit a cigarette and sat down on a deck chair. *He'll never catch anything out there on a lure...he should be using live bait.* After a few minutes, Le Guin mashed out his cigarette and walked over to the edge of his deck. He reached down, grabbed a rope and pulled up a bait bucket. As water streamed out of dozens of holes in the bucket, Le Guin shouted to the fisherman.

"Hey buddy...hey! I have some mud minnows and shad here...you're welcome to them. You'll have a lot better luck with live bait. Come on over."

Crap, thought Alexander. *He wasn't even supposed to notice me.* "No thanks, I prefer lures," he shouted back without raising his head to look at Le Guin.

"Suit yourself," Le Guin answered, dropping the bucket of thrashing bait fish back into the water. *Asshole.* Looking at his watch, he turned and went back inside. *Dammit! I'm going to be late! You know I can't stand being late!*

After a few minutes, Alexander heard a vehicle start and drive off, but he couldn't see if it was Le Guin. In a few seconds, he saw Le Guin's gold-colored Lexus going across the road at the end of the canal. He kept casting his line out until he could see the Lexus up on the causeway, heading toward Galveston. Picking up his cell phone, he called Doc Melton, who was waiting for his call at the golf course and told him to ring Le Guin's house phone from a phone at the golf course desk. That way, Le Guin's caller ID wouldn't register a number that would make him suspicious. Doc reported that it rang several times before the answering service picked up.

Ok, that's a good sign. Alexander patiently surveyed every house on both sides of the canal around Le Guin's to see if anyone was outside. Pulling up the anchor, he cranked up his motor and slowly idled over to Le Guin's boat ramp, which was between his house and his neighbor to the west. The second story deck cantilevered out over the ramp, exposing large support beams. Le Guin's boat was suspended on straps a few feet out of the water toward the front of the ramp. The location offered plenty of concealment from most of the other houses and canals.

His boat tied off to a cleat, Alexander slipped on a pair of tan leather gloves, switched his floppy hat for a yellow hard-hat, strapped on a utility belt and hopped up on the deck holding a clipboard. Anyone looking would see a utility worker checking on some problem. The first level of the house was half open deck and half enclosed. The second level was about twelve feet above the deck.

He casually walked to the backdoor and felt along the top of the transom—no key. *Crap!* He was fully prepared to break in if he had to. That's why the small pry-bar was in his tool pouch. Even if an alarm went off, he could run through the house and find the painting—if it was there—and get out before the cops could get there. *I have lost my ever loving mind!* Besides, if an alarm did go off and the pad was by the back door, he was pretty sure that he could guess Le Guin's security code. Instinctively, he grabbed the door knob and gave it a twist. To his shock, the door swung open.

My God...is Le Guin still here? Quickly but calmly Alexander walked to the corner and peered around to the front of the house...no Lexus. A wave of relief washed over him. Just in case someone was watching, Alexander stopped at the electric service meter next to the back door, tapped on the glass, and pretended to record the data on his clipboard. Instead, he wrote *I am not cut out for this sneaky-assed spy business!*

Then he walked into Le Guin's house. There was an alarm pad inside the door in the large garage and utility room, but it didn't appear to be armed. *MNIL, that's what I would have tired first,* Alexander thought as he walked into the room.

A white Ford van had been backed into the garage. Alexander opened one of the back doors and looked inside. It was immaculate. There were no back seats. There was a long, open, wooden box that appeared to be bolted down behind the front seats. Alexander crawled up inside the van just far enough to see into the box. It held a large roll of plastic sheeting, some rope, and a roll of duct tape. Then he noticed that the carpet on the floor of the van was not fastened down... just a large rectangle of carpet lying flat.

As he was crawling out, his eye caught a long strand of hair woven into the fibers of the carpet...black hair. *Like Shaneesha Riley's?* He plucked it out of the carpet and the second he did he was struck with a violent vision—three visions—each one a different young woman rolled up in the carpet, floating in the air, eyes wide open, staring at him helplessly. Clearing his head from the visions, he unconsciously stuffed the strand of hair into his shirt pocket as he staggered backwards a couple of feet. *That's how the bastard transported his victims...if anyone looked in his van, all they would see is a roll of carpet.*

When he turned around, his heart jumped up into his throat. *Holy Jesus!* He was staring into a blue jumpsuit. It took several seconds for Alexander to realize that there was no one in the jumpsuit. It was hanging on a clothes line that stretched across the back of the workshop. But he knew who *had* been in it... *Virion!*

Looking to his left on the east wall of the workshop, Alexander observed a clean rectangle about four feet by six feet with paint around all of the edges...the colors used in the fake Antoine paintings. Le Guin tacked canvases to that wall and did his paintings. Opening one of the cabinets against the back wall, Alexander saw numerous jars of acrylic paint, brushes, and other art supplies. There was also a box of ping pong balls. *We've got this sick sonofabitch now!*

Alexander quickly climbed the stairs to the second floor and was relieved to find that door unlocked, too. It opened up into the most bizarre living room he had ever seen. The sofa, chairs, and ottoman were black leather and almost invisible against the black walls and black tile floors. Every wall was plastered with posters of vampire and werewolf movies... *Nosferatu,* all of the Bela Lugosi movies, Christopher Lee, Jack Palance, and Gary Oldman as Dracula, Lon Chaney, Jr. as the *Wolfman,* and posters from *Wolf, Wolfen, Curse of the Werewolf, The Howling, Silver Bullet,* and *American Werewolf in London.*

How apropos, thought Alexander, *that Virion would relate to werewolves and vampires. He must think they are all brothers in the legion of many.*

But there was no Antoine painting.

The bedroom, he thought and climbed up the next level of stairs, which opened up into a studio-type bedroom. The bedroom was the same as the living room...black walls, black floor, black bed, and black-light posters of monsters.

There on the wall in front of the bed hung Antoine's painting...*The Face of Aids II*. Being brightly colored, it almost glowed, luminescent against the blackness. The rectangle at the bottom was filled with the filament-virus shapes, but no letters...the word *Virion* wasn't there. The orange ball shapes did literally glow against the greenish background. Unlike the forged copy that Le Guin painted, this painting was elegant... painted by a professional artist who truly had a passion about his subject. Alexander took a camera out of his tool pouch and snapped several pictures. Then he heard a most chilling sound...the front door opening.

Good God almighty! What is he doing back here? I'm a dead man if he catches me! Looking around frantically for options, Alexander saw the French doors leading out to the third floor deck. Quietly but quickly, he opened one of the doors, stepped out onto the deck, and closed the door behind him. *Thank God...an outside stair case off of this deck!*

But just as he started for the stairs down to the second level deck, he heard Le Guin come out onto the second level below him and he froze. Then the door beneath him slammed shut and he heard Le Guin walking slowing up the stairs to the bedroom...he also heard the unmistakable sound of an automatic pistol being cocked. *Naturally, my pistol is safe and sound in my nightstand.*

Alexander made his move toward the stairs, trying to be as quiet as humanly possible under the circumstances. Even so, some of the planks creaked under his weight. Reaching the stairs, he noticed that the railings were smooth and slick, painted with high-gloss enamel. Instead of running down the stairs, which would have undoubtedly made noise, he jumped on the railing and slid down to the second level deck. He repeated the maneuver and slid down to the first level deck. Reaching the first level deck, Alexander quietly ran over to the rope to which the bait bucket was tied, pulled it up, and poured most of the bait fish into his hard-hat. He heard Le Guin open and then slam shut the French doors on the third floor above. He lowered the bucket into the water and ran over to his boat as he heard Le Guin quickly walking down the stairs inside the house.

Thank God that he didn't come down the outside stairs or he would have seen me for sure. Alexander hopped down into his boat, untied the rope, and shoved off with all his might. The Baystealth slid quietly out into the main canal. Alexander grabbed an oar and gave a couple of mighty strokes to push him further out into the canal. Then he grabbed the floppy hat and shades just as Le Guin exploded out onto the lower deck.

Le Guin marched out to the end of the deck with his pistol down at his side, glaring hard at Alexander, who by that time was a good forty yards away.

"Hey neighbor," Alexander yelled with his best East Texas drawl, "There you are. I decided to take you up on your offer of the bait fish. I come up on your deck to ask you, and when I knocked on that there door, it come open. I hollered, but I guess you didn't hear me. So I helped myself. You was right...I couldn't catch a damn thing with them lures. Thankya much, buddy."

Le Guin kept glaring at Alexander for what seemed like an eternity. Stuffing his pistol into his pant pocket, he reached down and pulled up the bait bucket. When he saw that most of the bait was gone, he was satisfied that the dumb hick's story was true and was angry with himself that he didn't make sure his doors were locked.

On the other hand, he was pleased at paying extra so that his silent alarm sent a notification to his cell phone...money well spent. "You're welcome," he yelled back. "Hope you do some good." *Dumbass!*

It was all Alexander could do to not fire up his motor and get the hell out of there. But he calmly turned his back on LeGuin, picked up a second rod that was rigged up for bait fishing, grabbed a shad out of the hard-hat, put it on the hook, and cast out into the canal. *Thank you, Jesus!*

Le Guin walked back inside—having a heated conversation with himself about being careless and late—and made sure all of the doors were locked this time before getting back in his car to meet Doc Melton. As he drove past the end of the canal, he saw that the guy was still anchored in the same spot. *No reason to be upset at the dumbass...I offered the bait to him. He can just thank his lucky stars that I didn't catch him in my house.*

The second Alexander saw Le Guin's Lexus on the causeway, he pulled anchor, fired up his 150 horsepower Honda motor and gave it full throttle—*screw the 'No Wake' sign!*

43

By noon, Alexander was at Mario's Italian restaurant on 61st street waiting for Zapata. He was rehearsing how to tell him about his morning adventure when Zapata walked in and sat down opposite him.

"Alright, E.Z., I don't want any lectures because it's done and over," Alexander blurted out as Zapata sat down.

"What?"

"Not only does Le Guin have the original painting, he also has all of the art supplies, he forged the paintings, he kidnaps his victims in his van and wraps them up in carpet, and he has a thing for werewolves and vampires."

Zapata sat stunned for a few seconds. "You broke into his frigging house, didn't you?"

"No, I did not...the door was unlocked," Alexander protested, taking a big bite of pizza. He then proceeded to tell Zapata about his experiences that morning including his visions. "We have him E.Z.! Call Vincent and tell him to get out there."

"I did call Vincent, R.A. and he told me to fuck off. He isn't interested in harassing an upstanding UTMB scientist when all of the evidence clearly points to Antoine."

"But tell him about what I saw this morning...I have pictures!"

"Tell him about what you saw when you were trespassing on Le Guin's property...going through his house without a

warrant? Amigo, the only one who will wind up in jail is you…
not Le Guin. You're darned lucky Vincent didn't arrest you the
other night at Antoine's house."

Alexander put his slice of pizza down and wiped his hands
on a napkin. "E.Z., I know as sure as I'm sitting here—beyond a
shadow of a doubt—that Le Guin is Virion. I know that the
Gene Vincents of the world are not going to believe me, but I
would expect you to…and I would expect you to help me
prove it. His house is full of evidence and…wait! Speaking of
evidence…" Remembering the strand of hair he found in the
van, he excitedly plucked it out of his shirt pocket and told
Zapata where he found it.

"What if this is Shaneesha Riley's hair, E.Z.? If it is, then at
least you and I will both know the truth based on hard
evidence, not just my visions. And if it is, there are bound to be
more in that carpet. I saw a shop-vac near his van. What if he
vacuumed out his van and the shop-vac is full of more
evidence? We need to move quickly on this, E.Z., before he
realizes how careless he's been. What do you say, buddy…just
one quick lab test on this strand of hair?"

"Even if it is hers, R.A., how are we going to explain to
Vincent how it came into your possession?"

"We tell him the truth…I walked into Le Guin's garage and
found it in the carpet in his van…along with the art supplies
used to forge Antoine's paintings. I don't care if it does get me
into trouble as long as they can nail Le Guin."

"R.A., think about it…if you get arrested, what's that going
to do to you and Maggie? And not to mention that you'll most
likely lose your job."

"Yeah…you're right, E.Z.," Alexander answered after a
long drink of tea. "Let's you and I just wait and hope that Le
Guin screws up somehow and gets caught before he can kill too
many more women."

Zapata sat and stared at his enigmatic friend a few seconds
then held his hand out. "Give it to me. I'll run the test myself."

44

Right on schedule, Hurricane Michael rammed into Cuba around noon. Just as Franklin Buscanni predicted, the only Cubans to drown were the poor who had no means of escaping the wrath of the storm. He was, however, wrong about Michael. The forecast he was going by was over twelve hours old. The storm had been downgraded to a category two hurricane...but that was the day before. By the time it crossed over East Caicos Island, it had grown into a monstrous category four storm generating one hundred fifty mile an hour winds and numerous tornados.

At approximately 2:00 A.M. Monday morning, the roof came off of his two million dollar condo. About a minute later the storm surge finished washing the foundation out from under the building and it crumbled into the sea. At some point in that final minute, Franklin Buscanni surely regretted never having learned to swim...or fly.

45

Sheriff's detective Gene Vincent did not receive the news very well when Dr. Ezekiel Zapata told him that hair belonging to Shaneesha Riley was found in Dr. Lee Le Guin's van. It got worse when Zapata told him how he obtained the hair.

"Come on, Gene. It's not criminal trespass when someone comes to your house to talk to you and walks into your open garage to see if you're there," Zapata argued.

"Don't bullshit me, Zapata," Vincent snarled over the phone, "Alexander didn't go over there to chat with Dr. Le Guin...he thinks Le Guin is a killer. For all I know, Alexander planted the hair in the van. I say we let Le Guin decide if it's trespassing. Maybe he wants to press charges."

"Hey...you're forgetting the real crime here, Vincent. A murder victim's hair was found in Le Guin's van—not planted there—and I'm giving you the professional courtesy of telling you first...since these murders are part of your investigation. If you choose to ignore this and refuse to get a search warrant for Le Guin's house, I'll take it above you."

"Don't fuck with me Zapata...you will regret it!"

"Maybe, but you will regret that this phone conversation is being taped. And if another woman is murdered because of your inaction, you will be the one with even bigger regrets," Zapata fired back angrily.

The conversation ended with detective Vincent slamming his office phone down in Zapata's ear. But before he did that, he told Zapata that they would be sending a search team to Le Guin's house...and a deputy after Alexander.

46

It was Tuesday, September 2nd and while Zapata and Vincent were having their phone conversation, Alexander was meeting with his graduate students at the University of Houston at Clear Lake City to plan the new fall semester projects.

"Dr. Alexander," one of his male students spoke up, "I saw your name in the paper a couple of times this summer. What is this gift you have that's always getting you involved with murders and stuff? Sounds awesome!"

Alexander straightened up in his chair. *I knew this was inevitable.* "Ladies and gentlemen, what Patrick is referring to is an aspect of my private life that has no relevance to the University, this class, or the work that we all need to get done this semester. One of these days, I may be able to discuss it with you, but meanwhile, let's concentrate on your creative projects. No more questions about my personal life…ok?"

"Just one more thing, Dr. A," a female student interjected, almost in tears. "I knew Sabrina Williams. She was a friend and her death creeps me out. I hope you can help catch her killer… that's all."

"I think they are very close to catching him, Vicki…I really don't know what else to say," Alexander answered, now feeling like any further intellectual or creative pursuits were out for the day. He gathered up his notes and stood.

"So, Thursday, I want to see your sketches and ideas for your major projects. Also, this semester we will be trudging together through Heidegger's thoroughly abstruse essay "The Origin of the Work of Art." I want you tell me how the "thingness" of a work of art applies to contemporary art and especially what Heidegger meant when he defined art as *the becoming and happening of truth.*"

Ever since the arrival of the *Muse*, Alexander had a new understanding, respect, and awe for that definition.

As Alexander walked to his office, he read the PIN message from Zapata about his impending arrest. When got to his office, he was met at the door by the Dean of Arts and Humanities, Dr. Sarah Amadi. Amadi was tall and thin...not unattractive, but tried hard to be. She kept her grey hair up in a bun and wore bland suits that fit her in a way that sent out the message, *I'm a serious administrator and have no breasts and am probably a lesbian.* Some of that message was deceiving and some of it wasn't.

"Richard, I am greatly concerned that the Galveston Sheriff's office just called me to ask if you were here today. I'm also greatly concerned that you have produced no new work this summer. But mainly, I'm greatly concerned for your personal health and wellbeing."

"Sarah, besides my marriage falling apart and my being pursued like a common criminal, I'm doing just fine. I apologize for any embarrassment that I might inadvertently bring to the University and I understand the implications...and I thank you for your concern."

"Richard, you may not fully understand the implications... this could well be your last semester here at the University. Another major incident and it will be out of my hands."

47

"I understand that you're looking for me," Alexander announced as he walked into Gene Vincent's office.

"That's right, Alexander. Dr. Lee Le Guin has pressed charges against you for trespassing and vandalism...you know, the guy whose garage you broke into yesterday."

"I didn't break into his garage. I was out there fishing and he offered me some bait. When I decided to take him up on it, I went up on his deck to talk to him. I saw him walk into his garage earlier, so I tried the garage door...it wasn't locked. I walked in and saw his van. I got curious and opened the door...that's when I spotted the strand of hair in the carpet. Curiosity is not against the law." Alexander couldn't help but notice all the gold hanging off of Vincent's skinny frame as he waved his arms around.

"Maybe, maybe not...but jimmying a locked door is."

"I didn't jimmy that door...it wasn't locked."

"Well, it's sure as hell busted up, Mr. Alexander. We sent a team out to Dr. Le Guin's house and they found the garage door busted up. So is the door leading up to his living room. That's all they found in Le Guin's house by the way. There was no carpet in the van...no shop-vac...no strands of hair...no art supplies or any sign of Le Guin ever painting anything other than his furniture in that workshop...just two doors, both jimmied with a pry-bar...like the one my deputies found in your boat. That was pretty damned embarrassing for me and my men, Alexander.

"Dr. Le Guin is a very well respected scientist in our community. And you are under arrest...not only for breaking and entering, but for withholding evidence in a murder investigation. Where did you really get that girl's hair, Alexander...from your buddy's autopsy table next door?"

"Vincent, I've withheld no evidence and I damned sure did not break into Le Guins' house," Alexander argued as he was being fingerprinted. "Don't I get to see an attorney first, or did Galveston County secede from the United States?" he continued as he was being led in handcuffs to the holding cell.

So much for my job at the University, thought Alexander as the jailer shoved him in the cell with two other men, both of whom looked very much like they belonged there.

"I could swear that you already made your phone call, Alexander. In fact, I can find at least two witnesses who'll say you did. You'll get another chance in the morning."

"You're full of crap, Vincent...you know damn well I didn't make a phone call," Alexander hollered at Vincent as the section door slammed shut.

As soon as it shut, the larger of the men in the cell stood up and walked over to Alexander. "Looks like they got careless... didn't take yo belt. Yall know, a muthafucker could hang hisself with a belt like that."

Instinctively, Alexander's military training kicked in and he grabbed his belt, jerked it out of his pant loops, and wrapped it tightly around his right fist with about a foot of it, including the heavy metal buckle, hanging loose. "You're right, brother," Alexander replied, stepping back a few feet. "I'd better hold on to this and make sure it doesn't wind up around my neck."

Standing almost 6' 2" and weighing 210 pounds, Alexander was no easy prey. Working out in the YMCA weekly kept his sixty-three year old physique looking pretty buff.

Even though his aggressive cellmate was quite a bit larger,

he must have decided that an easier opportunity would present itself later. The big man grinned widely, reached out and slapped Alexander on the shoulder and said, "That's right, muthafucker, you best hold on to that belt. I'd hate for you to get all sad and wrap that thing around yo neck while we was sleeping tonight. Then again, if yall need any help doing that, yall just wake old Tyrone here and I'll be glad to oblige."

Tyrone laughed loudly and sat back down on the bench. The other man, a thin, gaunt, black man with an ugly scar across his face from his ear to his mouth, sporting a long goatee, just sat on the bench and stared down at the floor. Folks called him Toothpick because he was so thin and always had a toothpick dangling from his scarred mouth.

Around eight that evening, the jailers brought the three inmates dinner...a hamburger, some fries, and a paper cup of water. Alexander was starving. With his belt still wrapped around his fist, he took a couple of bites off of the cold burger and sat it back on the paper plate beside him. After munching most of the fries, he took a drink of water. It tasted metallic — bitter — but he drank it to wash down the fries.

Then, after a few minutes, the cell started spinning around him. He put both hands down on the bench to stabilize himself. Alexander fell to his hands and knees on the concrete floor, then, as if in slow motion, collapsed onto the cold concrete. His glasses fell off of his face...but he felt nothing as his world went black. The last thing he heard was the big man laughing.

Tyrone walked over and unwrapped the belt from Alexander's fist. He pushed the end through the buckle, making a noose, slipped it around Alexander's throat, and yanked on it a couple of times until it was snug. Then he noticed Toothpick picking up Alexander's hamburger and let the belt — and Alexander's head — drop to the floor.

48

On Monday, Lee Le Guin met Doc Melton out at the golf course and played a quick nine holes. But while he was playing, he grew more and more concerned about the fisherman and his own carelessness. Doc wanted to play eighteen holes just to give Alexander plenty of time, but Le Guin refused and left after the first nine holes.

When he arrived at his canal house in Tiki Island, Le Guin walked around to the deck door and pried it open with a pry bar. Then he went inside the garage, up the stairs, and pried open the door leading into his living room. Back down in the garage and workroom, he pulled the carpet, the rope, the roll of plastic sheeting, and the duct tape out of his van. He then vacuumed it out thoroughly with the shop-vac, opened the shop-vac, filled it with bricks, and dropped it over the edge of the deck into the canal. He packed up all of the art supplies and rolled paint over the wall where he had painted the paintings. He waited until dark and drove everything he thought incriminating over to a dumpster behind a local restaurant and disposed of it all.

Tuesday morning around 7:00, Le Guin called in to UTMB and took the day off. Then he called the sheriff's department and reported the break-in. He said that he never got a good look at the fisherman who he suspected, but he could describe his boat...down to the Texas Parks and Wildlife registration number and the name *In the Eye of the Beer-holder.*

Vincent's men arrived at his house with a search warrant later in the day—after he had spoken with Zapata and before Alexander turned himself in. When Vincent was informed about the reported break-in, he was elated...he had Alexander where he needed him.

49

Around ten o'clock the next morning—Wednesday, September 3rd—Alexander awoke in the county jail infirmary with a pounding headache and a very sore throat and neck. Other than that, his trip from the bench to the floor was slow enough that it didn't do any damage. As his eyes began to regain their focus, he saw a ceiling fan rotating overhead and an angel bathed in glowing white light standing next to his bed. After a few seconds, the angel turned out to be an orderly dressed in a starched, white uniform.

"What the hell happened to me?" Alexander asked the orderly who was holding a tray of food. "Where am I? What day is this? What time is it? Where are my glasses?"

"Relax man," the orderly answered. "You in the infirmary...but your ass is still in jail. So it don't matter what day it is. You just need to get down on your knees and thank the Man upstairs you still alive...you one lucky sonofabitch."

"Lucky that I'm lying in the county jail infirmary with a broken neck...maybe you can explain that to me."

"Look here, man, I gonna level with you...but you never heard this from me," the orderly said in almost a whisper, laying the tray down on the portable stand beside the bed. "And the only reason I'm telling you this is because God *gots* to be on your side. You come this close," the orderly whispered, showing about an inch between his thumb and forefinger, "to 'committing suicide' in that cell last night...least-wise, that what they was wanting everyone to think happened."

The orderly sat on the side of Alexander's bed, pretending to help him get ready for breakfast. He told Alexander what happened in the cell after he had passed out from the knockout drug that was in his water.

Toothpick grabbed Alexander's hamburger and began eating it as Tyrone started to strangle Alexander with the belt. Tyrone, being a large man with a large appetite, had designs on Alexander's hamburger and wasn't about to let the thin man eat it. So they got into a fight over the hamburger. Tyrone snatched the burger away from Toothpick and punched him in the face. Tyrone then ate the burger and turned his attention back to Alexander.

As he resumed choking Alexander with the belt, Toothpick grabbed Alexander's glasses, ripped off one of the ear pieces, jumped on Tyrone's back, and repeatedly jabbed it into Tyrone's throat until the big man was bleeding profusely. Tyrone managed to throw the thin man off of his back and kick him in the head a couple of times before blacking out. Tyrone then collapsed in a heap against the door of the cell and bled to death.

Turns out, Toothpick had the scar on his face because he and Tyrone had been incarcerated together a few months earlier and Tyrone, wanting the thin man's dinner, knocked him onto the floor and stomped on his face.

"What goes around comes around," proclaimed the orderly.

"Wait a minute," said Alexander, still groggy, "that answers the question about my glasses, but who's the *they* who wanted me dead? How did knock-out drops get into my water? I need some answers here."

"Hey man, we ain't playing no Jeopardy here...I done told you everything I know...and only because you be blessed! But like I said...you didn't hear nuttin from me 'cept one of yo cellmates killed the other one 'fo he could kill you! I needs my job, man."

The orderly stood and swung the arm of the portable stand around so that Alexander's breakfast was up against his chest. Then he turned and backed away, out of Alexander's limited range of focus, until he once again turned into a white glow.

Angels come in all forms, thought Alexander as he turned his attention to his breakfast.

By noon, Zapata had arrived at the jail with Alexander's son, Jeffery, and paid his bail. Alexander related to Zapata what the orderly had told him. *Sorry, angel, someone's got to answer for this.*

Zapata immediately got on his phone and called the sheriff. Then he took Alexander to the morgue and called in a phlebotomist to draw some blood and run a test for drugs.

"Damn, dad," Jeffery said as Zapata was driving them to Alexander's house, "when are you going to give this crap up and just do your art and your teaching?"

"I was just doing my art and my teaching, Jeff, when this crap, as you put it, crashed into my life. I can no more give this up than you can give up being you."

"Sorry, dad…I don't buy that. You have a choice whether to use one of the many talents you have. You don't have to go to anymore crime scenes, look at anymore dead bodies, identify murderers, put yourself and the rest of us in harm's way…you could choose just to be an artist. Had you made that choice earlier, you and mom would still be together…"

Jeff grew silent a second, then smiled and slapped his dad on the shoulder. "And you wouldn't have to go around looking like you just lost a cage-fighting match."

"Well, I suppose you're right, son. Maybe I could have ignored this freak ability…turn my back on all of this ugliness and just paint the pretty parts of life. At least four cold-blooded killers would have possibly still been on the streets — but that didn't have to be my concern. You're right...why should an artist care about all that...even if he has a rare, unique ability to do something about it? Why let moral responsibility and God's will spoil a perfectly comfortable life?"

A thick silence filled the car. Finally, after a few minutes Jeffery — ever the peacemaker — spoke up.

"Well, I hope your moral responsibilities have left some room for the Astros. I have three tickets for tonight's game against Cincinnati ...right behind the catcher. My boss scored the tickets from some client. I thought you, E.Z., and I could relax, watch the game, drink a couple of eight dollar beers."

"And eat a couple of twelve dollar hot dogs," Zapata chimed in, laughing.

By the time they arrived at Alexander's house, they were all laughing and telling stories about the ridiculous cost of beer and food at sports events and concerts.

"By the way, son," Alexander asked Jeffery as they pulled into the driveway," what brings you to town today?"

"Well Dad, it doesn't surprise me that you're not aware of this, but a major hurricane is headed our way and due to hit Galveston Saturday or Sunday. I came to help Mom get packed up. She's coming up to my apartment tomorrow. You need to do the same. I've only got one bedroom, but you guys can have it and I'll camp out on the couch."

Ever the peacemaker, thought Alexander.

"We can go to the game tonight," Jeffery continued, "and tomorrow I'll help you get packed, put up some window protection, and we can drive to my place tomorrow evening."

"I feel like crap right now and I'll have to think about going to your place," Alexander answered, "but I think going to the game tonight is a splendid idea. What do you think E.Z.?"

"We ain't left yet?" Zapata asked, laughing.

They all laughed and resumed their joking about the cost of mindless entertainment.

50

Later that afternoon, sheriff's detective Gene Vincent was not laughing...he was beside himself. *How could everything go to hell in one fell swoop? How could that drugged-up idiot Tyrone fuck up a simple assignment...and over a goddamned hamburger! It's not like this was his first time to assist with the 'suicide' of some rat or witness.*

Sitting in his car out at the east end of Seawall Boulevard, looking out at the sandy-green Galveston ship channel, Vincent was stewing about Tyrone screwing up and getting himself killed when he got the news about the death of Franklin Buscanni. Not that Vincent gave a crap about Buscanni personally, but Buscanni paid well — very well — when Vincent took care of special problems for him. Buscanni wouldn't be sending anymore payments.

The only good news about any of this was that Buscanni — psychotic asshole that he was — deserved what he got and secondly, Vincent wouldn't have to pay Tyrone what he had promised him.

But the bad news — the really bad news — was that the thin man called Toothpick, who killed Tyrone, was spilling his guts about the whole deal. He was supposed to have helped Tyrone lift Alexander's body up to make it look like a suicide hanging. But after Tyrone took the hamburger from him and punched him out, the thin man began fearing that Tyrone was going to kill him later...he had damn near done it a few weeks before.

Do unto others before they do unto you.

But Toothpick was now in the sheriff's office claiming that he and Tyrone were being paid by a detective to kill Alexander...and for a deal, he'd give up the detective.

Does he really know anything for sure? He's a worse dope-head than Tyrone was. I only talked to Tyrone and Tyrone would not have told him my name...or did he? And did he say anything incriminating to Alexander? What if Alexander used those freaky powers of his to uncover the whole plot?

Vincent trusted Tyrone to do what he was told because Vincent had too much on him. Tyrone even got himself and Toothpick arrested for fighting in a bar the night before so that they would be in the holding cell when Vincent had Alexander locked up with them.

It should have been flawless, like the other times, Vincent was thinking when his cell phone rang. It was the sheriff himself. He needed to talk to Vincent immediately. It was very serious. Alexander's blood test showed that he was drugged and the sheriff wanted to know why procedure was not followed in the jail. Why were the evening guards sent home early and why did Alexander have his belt and his glasses in the holding cell? And what about Vincent's business card in Tyrone's wallet?

Vincent stared out at the cargo ships and tankers coming in and out of the ship channel. Seagulls were flying high above a shrimp boat in a vortex and diving down in a frenzy after the detritus of shrimp, jellyfish, and other small sea creatures being dredged up by the nets. Occasionally a large brown pelican would drop out of the sky and hit the water like a bag of bricks, and coming up with a mullet between its beaks.

Vincent wished he could fly out there like a seagull and land on a freighter headed for South America. He turned his car around and drove toward town. After about a half a mile, Vincent stopped his car, stared long and hard at the Galveston skyline as if it was Sonny Corleone's fateful tollbooth in "The Godfather."

He turned his car around again and drove back toward the end of Seawall Boulevard. The east end of Seawall Boulevard was marked by a four-foot high concrete wall connected to an old World War II concrete artillery bunker. Beyond the wall, lay about twenty yards of granite blocks and then the ship channel about thirty feet below.

Vincent, tears flowing from his eyes, floored the accelerator of his Ford Explorer and by the time the front bumper struck the wall, it was going about one hundred miles an hour. For a few seconds, Sheriff's Investigator Gene Vincent did fly with the seagulls...but alas, he didn't land on a freighter bound for South America.

˙51˙

The next morning, Thursday, September 4th, Alexander awoke to the now forgivable barking of Rambo, the chattering of squirrels, and an unusually clamorous sound of traffic and excited voices. Rolling out of bed, he stuck his feet into his slippers and shuffled out into the front room in his boxer shorts to see what was going on. He regretted having stayed out so late, but at least the Astros beat Cincinnati and he, Jeffery, and Zapata had a really good time.

It was 7:00 AM. Lifting one of the slats in his blinds, Alexander saw neighbors up and down the street loading up their vehicles. *Oh yeah...the hurricane. They're getting the hell out of here.* Suddenly, his view was cut off as a piece of plywood slammed against the window with a bang. Alexander almost fell backwards. *What the hell...?* He opened the front door and stepped out onto the porch. Jeffery was holding the rectangular section of plywood up with his shoulder while zip-screwing it into place with a portable drill.

"Thank God we cut all of your window coverings last year and stored them in your garage," Jeffery hollered as he guided another zip-screw into place. "But I can't find any more zip-screws. Do you know where they are, Dad? By the way, you're standing out here in your underwear."

"Right...zip-screws...I gave them to Jack a while back when he was building the deck behind his house."

"Well, we need a shitload more, Dad, to get all of your

window coverings up."

Physically at least, Jeffery was the proverbial chip off of the old block. He stood around six feet tall, slim, muscular, with a head full of wavy brown hair. His face was long, chiseled, and tan, accented by a fuzzy goatee and mustache. Unlike his dad, however, he had almost no artistic or musical abilities; but calculus and physics flowed through his brain with the precision and rhythm of an Irish Riverdance. Also unlike his dad, he was a worrier and a linear thinker. Once he got onto a project, it was going to get done, step by step.

"I'll have to run over to Chalmer's Hardware and get what we need," Jeffery continued. "Meanwhile, you know how I like my eggs with that Owen's hot sausage. But first, while I'm gone, if you'll just set each section of plywood under the window where it goes, that'll save us some time. They're all numbered, remember. Oh, and Dad…really, put some pants on…those lily-white legs are scary."

An hour later, Alexander had the plywood sections in place and the sausage cooked and was waiting for Jeffery to get back before frying the eggs. Two hours later he was on his cell phone calling Jeffery, but getting no answer. Three hours later Alexander was at Chalmer's Hardware store.

Jeffery's car was parked down the side street. The store was packed with last minute shoppers who needed hardware and duct tape for window protection. But there was no sign of Jeffery in the store. As Alexander approached the checkout counter, he noticed a flat-panel TV on the wall tuned in to the Weather Channel. Hurricane Michael was entering the Gulf of Mexico off of Cuba and churning about fourteen miles per hour on a B-line toward Galveston. When he described Jeffery and asked if the clerk had seen him, she looked at him like he was wearing the orange pajamas from the psycho ward at UTMB.

"I can't tell you how many young men looking like that have been through here buying zip screws this morning," she said, motioning with her thumb back over her shoulder toward the TV.

Alexander left the store and jogged down 20th street to Jeffery's car. It was locked and everything seemed normal. On the passenger's seat was a paper bag full of zip screws from Chalmer's. He called Jeffery's phone again, but no answer.

This is very unusual...Jeffery always answered that phone. Ok...he went back inside the store...I just didn't see him... probably poor reception in there. I'll wait right here.

By 11:00, Alexander was convinced that Jeffery wasn't anywhere around. He thought about calling Maggie...then he thought about it again. She would only panic and blame him. Worse, she wouldn't leave Galveston until they found Jeffery and she needed to evacuate before the traffic made it impossible.

Alexander reached for the driver's door handle just to see if he could get into the car. *Maybe Jeffery left a note or something.* The door was locked, but something was very wrong...Alexander couldn't let go of the handle. It was as if an electric current was surging through the car, making it impossible for him to release his grip on the handle. Sweat began breaking out on his forehead as his arm shook violently. He saw his reflection in the window as he was struggling to let go of the handle—and then he saw the reflection of Lee Le Guin walking up behind him. His heart almost stopped as he jerked his cramped hand free and spun around.

There was no one there. Across the street a man and his daughter were walking to their car, staring at Alexander as if he was a lunatic trying to steal a car. To make matters worse, Jeffery's car alarm started going off.

"This is my son's car," Alexander hollered at the man who grabbed his daughter's hand and kept staring at Alexander as he picked up his pace. "He locked his keys in the car," Alexander lied in desperation. *Virion has Jeffery!*

52

By the time Jeffery had arrived at Chalmer's, stood in a long line of anxious shoppers, purchased the zip screws, and walked back to his car, it was almost 8:30. He opened the driver's door and threw the bag of zip screws onto the passenger's seat.

"Excuse me, young man…sorry to bother you."

Jeffery turned around to see a balding, middle-aged man driving a white Ford van that had pulled up next to him in the street. Droplets of sweat were running off of the man's forehead.

"Not a problem," Jeffery answered, smiling. "What can I do for you?"

"I live right around the corner on Ball Street," the rather large man began, pointing ahead. "I hate to bother you, but I really need a strong, young back to help me cover my picture window with plywood. I just need someone to hold the pieces in place while I fasten them. It shouldn't take long. I'll be glad to pay you for your time and trouble."

"No, I don't need your money, I'll be glad to help if it won't take too long. I'm helping my dad, too."

"You are a saint, my young friend. Tell you what…hop in and I'll drive you over and bring you back. It'll be over with before you know it."

Jeffery locked his car. *This should only take a minute.* He opened the door and hopped into the passenger seat. He noticed the van had a large roll of carpet in the back and right behind the seats was a large wooden box with a roll of duct tape and some rope. The huge driver reached out to shake his hand.

"Mark Legion, young fellow."

"Jeffery Alexan…" Jeffery started to say as the driver firmly grasped his hand and yanked him out of the seat with such force that his head snapped back, like he had been rear-ended. Before Jeffery could recover, the hypodermic needle was in his neck and he was being sucked down into a black whirlpool of dizziness. For a second, he tried to fight it, but unconsciousness was falling on him like a lead blanket. The last thing Jeffery heard was Le Guin's voice, coming from the top of the deep well into which he was now sinking.

"You and your dad will be my swine."

53

After the fourth trip inside the hardware store, Alexander drove back to his house. On the way, he called Zapata and told him that Jeffery had disappeared. He told him about his vision of Le Guin.

"Come on, amigo...he met some hot chick in the store and she asked him to help her and he took off with her. Jeffery is a big boy and he can take care of himself."

"No, Jeffery would have at least called me," Alexander answered, pulling into his driveway and hoping against all hope that Jeffery would be standing on the front porch with a story about how his car wouldn't start and his cell phone battery was dead. "Jeffery is a linear thinker and he was on a mission to help his old man. If anything interfered with that, he would have called me. I saw Le Guin in my vision when I touched Jeffery's car and there would have been no reason to unless he was involved. I'm getting my pistol and going out to Le Guin's."

"Whoa, buddy...you do not want to do that!" Zapata answered, now very concerned. "You wait right where you are and I'll be there in five minutes."

"Hold on E.Z., I'm getting another call...it's Jeffery! I'll get right back to you."

"Jeffery! Where the hell are you?" Alexander shouted into his phone.

"Shut up and listen carefully, Dr. Alexander," the voice on

the other end commanded. "I'm not going to repeat this and I think you can comprehend how serious I am because you have seen my work. Jeffery is resting comfortably at the moment, but he is one drip away from death. You will do exactly as I say or this catheter in Jeffery's arm will be his highway to heaven. Do I have your complete attention?"

"Le Guin, you sick sonofabitch, if you hurt my son, I will..."

"You will call me Virion...and threats will only reap deleterious consequences for your son, so I again emphasize the importance of your attention to my instructions," Le Guin said in a chillingly commanding but calm voice. "Do not provoke me, Dr. Alexander! I can very well carry out my plans without Jeffery or you, but you know what that means for Jeffery. Are we in concordance, Dr. Alexander, or shall I open the drip valve? You have five seconds."

"All right...I'm listening...I'm listening. What do you want?"

"First of all, we are not at my house, so do not waste time going there. Secondly, if I hear anything on the radio or TV about this incident, I will fully open the valve. Thirdly, I assume you have called your compadre, Dr. Zapata...call him back and tell him Jeffery is ok...he's simply helping a friend prepare for the hurricane. Fourthly, get a pen...here are the things I want you to do between now and Saturday morning. Drip, drip, Dr. Alexander."

·54

Alexander tried to ask Le Guin why he was the target of his wrath—even though he already knew the answer—but Le Guin cut him off, saying there would be plenty of time for questions and answers later. The one thing Alexander was not going to do was to lie to Zapata about Jeffery. *I need all the help I can get to think this through…and I may need E.Z. to be my tail-gunner.* He called Zapata back and told him about his conversation with Virion.

Thursday night was very dark with clouds rolling in from the Gulf and choking off what little light the quarter moon may have provided. Around ten that evening, Alexander turned on his small kitchen TV to the Weather Channel and watched the huge counter-clockwise pinwheel of Hurricane Michael surging across the Gulf of Mexico, halfway between Cuba and Galveston—25.5N, 90.4W. Knowing he was to sit and wait for that monster to come roaring over Galveston Island made the hairs on Alexander's neck stand and salute.

There were no lights on in the house, other than the range light in the kitchen. In the living room, the TV was on but muted. The door between the living room and the kitchen was closed. Alexander was wearing his .357 magnum pistol in a holster strapped to his belt. As he heard his back gate open and close, he reached up into his liquor cabinet and pulled down a bottle of 18 year old Glenlivet. He heard the footsteps up to his back porch and then gentle rapping on the kitchen door.

Alexander picked up a flashlight, pulled his pistol from its holster, moved the blinds aside with the barrel, and briefly flicked on the flashlight. He opened the door and Zapata and Doc Melton slipped in like a couple of cats with a junkyard dog after them.

"Goddamned!" Doc Melton said in a loud whisper. "First I thought Zapata was going to shoot my ass in the alley and here you are waving that cannon around."

"I told you to meet me at R.A.'s back gate, not jump out from behind the trash cans," Zapata retorted.

"Here, Doc," Alexander said, handing him the bottle of scotch. "Are you guys sure that no one could have seen you coming in?"

"No sweat, R.A.," Zapata answered, "I had Doc drive around the block once to see if Le Guin's van or car were anywhere around. Both of us parked a couple of blocks away in opposite directions and walked through the alley to get here. Sherlock Holmes couldn't figure out that we were here."

"Did Sandy and the kids leave?" Alexander asked, handing Zapata a beer.

"Yes, she and the kids and the grandkids left with our daughter and drove over to San Antonio to stay with her sister."

"I have never run from a damn hurricane and I'm not about to start now," Doc chimed in, pouring a glass of the single malt.

"Ok, let's do some brainstorming," Alexander said as they sat down at the kitchen table. "Did you check out his house, Doc?"

"Yep. I even walked up the outside stairs...banged on every door. His Lexus is in the drive, but the van isn't there."

"How could you be sure about that?" Alexander asked. "He keeps it in the garage."

"Easy...I busted out the driver's window of his Lexus and

punched the garage door opener," Doc answered, taking a long drink of scotch. "No van in the garage…damned alarm on that Lexus was irritating as hell, though."

They all had a good laugh.

"Ok, that confirms that he doesn't have Jeffery in his house," Alexander said. "So that means that they're either camping out in the van or in a motel…it's not easy keeping someone sedated while driving around in a van for a couple of days."

"What is it that he wants you to do, R.A?" asked Zapata.

"He told me to turn off my cell phone and leave it in my mailbox and gave me a shopping list…two utility bags with belts, four nine-volt batteries, a digital kitchen timer, and a large roll of electrical tape. While I was shopping, he came and got my phone and left that box in front of my door. It contained this envelop with two pills and this cell phone. The instructions said to take one pill at 7:00 a.m. tomorrow, one at noon, and wait for his call on this phone. He said he would know if I hadn't taken the pills …and if he suspected that, he'd kill Jeffery then and there."

"Ok," Zapata said, taking notes and thinking back on his time in Viet Nam as a demolition specialist, "he's probably making a timed bomb and either drugging you so he can come get you or he wants you to meet him somewhere, too spaced out to give him any resistance. Whatever you do, don't take the pills."

"E.Z., I have to take the frigging pills. He said he'd know if I didn't. I don't know what these pills do. I can't take that chance. That's where you guys come in…you're my tail-gunners. I've arranged it with Jack for you to stay next door in his house. He's already evacuated for the storm. You guys wait and watch. We can communicate by these walkie-talkies. Pull one of your cars into Jack's garage later…then whether I drive off or he comes and gets me, you follow."

"So, you're not supposed to do anything tomorrow except take the frigging pills and wait?" Doc asked.

"That's what he said."

"Let me have a look at those pills," Zapata said, slipping on a pair of latex gloves.

Alexander pulled a small white envelop out of his shirt pocket that was still sealed shut and handed it to Zapata. "I haven't even looked at them."

"Good, you shouldn't touch them...we can't rule out the possibility that this whole thing is just a plot to get you to take a tab of cyanide or something equally lethal." Zapata carefully tore open the envelope and very cautiously sniffed above the opening. Then he opened the envelope wider and peered inside. Smiling, he dumped the contents into the palm of his gloved hand.

"Alprazolam...better known as Xanax," he announced, holding out two small, orange oval pills. "This is a pretty strong dose...they will make you very mellow and keep you that way all day. I can't imagine that he's expecting you to drive anywhere."

"How long do they take to work?" Alexander asked.

"One to two hours usually," Zapata answered.

"Ok, then we can be pretty sure that he's probably going to pick me up here around two o'clock. That should give the second pill plenty of time to be in full effect."

"Good thinking, R.A.," Doc responded after downing the first glass of scotch.

"The hurricane should be blowing pretty hard by then. The wind has already begun to pick up out of the northeast. The streets will start flooding pretty quickly...could make it pretty difficult for you guys to do any tailing."

"That's why God invented the Hummer," Zapata replied, pulling his Glock 9 mm out of its holster and checking to see if he had a full clip.

"Has it occurred to anyone else that the cops ought to be involved in this situation?" Doc Melton asked, nervously eying Zapata's pistol.

"I am the cops," Zapata answered, taking a long pull off of his beer and pointing to the Galveston County Deputy Sheriff badge on his belt. "And after what we found out about Vincent —God rest his tortured soul—who are we going to trust? Besides, they're pretty preoccupied evacuating residents for the hurricane. Le Guin has his bases pretty well covered."

·55

Earlier that evening around 5:00, Karl Wayne Wagner sat at his kitchen table cursing the bill he got for fixing the damage caused to his car when Rose de la Rosa dove into it after being hit by the trolley. He threw his tenth empty beer bottle in the garbage can and made his decision.

"We are not pussies!" he slurred at his mangy cat who was hastily slurping up her Friskies out of a saucer on the kitchen floor. "Well o.k., maybe you are, but I'm not! We are not running from this goddamned storm."

Wagner had no way of knowing then that his decision was a fatal one.

An hour later, as he reached inside of his refrigerator for his twelfth beer, he was startled by a loud crunch of splintering wood. He opened the kitchen door to his back porch to see the last sight he'd ever see…a huge man in a blue jumpsuit walking toward him. Before he could protest, the pry-bar smashed into his left temple and Karl Wayne Wagner began his journey through eternity.

56

Jeffery Alexander was floating above a double bed staring dreamily at the ceiling fan turning above his head. He wasn't aware of his left arm being handcuffed to the side of the bed frame or the I.V. delivering the strong sedative into his bloodstream. And try as he might, he could not remember how he got there. Nor was he aware that he was in the house directly in front of his dad's house. Jeffery was aware that something was not right, but he just couldn't make himself care... he was enjoying his new ability to float in mid-air.

In the bathroom attached to the master bedroom, which was adjacent to the room Jeffery lay in, Karl Wayne Wagner was face-down in the bathtub, his throat slit ear-to-ear. In the darkened living room, Dr. Lee Le Guin was peering through the blinds at Alexander's house with a pair of binoculars. He could tell a TV was on by the changing shadows and colors against the blinds and radiating through the glass window on Alexander's front door, but could not make out any particular movement. So far, Alexander seemed to be following his instructions.

Le Guin was terrified of being on the Island when a hurricane was approaching—as any reasonable person would be. But he was on a mission. *I have to release my demons!*

He had visited the 1900 Hurricane Museum and had seen the terrifying photographs of Galveston Island in the aftermath. He had known all along that he was to be sacrificed for the cause, but not this soon...not this way...he still had much more work to do as Virion...too many swine to infect.

Yet God had challenged him...infected his program with a virus, so to say...*a Seer, of all things!* But no matter — Alexander would not be allowed to stop him, *storm be damned!* Nonetheless, the thought of drowning sent chills of terror up the huge man's spine, and by God, Alexander and his son were going to pay for this anxiety... *That's right Dr. Alexander...just like Abraham, you're going to sacrifice your only begotten son...only no angel is going save him...and you're going with him!*

57

In the Gulf of Mexico, there are more than 3,850 oil and gas producing platforms — the densest concentration being south of Louisiana. Many of the larger rigs are manned 24/7, year around. Hurricane season presents the gravest threat to production and profits for the oil and gas industry. Any hurricane heading toward Louisiana, Mississippi, or Texas can cause the evacuation of over 800 rigs.

Thursday morning, maintenance tech Wesley Allan Le Guin leaned against the railing on the top floor of a semi-submersible rig in the Garden Banks zone 515, around 260 miles southeast of Galveston, Texas. Wesley was one of a skeleton crew, the last men to have been evacuated.

But Wesley didn't want to be evacuated. He feared what would be waiting for him. He'd much rather take his chances with the hurricane. That's why he volunteered to be on the skeleton crew and then hid in one of the tool rooms when the last evacuation chopper came in. The operations coordinator even called out his name over the intercom for what seemed like an hour when they discovered that Wes Le Guin hadn't been checked off the evac roster.

"Wes Le Guin, this is your last call. We have to leave now! Countdown begins now...you have sixty seconds to get on deck...sixty, fifty-nine, fifty-eight..."

The evac crew had done a last minute sweep through the crew quarters and most of the rig and determined that no one was left. Le Guin had obviously got on an earlier flight without ever signing the roster. *To hell with Le* Guin, the operations coordinator thought, *he's a fucking weirdo anyway!*

The relatively small rig was already feeling the thirty foot swells as the last evac chopper grabbed pitch, lifted up into the stiff east wind, swung around and headed north toward Lafayette. After about thirty minutes, when he was sure that he was alone, Wesley Le Guin crawled out of the tool locker, made his way to the top deck and leaned against the railing to watch the huge swells being pushed up by Hurricane Michael. Rain was pelting the deck. He took a long pull on the bottle of Jim Beam that he had sneaked aboard the rig and stepped inside a tool room out of the rain.

He pulled out his cell phone and replayed the voice message his father had left three days earlier.

"Wes. I got the devices you rigged for me and the instructions. They're perfect. I know you have to evacuate your rig soon and I want you at my house Friday Morning. I need your help with this very important project. Do not fail me."

Piece of cake…this rig can ride out a hurricane, Wesley thought, hoping to convince himself. *There's plenty of food and water in the galley and I can hook up a small generator. When the crew gets back, I'll be a hero. I'll tell them I was in the electrical room on the A deck making sure the circuits were shutting down when I got shocked real bad and passed out… woke up under the workbench and I was all alone. Maybe I'll finally get some respect. Anyway, whatever happens—even prison—beats having to face him again!*

Wesley Allan Le Guin was the bastard son of Dr. Lee Le Guin and he had never figured out if he should love his father or hate him. One thing he was sure of…he feared him mightily. His mother had given Wesley up for adoption at birth—would have aborted the child had Le Guin not threatened to kill her if she did. Not having inherited his father's huge stature, Wesley

Allan was a thin man, stood 5′ 8″, and had the brown skin and black hair of his mother's Mexican heritage. He did, however, inherit his father's cold, blue eyes and balding forehead. What hair he had hung off the sides of his head, stringy and greasy.

Wesley was raised by his adopted parents in Arkansas for ten trying years. One day his adopted dad took Wesley duck hunting and Wesley 'accidently' shot him in the back at point-blank range with a twenty-gauge shotgun—twice. When the truth finally came out, Wesley admitted that he was angry because his parents wouldn't buy him a motor scooter.

After living a couple of years in a mental institution for youth, he spent his teenage years moving from foster parents to foster parents, constantly in trouble with school officials and the law. At the age of eighteen, he managed to get his GED certificate, dropping his adopted name and using the name Le Guin after discovering his biological father's name. He blackmailed a social worker into getting a social security card in the name of Wesley Allan Le Guin after discovering the social worker's little meth lab in the basement of his house. Instantly Wesley Allan's sordid past was deleted. That's when he felt it was time to meet his dad. That was to be his first real lesson in the true meaning of fear.

'58

It was the summer of 2006 when the lesson began. At first there was no emotion to be shared as Wesley Allan stood at Lee Le Guin's front door and told him he was his long-lost son. Two sets of identical blue eyes just stared coldly at each other. Wesley had known his share of bad-to-the-bones people, from whom he had suffered every category of abuse...but after about ten seconds, Wesley knew that he was staring into the very soul of Evil. And Lee Le Guin knew that the pathetic punk standing before him was indeed his bastard son. This was no joyous return of the prodigal son.

How timely, Le Guin thought. *Dracula had his Renfield, Virion shall have his!*

Le Guin took Wesley in with the understanding that Wesley had to agree to learn a worthwhile trade...he would not be allowed to live in Galveston with Le Guin. Le Guin enrolled Wesley in a proprietary school in Houston to learn instrumentation and electronics and set him up in an apartment close to the school. The day that Wesley got his certificate, Le Guin decided that it was time...*the preaching was over, and the lesson begun.*

Wesley's graduation was the excuse for a 'party.' Le Guin engaged a prostitute to entertain Wesley in the guest room of his house after an evening of heavy drinking. Le Guin waited outside the bedroom door until he determined that they were finished then barged in and jabbed a hypodermic needle into the woman's throat. He then instructed Wesley to drag the unconscious prostitute down to the garage. After they laid the woman's drugged body on the worktable, Wesley stood beside her in a stupor. Le Guin grabbed his right arm and pressed the handle of a straight razor into the palm of his hand.

"Have you ever slit a bitch's throat?" Le Guin asked in a voice that Wesley had never heard.

"What? What the fu..." Wesley started to ask when his dad squeezed Wesley's hand around the razor handle and in a powerfully smooth stroke, buried the blade of the razor into the woman's throat and slid it from one side to the next. For a brief moment, Wesley stared in disbelief at the sanguine line across the woman's throat and then gagged as the gash opened up with a burst of blood and the woman's body began to convulse. He dropped the razor and tried to run, but Le Guin grabbed his long hair and slammed him to the floor.

"Listen to me bastard child of Virion. You have just become a virion. You have just raped and murdered this bitch...your DNA is inside of her and your fingerprints are on the murder weapon. You belong to Virion. When I call, you will come. Whatever I ask of you, you will do. Or you will wind up on death row."

When Wesley awoke the next morning, the litany was repeated and Le Guin made sure that Wesley saw the dead whore again. Then Le Guin, in a complete change of personality, told Wesley that he had arranged an interview for him to work on an offshore oil rig.

"Don't fuck it up, Wes," was the last thing Wesley Allan Le Guin heard from his father—or as he called himself, Virion. As he stood outside the bus station on 25th street, waiting for the bus to Lafayette, Louisiana, he watched a homeless black man puking in the gutter across the street from the post office. *Which is worse...his life or mine?*

59

Wesley Allan Le Guin was now getting another lesson on fear. But in the words of Tom Paxton, *it was a lesson too late for the learning.* The winds and rain were conducting a cacophonous symphony of death and destruction throughout the steel structure of the drilling rig and the relentless swells were now beating violently against the bottom platform to provide the timpani drums...the fourth movement of Beethoven's Sixth Symphony as arranged by Hurricane Michael.

Wesley fought the wind and rain as he felt his way inside the control room. He walked down the hall to his cabin, took another long swig of whiskey and flopped down on his bunk. Even though the rig was shuddering like it was made from an Erector Set, Wesley fell into drunken slumber. When he awoke an hour or two later, all he could think about was how his father had made him participate in the murder of a prostitute... and then of his mother. He just wanted to meet her...see who she was...tell her he forgave her for selling him off like some used car.

But Lee Le Guin had other plans. "She knows too much," Le Guin said flatly as the woman he mistook for the mother of his son—Rose de la Rosa—walked into the kitchen of Derrick Antoine's house on the night of August 25th. Instead of the long-awaited reunion, Wesley found himself in another nightmare—totally controlled by the madman who called himself Virion. Rose's cousin, Gabriela, walked into the dark kitchen and laid Rose's keys on the butcher block table.

Before she could find the lights, Le Guin had her in a choke hold. She fought violently at first, but Le Guin smashed his huge fist into her face a couple of times until she was unconscious. He made Wesley help him carry her upstairs, take off her clothes, and lay her in the bathtub. As the tub filled with water, Le Guin instructed Wesley to cut her throat. Wesley couldn't do it, so Le Guin grabbed the knife and buried it Gabriela de la Rosa's throat. Wesley wanted to puke, but was afraid if did, his father would kill him, too.

That's when they heard movement downstairs and Le Guin went down and fought with Richard Alexander. Wesley slipped down the stairs during the fight and crept along the wall like a frightened rat. It was his silhouette that Alexander noticed in front of the window right before Le Guin charged the table under which Alexander was sitting.

Just before Zapata burst in the front door, Wesley hid in the front coat closet and stayed there until he heard Zapata and Alexander run upstairs. That's when he quietly slipped out of the closet, picked up the knife that Le Guin had thrown at Zapata, the shoes that Le Guin had taken off in order to sneak up on Alexander, and on his way out of the kitchen tore his father's partial portrait out Alexander's sketchbook. As Wesley left through the back door, Gene Vincent and his deputies came in the front.

I had no love for my mother, Wesley thought, lying on his bunk, *I just wanted to know who she was...but she didn't deserve...*

His thought was interrupted by the unmistakable sound of wrenching steel. The roar of the wind was like a jet plane hovering overhead. *What the hell was that,* he thought sitting up and feeling disoriented. *Too much whiskey.*

Then Wesley heard a sound on the floor of his cabin. He looked over to see one of his hardhats sliding across the floor and wedging itself under his bunk. It took a second for that to register, but when it did, the fear welled up in his throat like a volcano erupting, pushing the whiskey aside.

"Jesus!" he yelled. "The rig is listing...Jesus!" Wesley bolted up and scrambled through his closet to find his life-jacket. It wasn't there like it should have been. He ran out onto the deck and grabbed a floatation device out of an emergency chest. He looked around in a panic for the nearest SOLAS life-boat, but the rain beat against his face, almost blinding him. The roar of the wind and the scream of bending steel were deafening. Sparks were flying like Fourth of July fireworks. *Sparks?! My God,* he thought as his feet slipped out from under him and he started sliding toward the edge of the tilted platform, pushed along by one hundred twenty mile per hour winds...*I forgot to shut down the backup generator!*

Reaching out in a panic to grab something, he saw the 440 volt cable hit the deck in front of him, bouncing like an angry, writhing snake. The cable-snake bit into the metal plate of the deck with an explosion of sparks and steam just as Wesley slid into it. A few seconds later the bastard son of Virion flew off of the listing platform, a charred sacrifice to the angry sea below.

Neptune may have been appeased, but Hurricane Michael was not.

60

Around 2:00 A.M. Saturday morning, Doc Melton pulled his car inside of Jack's garage, next door to Alexander. Zapata was lying down in the back seat. Zapata used one of the walkie-talkies to notify Alexander that they were in place and would be inside Jack's house watching.

The maneuver didn't go unnoticed. Lee Le Guin squinted into his binoculars and wondered what was going on. He was certain that Alexander's neighbor evacuated that morning... *why would he come back?* The big man stepped back and plopped onto a sofa. *To hell with it. He isn't going to interfere with my mission. Gotta lay down and get some rest... Alexander knows better than to cross me.* Le Guin curled up on the sofa and instantly fell into a fitful sleep.

A moment later, Richard Alexander stepped out onto his front porch and a stared hard at the house across the street. *Jeffery and Virion are very close by...I know that as sure as I'm standing here!* Exhausted, Alexander went inside and laid on his bed fully clothed, his pistol close by.

61

It seemed only a few minutes later when Alexander awoke to the sound of wind and rain drumming against his window. He bolted straight up in bed as reality pushed its way through the fog of fatigue. It was seven A.M. He picked up one of the orange pills Le Guin had mailed him. *Well, let's hope E.Z. is right,* he thought and popped the pill in his mouth, washing it down with a glass of water on his night stand.

E.Z. wasn't right...not about how long the pill would take to work. By the time Alexander had made coffee and scrambled a couple of eggs, he could hardly keep his eyes open. There was a humming in his ears and it was very difficult to focus on anything.

Even though Le Guin had tried to assure Alexander that it wasn't his intention to kill him or Jeffery—"I need you both alive, for you're my herd of swine"—Alexander took Zapata's advice and strapped one of his friend's .32 automatics to his ankle. *Not that I think I could even aim at anyone, much less hit him in this state of mind.*

Maggie is probably going crazy by now, Alexander thought. *Funny that she hasn't called...oh yeah, I don't have my phone and I can't dare call anyone on this one...if Le Guin sees any activity on the call log, that'd be all for Jeffery.*

Zapata checked in on the walkie-talkie from Jack's house next door and Alexander mumbled that he was ok. Then he stumbled over to the couch and plopped down to read a book.

In a few seconds, he was sound asleep.

He dreamed there was a herd of pigs running through his living room. They had protest messages painted on their sides in neon green paint. *Jesus is a pig hater…The Lord hates lard… Drown the swine and pass the wine.* One of them stopped in front of Alexander, his snout only a few inches away, and started making strange electronic squeals. It morphed into sounding like a phone ringing.

Finally, Alexander woke up enough to realize that the phone Le Guin had given him was ringing on the coffee table in front of him. He quickly picked it up and dropped it. By the time he answered it, no one was on the line. He stared at it, the gravity of missing the call beginning to override his stupor. But the drug just wouldn't let him panic. Suddenly, it rang again and he answered it.

"Wake up, Dr. Alexander. It's twelve noon," Le Guin said. "Time to take your second pill. Answer me!"

"Ok, ok," Alexander slurred.

"Take it now while I'm on the phone with you. I'll know if you haven't."

"Ok, I said," Alexander answered and walked over to his night stand, picked up the pill, and stared at it. "Why the hell should I take this just to make it easier for you to kill me?" Alexander asked, suddenly feeling angry about the untenable situation he and Jeffery were in. "How do I know Jeffery is even alive?"

"I gave you my word, Dr. Alexander. If all I wanted was you and Jeffery dead, I would have killed the both of you long before this," Le Guin replied, on the verge of losing his temper. "How provincial, Dr. Alexander! This mission is much larger than the three of us! Like you, sir, I am an artist at what I do… that's why I was chosen to do it. Here…if I must prove myself to you…Jeffery, say hello to your father." Le Guin sounded genuinely hurt.

There was a moment of shuffling sounds, then Alexander heard Jeffery's voice...drugged, but unmistakably Jeffery. "Heeey, Dad...that you? Where you been, man? Did you know I can levitate?"

"Jeffery! Are you ok, son? What's he done to you?"

"Who? This is fucking cool, man, I..."

"There! May I now assume you are satisfied that I am not a liar?" Le Guin asked, angrily, after jerking the phone away from Jeffery. "I told you before that Jeffery is on a drip and that if you cross me, he will die on that drip. Now take that fucking pill and wait for my further instructions!"

"Alright, alright! I'm taking it," Alexander replied.

As he took a long drink of water, he could hear Jeffery in the background. "That's right, man...I'm on a trip."

"Have you taken the pill, Dr. Alexander?"

"Yeah...I've taken it already."

"Then relax. Do not make a call on that phone. If I see one call on that phone's call log...well, you know the consequences. I will call you when I'm ready."

As Le Guin broke the connection, Alexander began to regret that he had his house phone removed a while back and relied solely on his cell phone... *which, of course, Le Guin now has.* But he did have the walkie-talkie, so he updated Zapata and Doc Melton and told them to keep on their toes.

62

Alexander kept busy cleaning house, watching the Weather Channel on the TV, doing crunches and push-ups, trying not to fall asleep again. He was startled when the cell phone rang again after only thirty minutes and sprinted from the kitchen into the living room to answer it.

"Yes?"

"Dr. Alexander, pick up the bag with the items I told you to buy and walk across the street to Mr. Wagner's house and knock on the door. Bring the phone and do not come with a weapon. You have thirty seconds."

Alexander stuffed the phone into his shirt pocket, picked up the canvas bag, and ran for the door. Then as he stepped out on the porch, he remembered the small pistol strapped to his ankle. *Crap! I can't chance it.* He dashed back inside, ripped the Velcro strap from around his ankle, and tossed the pistol on the sofa. Snatching up the walkie-talkie, he shouted into it, "Across the street...Wagner's house!"

But the storm rains were now pounding the houses and the howling of the wind becoming more intense each minute. Zapata only heard "...cross the street...wag..."

"What the hell did he say?" asked Doc Melton.

"Something about crossing the street in a wagon. Quick, look out the door and see if he's out there."

"Those pills must have made him goofy as hell," Doc said as he cracked the door slightly to look out. But the rain pelted his face and covered his glasses. He had to lean against the door to keep it from slamming shut. He thought he caught a glimpse of someone dashing across the street, but couldn't make out where he was going.

Alexander ran up to Wagner's front door and knocked hard on it as instructed. He didn't even notice that he was totally soaked head to foot. Before Alexander could knock a second time, the door jerked open and a massive hand grabbed the front of his shirt and with unbelievable strength, pulled him inside.

There in front of him, still holding onto Alexander's shirt with one hand and a very large pistol in the other, stood the monster in the blue jumpsuit. His face was completely covered with green and black camouflage paint. Alexander's heart felt like it was crawling up his esophagus. *I'm a dead* man, he thought. Le Guin's iceberg blue eyes drilled holes into Alexander's skull. *This is the same man but a different person than the Le Guin I saw at UTMB*, Alexander thought.

Le Guin spoke, almost politely, in his rather high-pitched, effeminate voice as he stuck his pistol in his belt, took the canvas bag from Alexander, and proceeded to pat him down.

Le Guin peered inside the bag and sat it down. "You took thirty-three seconds to get here, Dr. Alexander, but I'm willing to forgive the three seconds considering that I have your full cooperation for the rest of the day. Kindly sit on the couch and lift both legs up toward me."

Alexander did as he was told and Le Guin felt up both pant legs. *Thank the Lord I shed that pistol!*

"Dr. Le Guin," Alexander started, showing Le Guin the same professional courtesy.

"You will call me Virion!" Le Guin snapped, in a different voice—a low, raspy, demonic voice. "Do not make me repeat that. Now, stand up and look me in the eyes."

Alexander obeyed, looking up to meet Le Guin's eyes. Le

Guin drilled deeply into Alexander's sleepy, heavy-lidded eyes. Alexander wobbled a little as he tried to stand still for what seemed an interminable amount of time.

"Hand me the phone," Le Guin ordered, holding out his hand. He took the phone and checked the call log. It was clear. "Very good, Dr. Alexander. And I see that you're appropriately sedated. Sit down before you fall down."

Alexander fell back on the sofa and closed his eyes for a few seconds. He heard the tree limbs beating against the roof of the house, a sure sign that the storm was intensifying. "I would like to see my son," he slurred.

"And so you shall in a moment. First, I'm going to brief you on today's events so that we can prevent any errors or misunderstandings. In a few moments, we will fetch Jeffery. I've already removed the shunt from his arm and he's sleeping peacefully. You will place him in the wheelchair next to his bed, sit the canvas bag in his lap, and roll him out through the kitchen to the back door. You will go out and open the side door of my van and place the bag in the wooden box behind the driver's seat. I will carry Jeffery to the van. There's some carpet that he can lay on. Then you will strap yourself into the passenger's seat and we will drive to UTMB. There is another wheelchair in the van. When we arrive at our destination, you will help me put Jeffery in the chair and roll him through the doors of the building. That will be the first leg of our journey. Do you understand what I have told you so far?"

Alexander squinted at the large man and noticed sweat streaming down his face. He nodded and said yes.

"I hope so for Jeffery's sake. I cannot abide stupid mistakes or having to repeat myself. This is an important mission and it must be executed smoothly. Now get up and follow me."

Alexander followed Le Guin down a hall, through the kitchen. The house smelled old and musty, like brittle wallpaper from the 1950s, and the kitchen reeked of rancid grease. He noticed a trail of blood on the filthy linoleum floor in the kitchen and followed it with his eyes into the bathroom. He saw a bloody body laying face down in the tub and held his breath until he turned the corner and saw Jeffery sitting up in a bed with his eyes half closed, snoring softly.

63

Zapata and Doc Melton threw on their rain gear and dashed out into the storm looking like a couple of Worster fishermen. "Are you sure you saw him out here?" yelled Zapata against the howling wind.

"I said I thought I saw someone run across the street," Doc replied, wiping at the torrent of water on his glasses to no avail. "I couldn't tell if it was Richard."

"Let's look in R.A.'s house...maybe he left a clue," Zapata yelled, dashing up on Alexander's porch, bracing against a burst of wind and rain out of the east.

Once inside, Zapata looked for clues while Doc found the bottle of Glenlivet and poured a glass. The walkie-talkie was on the coffee table and the .32 pistol was on the sofa.

Damn! thought Zapata, *now he's defenseless! Trying to arm that artist is like...pissing against the wind out there.*

Zapata snatched up the small pistol and threw it to Doc, who looked as if someone had just dropped a tarantula in his hand. Then Zapata pulled out his 9 mm Glock and headed for the front door. "Come on, Doc, we have to check the houses across the street!"

He turned the door knob and as the wind blew the door wide open, someone covered with a poncho came running out of the storm straight at Zapata. Zapata almost fell backwards trying to decide whether to get out of the way or shoot the caped intruder.

Maggie Alexander screamed when she saw Zapata aiming his pistol at her. "Jesus Christ...has everyone gone frigging insane? Where the hell is Rich and Jeffery?"

Zapata and Doc explained what they knew to Maggie whose freaking-out meter pegged with every detail. They calmed her down with a cup of stale coffee that Alexander had brewed earlier.

"Why are you still on the Island, Maggie?" asked Zapata.

"Jeffery was supposed to follow me to his place yesterday evening, but he never showed...and now they've closed the causeway. I've been burning up their phones all last night and all day today! What the hell are we going to do?"

She started crying as her anger finally surrendered to fear and despair. The increasing ferocity of the storm roaring through the oak and pecan trees outside the house didn't help. She slipped out from under the poncho that hadn't been very effective keeping her clothes dry. She wore a pink polo style t-shirt and white Bermuda shorts. Her shirt had the slogan "ASK ME ABOUT YOUR NEXT HOUSE!" printed on the back in one inch white letters. Her tanned, shapely legs were trembling from the wetness and frustration. She walked into the bathroom, grabbed a towel out of the closet and began drying herself off. When she came back into the living room, she was no longer crying.

"Why would Rich go across the street?" she asked.

"I have no clue," answered Zapata. "He said something about across the street...a wagon...made no sense to us."

"A wagon," Maggie repeated and was silent for a second. "Oh hell...I'll bet he said Wagner! That's the guy who lives directly across the street. Why would he go over there? Maybe Wagner is falling-down drunk again and called him for help! Let's get over there!"

"Rich didn't have his phone, Maggie," Zapata tried to explain.

But Maggie slipped into her poncho and was already out on the porch. By the time Zapata and Doc put on their rain gear and caught up to her she was beating on Wagner's front door. Pecan leaves and crepe myrtle blossoms were blowing past them, creating a surreal mosaic in the driving rain as Zapata and Doc reached Wagner's porch. Maggie was still beating on the door in panic mode when Zapata reached down and tried the door handle. The door swung open just as a rotten limb off of one of the pecan trees crashed down on the steps behind them sending missiles of bark sailing along the century old brick street.

Once they were all inside the dingy living room, Zapata smelled the familiar stench of blood and death and pulled back the hammer on his Glock. His stomach knotted up, hoping to God that his nose wasn't registering the remains of Rich and Jeffery.

"Wait here Maggie. Let Doc and I look a..." Zapata started to say, when Maggie darted down the hall toward the kitchen calling out for Jeffery and Rich. They caught up with her just as she stopped and looked in the bathroom at the bloody corpse in the bathtub. A scream caught in Maggie's throat as she stood rigid with her mouth opening and closing like a catfish freshly nailed to a tree. The three of them stood there long enough for Zapata to realize the body was neither Jeffery nor Richard.

Then the lights went out. The transformer in front of the house had exploded like a huge sparkler. The scream freed itself from Maggie's throat, startling Zapata, whose pistol discharged into the oak floor behind him. They all three screamed and jumped into one another, then fell into a shocked silence.

At first the dank darkness consumed them—like they had just been swallowed into the belly of a whale. Time ceased to exist. Their ears rang and the smell of the gunshot filled their nostrils. It took a moment for their eyes to adjust. It was only around 1:30 in the afternoon and it was still fairly light outside.

"Holy Mother of God...that was me...my gun went off," explained Zapata with the vibrating voice of an aging opera singer.

"Ya think?" Doc retorted.

"Is everyone ok?"

"No, I'm not frigging ok," whimpered Maggie.

"Doc, you ok?"

"Don't worry about me," Doc answered hoarsely. "I just pissed scotch all over myself."

After a moment they collected their wits and moved as a tight group into the kitchen, which had more light coming in the windows than did the other rooms. There they found a flashlight and a very frightened cat that came running in from the back porch with a shrill cry, causing the trio to once again jump and holler in unison. A quick pass through the rest of the house convinced them that no one else was there but the late Karl Wayne Wagner.

64

The University of Texas Medical Branch—UTMB—sitting on the east end of Galveston Island, one block south of the Galveston ship channel, is the oldest medical school in the state, founded in 1891. At that time, it comprised one small hospital and one main building, a Romanesque Revival style building built of red pressed brick, red Texas granite and sandstone by the architect Nicholas C. Clayton. The building—affectionately known as "Old Red"—still stands today, despite being severely damaged by a number of hurricanes, the first of which was the infamous 1900 hurricane. In 1891, UTMB had thirteen faculty members, and twenty-seven students.

Today, UTMB has over seventy buildings, 2,500 students, and more than a 1,000 faculty and researchers. One of its newest buildings is the National Laboratory, a BSL 4 laboratory built in 2008 in part by a grant from the National Institute of Health to examine the most dangerous pathogens known and that could possibly be used by terrorists.

What the university administration didn't know—couldn't possibly have known—is that one of the Ph. D. researchers who worked in the lab was a serial killer and attempting to become a terrorist on a much grander scale.

Richard Alexander sat shivering on the floor in a lab on the top floor—the 8th floor—of the National Laboratory. His left arm was handcuffed to his son Jeffery's right arm and the chain of the cuffs was behind the metal leg of a stainless steel work table bolted into the concrete floor against the left wall. According to a round clock on the wall in front of him, it was 1:33. He and Jeffery were both wearing blue jean cut-offs. Alexander had on a typical Hawaiian shirt and Jeffery a Texas A&M t-shirt, all soaking wet. Jeffery was still mostly out of it, nodding off then waking to wipe the drool from his chin with his free arm. Alexander, not having taken the second Zanax, was not as out of it as he had pretended to be.

The sterile, ochre-colored room looked like a laboratory out of the science fiction movie *The Andromeda Strain*. The part of the lab he and Jeffery were in was a twenty-foot square. It was separated from the rest of the lab by a thick glass wall and a couple of glass-enclosed booths beyond that. There was a refrigerator and several glass shelves on the back wall that were lined with beakers, vials, Bunsen burners, and normal lab paraphernalia. Overall, Alexander estimated, the lab was about 20′ x 40′.

The door was several feet to his right front. He would have felt much more nervous being in such a lab, but for three things he noticed as Le Guin had him wheel Jeffery into the room; the sign above the door said BSL 2 and there was not a double-door entry or any air locks or any shower equipment like most labs would have that handled the really dangerous bugs; the room had an outside window. Doc Melton had briefed him on the requirements for a BSL 4 lab when they came to UTMB a few days ago to scope out Le Guin.

What did make Alexander nervous and sick to his stomach was the fact that when Le Guin—wearing a traditional white lab coat over his blue jumpsuit—gained entry into the building he pointed an electronic device that looked like a large cordless drill at the security camera, causing the lens to shatter in a burst of smoke and disabling it. Then he walked over to the bewildered guard who had stepped out from behind the security desk and with a silencer-mounted 9mm automatic, shot him in the chest and then the forehead. He then quickly picked up the body with one arm like it was a bag of leaves and dragged it behind the counter before the blood started pouring out of the wounds.

Le Guin was now in the other room and was wearing one of those white space-man-looking outfits that was tethered to a yellow oxygen line coiling down from the ceiling. His head was covered with what looked like an inverted round, clear plastic trash can. Alexander couldn't believe his eyes because the outfit looked exactly like the lab suits worn by Dr. No and his men in the first James Bond movie. He remembered thinking how cheesy and fake they looked at the time.

Le Guin was digging around inside some kind of freezer, pulling out various vials and placing them inside a plastic test tube rack. On top of the table to which Alexander and Jeffery were handcuffed was a brown leather case that Le Guin had taken out of a cabinet in the lab. After a few minutes, the glass door separating the two areas hissed open and Le Guin—sans the Dr. No suit—walked into the section where Alexander and Jeffery sat.

"Listen," Le Guin said smiling, cupping a hand behind one of his ears. "You can barely hear the storm outside even though we're on the top floor, right? That's because this building was built to withstand a category five hurricane…winds of over two-hundred miles per hour. Unfortunately, while that complicates my plan, the architects having over-done everything in this building will actually help me with my mission.

"Take this lab for example. It's a level two lab but it has negative air pressure and it's vented to the outside as if it were a level three or four. Entering one of the level four labs would have notified security when I brought you two into it and we couldn't have that. No one cares who comes and goes inside this level two lab unless specific work is going on. This is perfect for our mission."

"So…Virion…, what exactly is *our* mission?" Alexander asked, no longer bothering to feign the effects of the Xanax. "I don't recall you explaining that detail."

"My, it seems the perspicacious Dr. Alexander isn't quite as susceptible to the soporific effects of tranquilizers as is young Jeffery. Dare I assume you didn't follow my instructions? Oh, well, perhaps it's better that you are more clear-minded than my original plan would have had you be. What is our mission, you ask?"

Alexander nodded, noticing the streamlets of sweat beginning to roll down Le Guin's massive face and neck, even though according to the thermostat Alexander saw on the wall to the right of the door as they entered, the lab was kept at a constant sixty-nine degrees.

"Our mission, Dr. Alexander, is one of biblical proportions. Do you read the Bible, Dr. Alexander…are you a believer?"

"I'm a Christian, if that's what you're asking. And yes, I am familiar with the Bible."

"Ah, splendid! Then you shall indeed appreciate our mission. To be fair, it really isn't *our* mission…it's *my* mission since you and Jeffery had nothing to do with its conception and are merely serving as my herd of swine, so to say."

At the opposite end of the lab, a flat-screen TV was bolted onto the center of the wall and was tuned into the National Hurricane Center. The Doppler radar showed that the center of Hurricane Michael—now a relatively small category 2 storm—was only twenty-five miles to the south-east of Galveston Island, moving to the north-west at twelve miles per hour. Landfall would be around the San Luis pass on the west end of the island in approximately two hours. After the eye passed over the island, the 95-100 mile per hour winds of the eye wall would begin blowing out of the west-southwest, eventually wrapping around the Greater Houston Metroplex. Le Guin watched the screen for a few minutes, checked his watch, then said something about having plenty of time.

Le Guin pulled up a folding chair in front of Alexander and straddled it backwards, folding his arms on the back of the chair and staring intensely at Alexander, a slight, self-appreciating smile on his purplish lips. Then he pulled out a pack of cigarettes, jolted it upwards, and snatched one with the side of his mouth. As he lit the cigarette, he looked up at the smoke alarm as an afterthought.

"Smoking is strictly prohibited in this building," Le Guin said glibly as he reached for the cordless drill device and pointed it at the smoke alarm above the door. When he pressed the button, the device vibrated with a high-pitched hum and emanated a thin, red line terminating as a red dot on the smoke alarm. The alarm managed to release one shrill beep before the laser beam melted through the cover and destroyed its circuitry.

"My God," Alexander remarked. "How can that small a device be that powerful?"

"Impressive, isn't it? My son made all of the electronic devices I'm using today. Did you know I, too, have a son, Dr. Alexander? Bless his little bastard heart. He's what they call an instrumentation and electronics specialist. He's what I call a cowardly ingrate. He was evacuated from his offshore drilling rig because of the hurricane and was supposed to be here now to help me carry out my mission. Can you comprehend how important this hurricane is to me, Dr. Alexander? Anyway, he never showed. But he will still play a part in my mission...he just doesn't know it yet. He called me an evil man, but he's wrong...I'm not an evil man, Alexander, I'm Evil's man...there is a difference...I am but a virion."

Jeffery yawned widely and looked around with puzzled eyes before nodding off again. Alexander studied Le Guin's smug face a minute, trying to assess the situation. *In a major virology laboratory with potentially explosive devices...release his brethren... biblical proportions...his herd of swine...the importance of the hurricane...Evil's man...a virion?* He was afraid that he knew what Le Guin's mission was...and what his and Jeffery's role was to be.

65

Zapata, Doc Melton, and Maggie Alexander had run back through the storm to regroup in Alexander's house and were sitting around the kitchen table trying to decide their next move. A large palm tree collapsed onto a garage a couple of houses away and someone's unsecured garbage can was tumbling noisily down the street. Zapata called the sheriff's department to report finding the body of Karl Wayne Wagner but got put on automated hold. He tried 911 and got the same results. Both numbers were probably getting inundated with calls from panicky islanders who had chosen not to evacuate and were now, as streets were beginning to flood and Galveston Bay was rolling into their back yards, regretting their recalcitrance.

Doc Melton poured a shot of scotch and said, "Why don't we just call one of their cell phones and see if someone answers?"

Zapata looked at Doc as if he had just suggested they all go up on the roof and dance the Boogaloo naked.

But Maggie stood up and said excitedly, "That's it! Jeffery's cell phone!"

"You want us to call Jeffery's cell phone, Maggie?" Zapata asked, his frustration growing. "And what...he's going to answer and say 'Hi, mom, I'm with dad and this insane killer who calls himself Virion'?"

"No, smarty-ass," Maggie replied. "Jeffery's cell phone has

a GPS feature and he always keeps it on. I can track it with the GPS unit in my car. You said that Le Guin was using it to contact Rich. Maybe they still have it. Come on, let's try it. What do we have to lose?"

"Indeed, my dear," Doc interjected, raising the glass of scotch in a toast, "What do we have to lose?"

The trio suited up again and ran out to Maggie's car, which was parked in front of the house. Once inside, Maggie started the car and keyed Jeffery's phone number into her automobile's GPS system. The system struggled because of the storm clouds overhead as the wind rocked the car back and forth. Finally a dot began flashing.

"Yes!" yelled Maggie. "It's working! Can y'all tell where that dot is on the map?"

Zapata looked at the screen for a second before it went blank. "We may have to wait until the eye is over us to get better satellite reception. But I think that dot was not too far from where we are...to the east...maybe over in the UTMB area."

"My guess is the National Laboratory where that lunatic Le Guin works," added Doc.

"Well, let's get the hell over there," Maggie said with the urgency that only a mother can muster. She jammed the car in gear when Zapata spoke up.

"Wait! The streets are starting to flood pretty bad and this car isn't going to get very far. Let's take my Hummer. It has a GPS system, too. You can program it, right Maggie?"

"Damn straight! Let's hit it!" Maggie replied as she dived out of her car, looking for the Hummer. The wind caught her and she started running backwards to keep her balance, screaming to high heaven.

"In the garage next door!" Zapata shouted as he and Doc jumped out of the car and grabbed her arms.

Once they were all in the Hummer, Doc Melton leaned up

from the back seat with his head close to Zapata's right ear and said with no lack of sarcasm, "Smarty-ass!"

66

"You say you're familiar with the Bible, Dr. Alexander. What do think of when I say Genesis 7:22?" Le Guin's eyes were cobalt blue, devoid of human feeling, and boring deeply into Alexander's hazel eyes. What may have passed for a small degree of levity earlier had been replaced by sheer malevolence.

Alexander tried to hold back the involuntary shudder set off by Le Guin's inhuman gaze. "I believe that's telling of the great flood…Noah, etc."

"You are correct, sir. What it says exactly is, 'All in whose nostrils was the breath of life, all that was in the dry land, died.' Now, let's jump to other end of the Bible to Revelation 16:17. Are you familiar with that?"

"No," answered Alexander, wanting to avoid his gaze but not daring to show any weakness.

"Well sir, it's about the seventh bowl of wrath being poured out upon the earth. 'And the seventh angel poured out his bowl into the air, and there came a great voice out of the temple of heaven, from the throne, saying, It is done.' Do you see the connection between alpha and omega, Dr. Alexander?

"The air that we all breathe," Alexander replied, "and the storm that brought death to all living things. You intend to release deadly airborne pathogens into the storm tonight."

Le Guin rose from his chair, smiling again, and began clapping his hands loudly. "Splendid, Dr. Alexander! Splendid!

The seventh bowl of wrath would be airborne pathogens. You are indeed perspicacious. Bravo! Bravo!"

Jeffery looked up from his drug-induced slumber and mumbled, "Thank you, thank you very much."

"The world will know and fear the name Virion. It will become synonymous with the name *Legion*," Le Guin pronounced as he took a long draw off of his cigarette and flicked the ashes on the otherwise pristine floor. "What I am about to release upon the world today will make cholera look like a summer cold. It'll make the deadliest hemorrhagic fevers seem like mild nose bleeds. It will put AIDS in the shade. I am releasing my brother virions. Actually, they're my children...I made them...right here under their national security noses."

"Why do you feel the need to do this, why do you consider yourself but a virion, and why me and Jeffery?" Alexander asked, mentally shaking his head in disbelief, but physically trying to appear genuinely inquisitive.

"Don't be obtuse, Dr. Alexander. I just told you why I'm doing this. It's not by *my* design. It's been *prophesied*. Only my bowl of wrath is a twenty-first century upgrade of whatever the author of Revelation had in mind. I consider myself 'but a virion' because that's exactly what I am.

"Why you and Jeffery? Thanks to you, Jeffery is just a pawn...a sure way of getting your attention. I believe the in-phrase is 'collateral damage'. That brings us to you, Dr. Alexander. At first, I was simply concerned that you would use your unusual gift to discover Virion's identity. Since then it has occurred to me that you pose a threat to Evil in general. All of we virions have work to do, Dr. Alexander, and we can't have agents of Jesus running around with spiritual powers interfering with our work."

"Agents of Jesus...spiritual powers? My Muse is the result of a physical aberration caused by a bullet fragment in my brain. What are you talking about?"

Le Guin stood silently at the table pulling objects out of the brown suitcase, seemingly ignoring Alexander's question. He turned up the canvas bag and poured out the items that he had instructed Alexander to purchase...electrical tape, digital timers, utility bags. He kept looking over his shoulder at the flat-screen TV, checking the progress of the hurricane. He abruptly stopped and sat back down in the chair in front of Alexander, clearly aggravated, as if suddenly distracted by an unpleasant afterthought. He shook his finger in Alexander's face and spoke in that low, demonic voice like he did at Wagner's house.

"Physical aberration...you are being obtuse, Alexander. And don't you dare think for a second that I'm just another pathetic religious nut hiding behind the Bible to justify my worldly perversions! You would be...you are...you have no idea!" Then finally in his regular voice, "You really don't know what this is about, do you? Can you not appreciate *my* art, Dr. Alexander? Perhaps I've assumed too much about your 'mystical powers,'" Le Guin said, at the same time patronizing and slightly apologetic.

To buy time, Alexander wanted to keep the discussion going on a philosophical plane because Le Guin seemed to appreciate more intellectual and less emotional responses.

"I believe that I'm becoming cognizant of your means, but you are correct saying that I don't know what this about. Heidegger said that art is the becoming and happening of truth. What is your truth, Virion? What do you hope to accomplish?"

"Heidegger was a pompous Nazi-sympathizing ass and hope is the opiate of the powerless. Are you familiar with the fifth chapter of Mark, starting with verse eight? This will give you some insight into what I will — not hope to — accomplish."

"My name is Legion, for we are many," answered Alexander, already knowing what this was about. "But that is really about Jesus demonstrating that He is the protector of humankind from evil. It seems that you are equating your deadly pathogens with Legion's demons and that not only Jeffery and I but also the general population will be your herd of swine."

"Very astute, Dr. Alexander. Evil—with a capital E—is the key word here. The demons Mark wrote about were a metaphor for Evil. But answer me this, Dr. Alexander, why could Jesus not destroy Evil? Why did he instead send its demons into the herd of swine?"

Alexander thought back on what his pastor friend told him and on the conversation that he, Doc Melton, and Zapata had sitting outside of the coffee shop a few days ago. *I cannot believe that I have already thought about all of this...that Virion and I share the same thesis about the nature of evil! But then again, that's how the Muse often works.*

"I think we can find the answer to that in Isaiah... the 45th chapter, I believe."

"My word, Dr. Alexander! I am impressed! Good and evil already existed in the universe when God created the Earth and man. He tells us so in Isaiah 45, verses six and seven. He says '*I am the Lord and there is none else. I form the light and create the darkness: I make peace*'—that is to say, good — '*and create evil.*'

"That means he created both good and evil before he created man. Who do you think God was talking to when he said 'Let *us* make man in *our* image, after *our* likenesses? He was talking to Good and Evil—Jesus and Satan! All humans have good and evil in them. We're made in *their* images! God is omniscient! He already knew that humans would be weak and disobedient. God had to do that! Otherwise, to choose to do good over evil would not have been an act of will...would not have been a testimony of love and fear of God. There would be no sin, no original covenant, no new covenant with Jesus, no need to repent. God set Adam and Eve up for failure by allowing Satan to enter the garden. It was a set-up! A game just like he and Satan later played with Job! It was Satan who infected the first two humans and inflicted pain and suffering upon humankind. Evil was the first virus released upon the Earth!"

Alexander struggled against the chaffing of the handcuffs and the hard concrete floor. He shifted his rear around to relieve the dull pain. "Are you saying that evil people—say serial killers like yourself—are the way they are because they have a virus?" asked Alexander, knowing that wasn't what he meant.

"No, I'm not saying that," shouted Legion impatiently, looking back at the TV screen and continuing to work with the vials and other objects. "That's an oversimplification of pedestrian dimensions. I thought you were getting it. I'm talking about evil in general...evil all over the world...all over the universe. I'm talking about the fountain of maleficence ...all kinds of murderers, genocidal tyrants, suicidal bombers, rapists, war-mongering politicians, wife beaters, child molesters, abusers and cheaters of every ilk. Being a serial killer is simply one manifestation of evil.

Again, I'm talking about Evil with a capital E...the force that you good Christians refer to as Satan, Lucifer, Beelzebub... the Devil! Oh, the Devil is real alright...the fallen angel. But he's not the winged red monster with a dragon's tail that William Blake painted. He's much more ominous than that. Satan is the aggregate of all the evil in creation and Evil is a virus! That's what I'm trying to teach you here! Evil is a virus! Evil people are the virions! Evil people aren't evil because they *have* a virus...they *are* the virus! Virions...human particles of a virus!" Legion exclaimed, almost trembling with the excitement of epiphanic insight.

Alexander felt Jeffery stir and looked over at him to see

that his eyes and mouth were wide open with astonishment. The drug was beginning to wear off. He almost wished that Jeffery would stay asleep, knowing his proclivity for mouthing off when he became defensive or angry. To Alexander's relief, Jeffery shut his eyes again.

Le Guin held up one of his sealed glass vials that contained a thick, cloudy liquid. Alexander estimated that it was about six inches long and about ¾ of an inch in diameter. It had a two inch red stopper that had been pushed in at least a quarter of an inch below the lip of the vial. There would be no pulling out that stopper without the aid of a drill bit…*thank God!*

"These, too, are but virions…just microscopic versions of evil people. They'll each do what they're programmed to do to see that Evil is served."

Then as Le Guin started to replace the vial in its holder, it slipped out of his sweaty fingers, struck the side of the holder, and clattered down on the stainless steel table top, still intact. The test-tube shaped vial rapidly rolled away from Le Guin toward the edge of the table directly over Alexander and Jeffery. Le Guin tried to scream but it caught in his throat and only made a gurgling sound as he lunged for the vial.

Alexander couldn't see what had happened but he surmised it from the sounds and from the ashen look of terror on Le Guin's face. He looked up at the edge of the table, praying to God that the cloudy liquid wouldn't start raining down on him and Jeffery. Instead he saw the glass vial fall off the edge of the table directly to the left of Jeffery. He and Le Guin watched in helpless terror as the glass container filled with the deadly virus seemed to fall in slow motion.

Just as the vial was about to strike the concrete floor and surely shatter into pieces, Jeffery stretched out his left arm, opened his palm, and caught the vial. Both Alexander and Le Guin let out yelps of relieve and disbelief.

Jeffery didn't say a word — he just furrowed his brow and

looked incredulously at the glass container in his hand and then at his dad and Le Guin.

Le Guin quickly — but gingerly — plucked the container from Jeffery's hand and carefully replaced it into the holder. Then he walked over to a sink, splashed water on his huge face, toweled himself off, walked back to the work table, and continued assembling and talking as if nothing had happened.

"You must not assume that all viruses are microscopic bits of protein and nucleic acid," he said, looking down at his two captives. "Second, you must not assume that a virus is a physical entity alone. The root of the word *virus* means toxin or poison, referring to the deleterious effects of an infection, not solely the entity that caused the infection. In other words, a virus is a combination of virions and their patterns of infectious behavior *and* the toxic results."

"But not all viruses are harmful," Alexander blurted out, trying to make sense of Legion's diatribe and hoping to buy more time.

"Wrong," asserted Legion with the arrogance of certitude, stooping down within inches of Alexander's face. "All viruses are harmful to something…all viruses must find host organisms to stay alive and replicate, and in doing so, they alter or destroy the host…could be a bacteria…could be a human cell…could be a slutty teenage girl…could be a meddlesome artist freak and his son."

Alexander's mind was racing…his eyes recording every detail, searching for a plan of escape. Of course, he would first have to become Houdini and get out of the handcuffs, which were about to cut off the circulation in his left hand.

"So what would have happened if that test tube had hit the floor and shattered, releasing your…brethren?"

"Well, let's just say that the three of us would have had a very unpleasant week while our skin sloughed off and our lungs disintegrated."

67

It was now 2:00 and the ferocity of Michael was picking up as the center of the storm crept closer to the island. Shingles from a damaged roof blew across the street in front of the Hummer as Zapata, Doc Melton, and Maggie drove slowly up 14th street and turned right on Mechanic Street toward UTMB. Water was up to its hubcaps in some locations. Zapata's GPS unit had picked up Jeffery's cell phone for a second, then lost it again. He was positive the blip was smack in the middle of the UTMB campus. So was the National Laboratory, Doc Melton reminded them. The trio tried to spot Le Guin's van or Jeffery's car. The torrents of rain made the task almost impossible, not to mention that Le Guin could have parked inside one of several parking garages on the campus.

Lightning bolts were streaking across the sky like a fireworks display. Doc Melton, who had been through several hurricanes, would later recall thinking that he never noticed lightning like this in the other storms.

Then without warning, a large palm tree came crashing down, blocking the street a few yards in front of the Hummer and bringing down some power lines with it. Sparks exploded and the tree started burning in spite of the driving rain.

"Crap!" hollered Zapata and Maggie at the same time.

"Don't touch anything metal. If the water is up to the hubcaps, we could be getting some of that current. I'll have to back up to 14th street and try Market Street," Zapata said, thinking how nice it would be to be sipping on a margarita while strolling around the River Walk with his family in dry, sunny San Antonio.

"It's ok, the pole breakers up there just blew ...that line's dead now. Market street will work," Doc Melton offered. "The National Lab is right behind the Moody Medical Library. Even if we don't spot one of the vehicles, I'm betting that's where they are."

68

"Oh, I know…I know," Legion continued, checking some sort of blueprint and assembling the items on the table, "Hollywood and hack novelists preempt our imaginations with their banal, imitationalist explanation for what makes a criminal mind — such as a serial killer."

He stepped directly in front of Alexander, shrugged his shoulders and raised his bushy eyebrows as if waiting for Alexander — the unprepared student — to volunteer the answer.

Only Alexander was prepared, having studied serial killers for years.

"Your mother," he volunteered with a perceptible degree of impudence, enjoying the double entendre.

"Yes, very good!" shouted Legion, almost gleefully, ignoring the insolence. "It's the mother…always the mother! She went Joan Crawford on them and she fed them rats. She turned Black Widow and ate the old man. She fucked the mailman, milkman, the man in the moon, and the man in the grey flannel suit. She seduced young children with gingerbread and baked them in her oven. She was a whore, a witch, a first class bitch, and worst of all…she refused to breast feed her innocent little angels.

"Bullshit," Legion concluded quietly, again stooping only inches from Alexander's face, staring intently into his perplexed hazel eyes, as if the key to Alexander's psychic powers lay somewhere just behind his retinas. Beads of sweat were falling from Le Guin's face onto Alexander's now half dried shirt.

"My mother was a decent, loving, hard-working, Christian woman who loved her family and treated all of us with dignity and respect. And we loved her. Sorry, but we have to leave Mother out of this equation. My father was pretty much a worthless drunk and died when I was very young. He was never in the picture."

"So," Alexander replied calmly, trying not to show fear but trying not to be antagonistic, "you're saying that early childhood experiences play no role in the making of a serial killer...that it's not a psychological disorder?"

Legion seemed to appreciate the question. He backed up a couple of steps and caressed his chin as he mulled over his answer, as if in a scholarly debate with a panel of scientists.

"No, I'm not ruling out anything of the sort. But let's dissect the 'mother' theory, though granted, very briefly, for time is of the essence. Let's suppose that with some serial killers — most, if that's more reassuring — the quintessential evil mom is the cause — the raison d'être — of her offspring's unquenchable desire to kill other humans." He sat down in the chair in front of Alexander and looked down at him with a slight smile.

"Once again, the key word here is *Evil*, don't you see? Evil is what we are discussing here today. It would take an evil mom to abuse her child to the degree of destroying his soul and creating a serial killer. Therefore, the mom would have to be a virion. She, being a single, infectious particle of the virus — Virales Satanicus, let us call it for the lack of an actual classification — must invade a host to survive — her son, let us suppose, since most serial killers are males. She subsequently reproduces the evil inside the host, which then takes over the characteristics of the host, destroying what it was and turning it into something else...something perhaps even more evil than she. But my point is, my learned friend, that it makes no difference whether the virion was the evil mother, the asshole father, the coke-snorting uncle, or the sick child molester down the street. They are all part of the same entity…Virales Satanicus… Evilness."

"I see," Alexander responded. "That's a fascinating theory. But if it takes evil to create evil, doesn't that rule out the possibility that a criminal mind could be the result of genetic disorder or brain trauma or a tumor…something strictly physiological?"

"Do you believe that those things just happen for no reason?"

"Are you suggesting that someone is born with a rotten gene because of the inequities of his or her ancestors?"

"No, I am not suggesting any such thing," Le Guin responded testily, checking the weather radar on the TV, "although I suppose that's a possibility. What I am suggesting is that God is not the only one who acts in mysterious ways… so does his creation, Satan. And Satan needs no reason to strike. He might plant a virion in an embryo's DNA just to watch him grow up to be a monster."

"So, what was it that infected you…and at what age?"

Alexander immediately regretted asking the question. Le Guin turned and glared at him with eyes molded out of magma from hell, his voice like an echo from the cellar of hell.

"Virion has revealed the truth of Evil to you, Dr. Alexander. He does not intend to reveal himself. This conversation is over."

69

Le Guin busily assembled his apparatus in a cloud of icy silence that fell on Alexander like a suffocating fog. Jeffery began to stir and looked at his dad with heavy eyelids.

"What the hell is going on? Who is this asshole? Why are we handcuffed here? Where the hell is here?"

His dad shushed him and wished he would go back to sleep.

Alexander thought it was important to keep Le Guin engaged in some kind of conversation…especially because ever since he had entered Wagner's house, he had been recording everything said on a small digital recorder that he had clipped behind his belt buckle. He figured that the battery ought to last for three or four hours.

"Virion, why did you kill Derrick Antoine and Doug Millsome? How were they a threat to you?"

Le Guin kept working, ignoring Alexander's question. After a few seconds, Virion answered. "I needed no reason to kill that degenerate artist and his little faggot friend…but obviously, I wanted the police to think Antoine was Virion for a while longer. Also, he knew too much about Le Guin, Rose, and the bastard son. His little he-bitch was just in the wrong bed at the wrong time.

"And of course, Rose…she knew that I had that painting of Antoine's. Then out of the blue, she started threatening to tell UTMB that I forced her to give her son up for adoption unless I gave her a ludicrously large sum of money. But I only killed her in effigy you might say, since she sent her look-alike cousin — her late look-alike cousin — to Antoine's house the other night."

"And Clint Westwood…was he the victim of one of your concoctions — the super staphylococcus?"

Le Guin glared at him again and angrily replied, "That phony whoremonger deserved every agonizing second that he suffered. He could have — would have — spread his AIDS demons to…well, let's just say that I stopped that little epidemic-to-be."

Alexander was desperate to keep Le Guin talking in hopes that someone would detect their presence there. He hoped that his little recorder was picking up all of the conversation. "I have to say I do admire your artistic talent, forging Antoine's paintings that your two victims' bodies were wrapped in. But your first victim wasn't wrapped up in a painting…why not?"

"My first victim?" Le Guin sneered. "You have no idea how many victims have fallen prey to Virion. Do you have any idea how many young women — and men — have disappeared along the I-45 corridor between Houston and Galveston in the last two decades?"

"I've read about quite a few disappearances and bodies found in that area. But you've never left clues. I've never seen the name Virion before. Why now?"

"Why now? Because of you…that's why now. I have had this event — the freeing of my fellow virions — planned for some time and then you come along with those freak abilities of yours and threaten to expose me. I knew that if I could throw suspicion onto Antoine for a little while, that would give me time to finish my preparations. But that didn't fool you, did it, Dr. Alexander?"

"I wouldn't even have known about you had you not left those women's bodies where they could be easily spotted — wrapped in artwork! Maybe my friend, Dr. Zapata, was right…

maybe you wanted to get caught and end all of the killing. But it doesn't have to end this way!"

"You're boring me now, Dr. Alexander. Enough questions."

At that moment, the Weather Channel announced an update on Hurricane Michael. The storm—just a few miles offshore at 28.7N, 95W—had changed its course slightly toward the west, and would be coming ashore just west of the Port Arthur-Lake Jackson area. That still put Galveston on the dirty side of the storm with winds coming from the south-southeast, now gusting over 80 miles per hour.

Le Guin turned and watched the report, then resumed his assembling for a few more minutes. Finally, he looked down at his two captives and spoke. "This storm is cooperating better than I had anticipated, Dr. Alexander. Now I don't have to wait for the center of Michael to pass over the island...the wind is going to blow my brethren directly over the Houston area and deep into the heart of Texas...then the infected ones shall spread them all over the country. Even the sober and vigilant won't escape—for as Peter warned, my master walks about like a roaring lion, seeking whom he may devour.

"Now, if you both will kindly indulge me in complete silence," he continued, giving Jeffery a stern look, "I will explain what is going to happen in a few minutes. Do I have your complete attention?"

Alexander nodded. Jeffery started to object but quickly shut up when his dad gave the handcuffs a hard yank.

"Ouch...shit!" Jeffery uttered quietly through clinched teeth.

Le Guin held up one of the utility belts. "As you can see, each utility belt now holds a six volt battery, a timer, and four vials of fluid. I won't bore you with the details of which vial carries what virus, but rest assured each is enough to start a deadly epidemic. You'll see here," he continued, lifting up one of the vials, "that each vial is encircled with a very thin ring of plastic explosive and that embedded in each ring of explosive is a small blasting cap, which in turn is wired to the timer. When the timer goes off, the caps will explode, shattering each vial. The explosions will not in themselves do you any damage, except perhaps cause some glass cuts. I recommend that you don't look down at them until they've exploded. However, that will be the least of your worries."

Le Guin then picked up a one-foot long thin rope of plastic explosive that was about the diameter of a pencil and pressed it against the window so that it looked like a grey wreath of silly putty. He inserted a blasting cap into the wreath and connected the wires to a timer and battery that he had set on the window sill. He set the timer and started it.

"A few seconds before the vials explode this window will be blown out, activating the emergency air exhaust system. The negative air pressure in the lab will assure that all the air in the lab is sucked up through the super HEPA filter system at the base of the air duct there." He pointed to the air duct in the center of the ceiling. Under ordinary circumstances those treated filters will capture and destroy any bacteria or virus in the air. However, thanks to my absentee son, this laser devise will burn a hole straight through the filters."

At that, he slipped a pair of safety glasses over his massive head, pointed the laser gun up at the air duct and pulled the trigger. First, the thin, metal grate fell to the floor as if it had been cut out by a welding torch—in effect, it had been. Then there followed five minutes of sizzling and popping as smoke poured out of the duct. *His real reason for destroying the smoke alarm.* Finally a large section of charred filter fell to the floor, smoking. Le Guin kept this up until several more similar sections fell to the floor. Then he smiled with satisfaction, put the laser gun on the workbench and walked over to a heavy, stainless steel rolling rack stand that was about thirty inches tall, four feet wide, and twenty-four inches deep.

Le Guin rolled the stand over Alexander's and Jeffery's legs until it rested over their thighs, pinning their legs to the floor with very little wiggle room. He grabbed two more pairs of handcuffs and secured Alexander's and Jeffery's free hands to the rolling rack. Then he picked up the duct tape, and his pistol. With surprising agility for a huge man, Le Guin sat on the floor and scooted under the work bench behind his captives. Jeffery only stopped his protesting when Le Guin pressed the silencer barrel against his temple. Ripping off sections of the tape, Le Guin bound their heads to separate table legs, wrapping the tape over their mouths, so that couldn't bend over or to the side or call out. Then he strapped a utility belt on both of them from behind and set each timer for twenty minutes, scooted out from under the workbench, and stood up.

"There now…You be good little pigs. I was exaggerating earlier about your skin and lungs deteriorating in a week. That will take around three weeks. You won't feel any effects for at least two days, at which time you will be afloat in the sea of a puzzled medical world and will have infected numerous well intended care-givers before they find out what demons have jumped into this little herd of swine."

70

When Zapata, Doc Melton, and Maggie reached the intersection of Market and 10th street, they caught a break in the rain for brief moment. It was long enough for Doc to spot the rear of a white van parked on the side of the National Lab building.

"Stop E.Z.! Back up a little. See the van? I told you they'd be there."

"Let's hope you're right, Doc. How do we get over there?"

"Pull up on the sidewalk and drive around the library... just stay on the sidewalk until we get close to the van."

The black Hummer rolled slowly up the sidewalk next to the Moody Medical Library just as another rain band hit with hard gusts of wind.

"Did you see that window up there on the top floor?" Doc asked. "That's the only light that's on up there. They must be in that lab."

"How are we going to get into the place, Doc?" Zapata asked, zipping up his rain coat.

"A friend of mine told me the guest code...it's UT449 this month. There ought to be a guard on duty, though. If that code doesn't work and we can get his attention, maybe he'll let us in. I still have an old ID card on me."

"Doc," Zapata replied, "If there's a guard on duty, how could Le Guin get R.A. and Jeffery into the lab?"

"Le Guin could have just told him he wanted to show his

friends some of the lower risk labs."

"During a hurricane? When everyone is supposed to be evacuated?"

"Hell, I don't know. What do you want from a Ph.D.? Let's just go see."

"Ok, Maggie you stay in the car and keep trying to get through to 911 and tell them what's going on and where we are. Doc and I will try to get in the building and find Rich and Jeffery. If Le Guin comes out call me...and don't let him see you."

"I want to go in, too!" Maggie protested.

"Maggie, we need you out here to watch the entry and to try to reach the cops. Please do that for us...or the whole thing could go to hell in a flash."

"Ok...but if you guys aren't back out and I don't hear from you in twenty minutes, I'm coming in."

"No, Maggie!" Zapata argued, "Do not go in there. We need you on the outside!"

"Ok, ok," Maggie agreed, resignedly.

Doc and Zapata ran around to the entrance and Doc punched in the visitors code...the doors hissed open. Zapata held his pistol at ready and went in first. The corridor was vacant and relatively dark. Only the emergency lights were on. No guard at the desk. They ran over to one of the elevators and Doc inserted his old card...nothing. The card reader would not accept it and therefore, would not signal the elevator doors to open.

"Damn!" Zapata said quietly. "I wonder if we can use the stairs."

"Nope," answered Doc, "there's an ID card reader on that door, too."

"Maybe the guards left a card behind the counter over there," Zapata said as he hurried over to the reception area. "Jesus Christ, Doc...the guard is back here...dead. God, this is bad…very bad!"

"Well, I don't mean to sound calloused," Doc replied as he walked behind the counter, "but the guard has an ID card there on his shirt. That'll get us in the elevator."

Zapata reached down and unclipped the guard's ID badge. It was half covered with blood, so Zapata wiped it off on a towel that was laying on the counter. The two ran back to the elevator and inserted the card. The pistol in Doc's hand was shaking so badly that Zapata was tempted to take it away from him, but decided that they may need two guns, even if one was just bluff. As the elevator doors slid open Zapata told Doc to stand to the side and crouched down on one knee, pistol pointed at the elevator. It was empty.

They got into the elevator and punched number seven. The second they did Zapata wished they had taken the stairs. He felt like a very large target in a very small shooting gallery. Then when the elevator passed the second floor he heard the ding! Now he really felt like an idiot. It dinged six more times before it stopped on the seventh floor with a final ding. Zapata told Doc to stay in the right front corner away from the opening and assumed the crouched firing position. As the doors slid open Zapata cocked his pistol and prepared to fire. All he saw was an empty hallway.

71

Did I just hear the elevator? Yes! There it is again...on this floor! Le Guin cocked his pistol and turned off the lights in the room. He crouched down to the left of the door and listened for footsteps. There was a little ambient light coming in from the window in the lab and the one at the end of the hallway to the left of the lab door.

Alexander also heard the dinging of the elevator...*E.Z. I can feel his presence!* He followed Le Guin with his eyes. For the first time that day, he felt a glimmer of hope. But he knew that if anyone walked in the lab, Le Guin would kill him. Then in the dim reflection of the clock on the opposite wall, Alexander saw the reflection of someone in the hallway slowly approaching the door.

It is Zapata!

Just as Le Guin raised his pistol to fire, Alexander pushed the rolling stand as hard as he could and the cuffs made a loud clatter against the railing of the stand. It startled Le Guin and he jumped to his feet, pointing his pistol at Alexander.

Zapata fired the first shot at Le Guin's back, but the glass in the lab door was reinforced and the bullet was deflected. Le Guin whirled and returned fire with the muffled *fap-fap-fap* of the silenced 9mm. This time the glass disintegrated as Zapata dove out of the way to the left of the door.

Doc Melton, standing back on the far side of the elevator, could see the clock in the lab through the shattered door. He fired several shots at the clock just to make noise and to keep Le Guin pinned down. He missed it altogether, but it kept Le Guin inside the lab until Zapata could get back on his feet.

"Le Guin!" Zapata shouted, pressing his back against the wall. "The building is surrounded and more police are coming. Throw your gun out and give it up."

"I doubt that very much," Le Guin said under his breath as he crouched against the wall a few feet from Alexander. Le Guin quickly discarded the silencer and fired several shots at the glass wall in Zapata's direction to keep Zapata in place. Glass shards flew out into the hallway with a deafening racket. Then, he stuck his pistol out of the busted door in Doc's direction and fired a couple of more rounds. Satisfied that his adversaries would hold their places for a moment, he scooted under the workbench behind Jeffery, unfastened the utility belt, and pulled it from around Jeffery.

"Change of plans," he announced as he scooted out from under the bench, holding the utility belt-virus-bomb. He reached in and stopped the timer. "Your bag of goodies should be enough for both of you," he said to Alexander, whose ears were ringing and mind reeling. "But just in case Murphy 's Law kicks in, I'm going to relocate these brethren to another launch pad. "From the sound of things, you have only two heroes in the hallway attempting to rescue you and who will very shortly be dead. And Dr. Alexander...be assured that if you do not serve as my swine this afternoon—in about eight minutes to be precise—I will be visiting you. Perhaps I'll take you for a boat ride...tied to my transom."

At that, Le Guin stepped out into the hall with his gun pointed in Zapata's direction and began firing. Zapata, not expecting that, was caught off guard. He tried to jump out of the way, but his bum leg was throbbing and weak after hitting the floor and he couldn't move fast enough. Two of the bullets struck him and he flew backwards in the hallway, landing on his back. He lay motionless as a pool of blood began to seep out from under him.

Le Guin took a couple of steps toward Zapata and took aim at his forehead. But then he turned as Doc Melton screamed, "Die you son of a bitch!" and emptied the little .32 pistol in the direction of the blue jump suit, hitting nothing but walls and ceiling. Doc threw the pistol on the floor and ran to the dark end of the hallway where the stairwell door was. Le Guin fired three rapid shots at him in the shadows and Doc yelled out in pain as he pushed through the stairwell door that he had earlier propped open with one of his shoes—just in case. Le Guin ran over to the door as it slammed shut, locking automatically. He looked down and saw drops of blood.

I hit him...he's out of the picture. Le Guin quickly stepped over to the elevator and punched the down button.

72

Doc Melton crouched down in the stairwell, out of view of the little square window in the door. He was horrified that Zapata was dead...or worse, bleeding to death when he could be out there helping him. *But two dead men aren't going to save the day.* He ignored his own pain, knowing that it was just a flesh-wound. He couldn't believe Zapata was gone and he felt a terrible rush of guilt. *If only I could have hit that bastard with one bullet...at least that would have been revenge for Zapata's death.*

After hearing the elevator open and close, Doc waited in the stairwell for another minute then carefully peeked through the window in the door. He couldn't see anyone so he slowly opened the door with the dead guard's ID card. He quickly walked toward Zapata, looking back over his shoulder every other second. He stopped briefly to look inside the lab where Alexander and Jeffery were making a racket trying to get someone's attention. They saw Doc and settled down, their eyes wide with anticipation. Then Doc heard loud moaning at the end of the hall and ran down to see Zapata rolling around on the floor in a puddle of blood, holding his chest.

"Got-dammed that hurt!" Zapata groaned as Doc helped him sit up. Then he crossed himself with his left hand because he couldn't move his right arm. "Thank you Lord for Kevlar vests!

"That maniac hit me right in the middle of my sternum...I

would have been dead meat without this," he continued, pulling his shirt apart and pointing at his bullet-proof vest.

Doc had forgotten all about the Kevlar vests that Zapata insisted they wear. "Fat lot of good the damned vest did me!" Doc replied, holding his rear end. "He shot me in the ass! Just a graze, but it hurts like sin!"

"He got me through the right shoulder. That's what's bleeding all over the place. Here, tear a strip out of my shirt and tie it tightly over this wound."

"I'll do you better than that," Doc replied and ran into the lab holding onto to his rear. Doc tried pull the cart off of Alexander and Jeffery—both of whom were going nuts because they were still handcuffed to the cart. Doc reached down and yanked the duct tape from around Alexander's head, almost pulling his off his lips.

"Shit!" hollered Alexander. "Bring me back my mouth when you're through with it! What's going on out there? Is E.Z. alright?"

"E.Z. will live if I can get out there and stop the bleeding. Hey! Is that a fucking bomb strapped to you!"

"Yes! It's a fucking bomb! Get Zapata in here to disarm this thing. We have about two minutes then we all get a dose of deadly virus!"

"Crap!" We'll be right back!"

Doc applied the duct tape to Zapata's wound and pulled it tight around his shoulder to cover the exit wound. Then he helped him to his feet and they both limped into the lab. Zapata sat down next to Alexander, holding his chest and trying to catch his breath. He studied the crude bomb for a few seconds. Then he fished a ring of keys out of a pocket that had a handcuff key on it and started to unlock the cuffs on Alexander while Doc untapped Jeffery.

"E.Z., this thing is going to explode in about one minute," Alexander said quietly but sternly. "Disarm this thing first, then worry about freeing us. Whatever you guys do, do not break one of these vials! They are loaded with Satan himself!"

"Not to worry, buddy. This is simple. Only I can't move my arm. Doc, pull out the blasting caps from the rings of explosive then push that power button on the timer."

The word *timer* had no sooner come out of Zapata's mouth when the wreath bomb on the window exploded, sending shards of glass all over the lab. A violent rush of air blew in the window and the emergency air evacuation system came on. So did an amazingly loud alarm. Zapata and Doc fell on their sides. Everyone's ears were ringing.

"Doc!" Alexander hollered, "We have less than thirty seconds!"

Jeffery sat perfectly still, not daring to breathe, his eyes wide open. Doc sat up and shook his head to clear his thinking. He felt around on the floor for his glasses. Bits of broken glass were embedded in his beard, which was twinkling like a Christmas ornament. He fit his old trifocals over his ears, then casually reached over into the utility pouch and punched the power button on the timer. It stopped with seven seconds to spare.

73

Maggie sat in the Hummer, biting her nails, trying to see through the rain that was slamming relentlessly against the windows and windshield. The heavy vehicle was rocking back and forth as the gusts of wind from Michael whipped around the buildings. She thought about the movie, *Jurassic Park*, when the people were trapped in the stalled tour cars in the midst of a hurricane and the Tyrannosaurus Rex started tearing down the containment fence. *I'd much rather face a T-Rex than this!*

Even though she began feeling terribly apprehensive, Maggie sat as patiently as Maggie could be patient...until she heard the gunshots—more like firecrackers in the distance through the roaring of the storm, but they were definitely gun shots...a lot of gun shots.

She flung open her purse and snatched out a little .32 automatic pistol. Her real estate firm had insisted that all of the female agents carry a pistol and get a concealed weapons license. Maggie opened the car door and pushed it with her shoulder. The wind grabbed it and blew it away from her, almost ripping it off of its hinges. She tumbled out of the Hummer and fell face down in six inches of water. The little pistol went flying. It took Maggie several minutes sloshing through the water on her hands and knees to find the weapon. When she did, she sprinted to the door of the National Lab building and punched in the visitors code that she remembered

Doc saying...UT449. The doors slid open and Maggie ran in sideways, holding the gun straight out across her body, her left hand propping up her right hand—just like her training taught her and just like she had seen in a hundred cop movies.

A few seconds after she was inside she heard three rapid shots—very distinct now. But immediately afterwards, an ominous silence filled the building—so thick that it muted the roar of the storm outside.

Luckily, Maggie didn't see the dead guard behind the counter; otherwise, the silence would have been shattered like thin glass by her screams. The sight of blood made her sick...a bloody dead body would have done her in. She hurried over to the elevators and noticed that both cars were on the seventh floor. Just as she reached out to punch the button, one of the cars started down.

Thank God! she thought. *At least the elevators are working!* 6...5...4...3...2...1...Maggie nervously watched the elevator car descend. She was shaking with fear and anxiety. *God, let Jeffery and Rich be ok!*

When the elevator doors finally parted, Maggie gasped and jumped out of her skin. There in the elevator stood a huge man in a blue jumpsuit with his face painted green and black. He had a canvas bag over one shoulder and held a utility belt in front of him with both hands. It had a battery and test tubes and wires stuffed in it. He had a pistol handle sticking out of a front pocket. Le Guin stared at the muddy, soaked-to-the-bone woman with surprise and amusement.

Maggie backed up a couple of steps, pointed her pistol at Le Guin and yelled, "Freeze, sucker!" *Freeze sucker? God! What am I doing?* Mud and water dripped from the barrel of her pistol.

Le Guin raised his free hand over his head and slowly stepped out of the elevator and calmly sat the utility belt on the floor. He straightened up and smiled at Maggie. "Well, well...

Mrs. Alexander. We meet again," he said with some consternation in his voice.

Maggie stared at him with a confused expression on her face. His somewhat effeminate voice was familiar, but it didn't register with her that this giant joker with green and black sweat dripping off of his chin and her bogus client, Dr. Mark Legion, were one in the same.

"I wouldn't fire that pistol if I were you, my dear. The barrel is clogged with mud and the little thing could explode in your hand," Le Guin offered with a smile, pointing at the gun.

Maggie ever so slightly bent her head to one side trying to see the end of the barrel. That was her mistake. As rapid as a rattle snake striking, Le Guin reached out and yanked the gun out of her hand. Before she could react, he jabbed her in her solar plexus with his fist and Maggie collapsed in slow motion, much like a high rise building being imploded, and passed out.

"Come, my dear. We haven't any time to tally here," Le Guin said. He reached down and gingerly picked up the utility belt bomb with one hand, lifted Maggie up by her waist as if she were a rolled up throw-rug and exited the building with her tucked under his arm.

A little more insurance can't hurt.

74

Doc took Zapata's keys, uncuffed Alexander and Jeffery, and rolled the cart off of their legs. Rain was furiously blowing in the window opening and the siren was screaming like a fire truck on steroids. Jeffery staggered to his feet and stretched his arms and legs

Alexander remained sitting in a daze for a few seconds. For that few seconds, his mind flashed back to Viet Nam. He was sitting in a make-shift bunker of sandbags on the perimeter of their base in Phu Loi, about forty miles north of Saigon. The monsoon rain was pouring down on him, drops as big as .45 rounds. Although it was eighty-five degrees, he was shivering from the drenching and from raw fear. The incoming siren was wailing somewhere behind him in the camp. He could hear the cries of wounded soldiers, but it sounded like they were at the far end of an empty auditorium. The blast of the 122 mm rocket that just landed in front of him was still ringing in his ears...it would ring in his ears for the rest of his life.

"Dad! Dad, are you ok?" Jeffery asked.

Alexander looked at his son for a second, and then his mind segued back to the current scenario of sirens and soaking rain. "I'm fine, Jeff. Are you ok?"

"You mean other than having been kidnapped, drugged senseless, waking up in Jekyll and Hyde's lab with a headache that could power the space shuttle, about to have the Andromeda Strain blown up my nose, drenched, covered with glass, both wrists worn to the bones, and having to piss like a stowaway in a brewery? Yeah...I'm fine."

"R.A.," Zapata said urgently, still sitting on the floor, "Maggie is down in the Hummer trying to contact the police. We need to get our asses out of here in case that freaking maniac set other bombs."

"E.Z., we have to try to stop that freaking maniac. He's going to let loose those viruses."

"What are we going to do about it, amigo? We don't know where he went. Anyway, if I don't get this bleeding stopped, there won't be nada about viruses on my tombstone."

"Oh God...you're right. Well, we're at UTMB...there's three or four hospitals here and a huge emergency room. They have to have kept something open. Doc, I know you're wounded, too, but if we get E.Z. in that wheelchair over there, do you think you can push him over to the emergency room?"

"Yes, I think so. I don't seem to be bleeding anymore. We can use the interconnecting hallways to get over there."

"What you mean...wheelchair...I don't need a fuuu...," Zapata's eyes rolled back in his head and he fainted, falling over on his side.

Alexander and Jeffery picked up Zapata and put him in the wheelchair that Le Guin had used to haul Jeffery from Wagner's house. As the four of them started to leave the lab for the elevator, Jeffery patted himself down and looked around the room.

"Well, apparently Mr. Hyde stole my cell phone...not just a murdering bastard...he's a thieving bastard as well!"

The elevator door opened on the first floor and Doc wheeled the semi-conscious Zapata out first. As the chair exited the elevator, it hit something in the floor, stopping abruptly and almost catapulting Zapata out on his face.

"Goddammit!" Doc yelled. Someone left a fucking pistol on the floor...must have been the Mad Scientist."

"Let me see that!" Jeffery barked. "Holy Christ! That's mom's pistol...see, her initials are in the handle!"

"And that's the cap she was wearing," Doc said, pointing to Maggie's wet 'gimmie' cap on the floor.

"I thought you said Maggie was waiting in the Hummer!" Alexander shouted to Doc.

"E.Z. told her to stay put and try to reach the cops. She promised she would."

"Right!" they all three said together.

"Maggie!"

"Mom!"

Alexander and Jeffery hollered down the hallway. Jeffery ducked inside the public restrooms...no Maggie.

"Jesus, you don't suppose...?" Jeffery asked, pacing back and forth in front of the elevators.

"What else can we suppose?" Alexander answered. "Unless...let's go see if she's in the Hummer, son. She may have come in, got frightened, and ran back to the car."

They weren't gone forty-five seconds before Doc Melton opened the front door for them to come back in. They looked like drowned wharf rats.

"Maggie's not in the Hummer. Le Guin's van is gone. I don't know how far he can get with the streets flooding as bad as they are," Alexander said. "We can't just stand here...Doc, you wheel E.Z. to the emergency room and Jeffery and I will take the Hummer up and down the streets and do a systematic search. If we can't reach the cops, that's all I know to do."

"Wait a minute, Dad! That thieving bastard Le Guin has my cell phone!"

"Christ, Jeffery! You can get another frigging phone. We have to find your mother!"

"That's my point, Dad...my phone is..."

"Traceable!" shouted Doc. "Zapata's GPS! That's how we tracked you guys here! It's still on the screen!"

"Let's move!" Alexander barked.

As Alexander and Jeffery started for the front door, Doc threw Zapata's cell phone and Hummer keys to Alexander and yelled over his shoulder at them.

"Call us and let us know what's going on...if this damn phone works in a hurricane."

A limping Doc Melton started pushing Zapata toward the interconnecting entrance of the National Lab. UTMB had a labyrinth of hallways that connected most of the buildings on campus. It took weeks of wandering around lost — or extrasensory perception — to learn the routes, but they provided very handy inside access to most hospitals, clinics, the cafeteria, offices, etc. This was most appreciated in inclement weather as well as the quickest way around...and Zapata had little time to lose.

75

Once outside the National Laboratory building, Le Guin caught a glimpse of Zapata's black Hummer parked around the corner. *The perfect vehicle to drive in a hurricane.*

With Maggie under his arm, he hurried through the driving rain over to the Hummer, only to discover that there were no keys in the ignition. Cursing, he turned and sloshed through ankle-deep water to the front to where his van was parked. He deposited Maggie in the passenger seat and slammed the door. The slamming of the door began to bring her around.

"You're a member of a unique group, my dear," Le Guin uttered sarcastically as he shook the water off of his hands. "Many misguided young women have taken their final ride in my chariot...and you won't be the last," he added with a sinister sneer.

He started the Ford van, jammed it into drive and roared off down the wide sidewalk and down a series of concrete steps toward the pavilion in front of Old Red so he could gain access to Strand Street. He turned left, drove up on the opposite sidewalk in front of the Student Center to avoid the vehicle barriers, and swerved onto the Strand. The water in the street was now well over the van's hubcaps. The street flooding wasn't from Michael's storm surge, which would prove to be not that extreme; the east end of Galveston — especially the downtown Strand area — flooded during almost any unusually hard rain...and Michael was dumping rain onto the Island at about six inches per hour.

Le Guin turned right on 13th street and then left on Harborside Drive, next to the ship channel. The water was even deeper there and it began to pour in the bottom of the doors as he kept pushing the van forward. Finally, just as they passed 14th street, the van jumped forward a couple of times, choked, and died.

Le Guin sat there cursing and grinding the starter to get the van going. He looked over at Maggie, who was now fully cognizant of her situation. Then his gaze zoomed past her out at the ship channel as the rain and wind let up for a brief moment.

"Perfect! If this is not a divine sign, I don't know what is!" he said, staring out at an offshore drilling rig that had been moored on the dock of the ship channel for repairs. The rig was lit up like a Christmas tree in spite of the battering it was taking from Michael.

Maggie looked out of the passenger window to see what Le Guin was talking about.

"You better let me out of here this instant," she demanded, turning back toward Le Guin, only to be staring down the barrel of his 9 mm automatic.

"Well, my dear Mrs. Alexander, I'd love to have taken you on a boat ride, but I fear circumstances have dictated otherwise…so this will have to suffice."

Maggie gaped at the pistol in muted disbelief as Le Guin pointed it at her forehead and pulled the trigger.

76

With the eastern edge of Hurricane Michael's eye barely brushing Galveston Island, the rain and wind had abated just enough to allow a glimpse of blue sky to appear above the Island. It would be a brief respite. Alexander and Jeffery were ecstatic to see the small red blip that signaled the whereabouts of Jeffery's cell phone blinking on the GPS unit. Fortunately, Alexander had followed his intuition and had started driving west on Market street toward the downtown area. They reached 13th street when the red blip pinpointed Jeffery's phone one block west on Harborside Drive. It didn't appear to be moving. Alexander took a right at 14th street and proceeded as fast as he dared in the high water toward Harborside Drive. The Hummer was having no trouble navigating through the water, as it sat up high on large tires, but the last thing Alexander wanted was to stall out before he got to Maggie.

Jeffery hollered out as the red blip began moving very slowly toward the north. "How can that be? There's no road there. They'll go into the ship channel!"

"No, look...the van isn't moving at all. It's stalled out," Alexander replied as the Hummer pulled up to the intersection.

The van was sitting in water up to the bottom of its doors in the middle of the next block, to their west. The blue sky was beginning to be blotted out with clouds moving rapidly from the southwest and the rain and wind started picking up again as Alexander slowly maneuvered the Hummer behind the van.

He flicked the headlights on bright, pulled Maggie's little .32 automatic out of his pocket, and cocked it as he focused intently on the interior of the van for movement.

"Careful, son...I can't tell where Le Guin is. I'm getting out to see if your mother is in the van."

"Dad, look...the blip is still moving to the north...over there," Jeffery said, pointing toward the rig. "That means that Le Guin still has my cell phone on him and is walking or running toward the ship channel...maybe near that offshore rig."

Alexander, using the reconnaissance technique he learned in the Army, searched the area of the rig methodically with his eyes. Then, through the rain and blowing debris, he saw what appeared to be some sparks over by the rig. Finally he spotted Le Guin's huge frame kicking open a gate to the repair yard about seventy yards to the north. *He must have that damned laser gun with him.*

Alexander and Jeffery jumped out of the Hummer into water up to their knees and rapidly sloshed over to the driver's side of the van. They saw Maggie slumped over in the passenger seat, leaning against the door.

"Mom!" Jeffery cried out.

Alexander held his breath as he swung open the driver's door. Then his heart sank as he saw the bloody wound on Maggie's forehead and the blood running down her face, soaking her T-shirt. He crawled into the driver's seat and reached over and put his hand on her shoulder.

Holy Mother of God...Maggie's dead and it's my fault! I killed her by using my freaking powers! Jeffery will never forgive me.

"Dad, is she alright?" Jeffery asked quietly, trying to remain calm as he pushed himself into the van behind the driver's seat. He stared at his mother, unable to say anything. Tears started filling his eyes.

Richard Alexander couldn't answer his son because his throat was paralyzed with grief. Then, quietly at first, but rapidly getting louder, he started saying "Yes! Yes! Yes!" He smiled for the first time that day. "I see a pulse on her neck... she's breathing...she's alive!"

At that, Maggie groaned and slowly sat up in the seat. She reached up to the wound on her head and stared in bewilderment at the blood on her hand. Alexander touched her shoulder again and she recoiled in fear, throwing her hands up to protect her face. It took a few seconds for her to realize that it was Rich and Jeffery in the van with her. They were both about to pass out from the tension and relief.

"Oooh...that big asshole," she finally managed to moan. "He was going to shoot me...but his gun was empty. So he got mad and smacked me on the head with it." She started crying with big snuffing sobs. Then she bent over and threw up between her legs.

Alexander stifled a smile of relief, knowing that Maggie was in pain and very upset. She could have easily been killed by Le Guin.

"Jeffery, let's get your mom into the Hummer and take her to the emergency room. She needs immediate medical attention. More than likely, she has a concussion."

Alexander jumped out of the van, waded to the passenger side, opened the door and grabbed Maggie under her arms. Jeffery exited by the side sliding door and supported his mom from the other side. Together they carried her to the Hummer, her feet dragging through the water, and helped her into the passenger seat.

"Ok, son, drive her straight down Harborside Drive to the emergency room at UTMB. And see if you can get through to the police." He handed Doc Melton's phone to Jeffery and closed the door beside Maggie.

"Wait, Dad...where are you going?" Jeffery hollered out of

the driver's window.

"I've got to try to stop Le Guin before he releases those viruses. You have to take care of your mom. Now go! Get her out of harm's way!"

77

Dr. Lee Le Guin—the man who knew himself as Virion—was immersed in a state of revelation as he began climbing the moored rig with the virus-laden utility-belt strapped to his waist, oblivious to the assault of the storm. He now more than ever understood his destiny. Once he was at the top of the rig, he would hold in his hand the Seventh Bowl of Wrath and release the wrath of God into the air.

"For I am the Seventh Angel...an Angel of Death! Death cannot touch me...my viral brethren will not harm me. And it will be the great voice of Satan out of the temple of Hell that will say 'It is done! Well done good son...good soldier...good virion. Good little bug! What? I...I'm not a mere bug. Oh but you are...you are spider crawling up to kill its prey...a praying mantis poised to pinch off the head of humanity. No, I'm a good soldier...my name is Legion...I am Virion! You're right, you're not a bug...you're less than a bug...you're a germ...a submicroscopic spec! Fuck you...I'm the one doing this...who else will do it...who better knows the appetites of my brethren...the needs of my children...I am a human reservoir of death...I am destined to be...I am Virion! You are destined to be thrown in the lake of fire, germ!"

Le Guin continued to climb up the steep ladder that led to the upper platform of the rig, mumbling to himself and stopping occasionally to wipe the rain and camouflage makeup out of his eyes. He was excited again about his mission and couldn't help but smile as the hurricane force winds pressed his body against the metal structure.

"God sent me this hurricane to spread my brethren far and wide because he knows this has to be done! It has been prophesied!"

Richard Alexander waded off of the road and found that the water was not nearly so high on the parking lot of the rig repair service. He looked over his shoulder to make sure that Jeffery got the Hummer turned around and moving toward UTMB, then attempted to sprint over to the first gate that cordoned off the property. The wind pushed him forward and to his right like he was a scrap of paper. Twice the gusts blew him down. When he finally reached the gate, he saw that the lock had been cut off with the incredibly powerful laser device that Le Guin's son had made for him. He stood a minute with the wind and rain beating at his back, trying to see if he could locate Le Guin before he ventured into the yard. Suddenly he heard a clattering racket to his left rear and turned just in time to see a sheet of tin that had been torn off of some roof sailing through the air right toward him. Instinctively, he dove to the ground inside the fence a fraction of a second before the tin missile smashed into the gate, crumpling up a bit, flipping over the gate post and then wrapping itself around a utility pole. It would have sliced off his head had he not moved when he did.

That was the good of it...the bad and the ugly of it was that when he fell to the soggy ground, the cocked .32 he was holding discharged and hit a small butane tank next to a tool shed. The tank exploded with a roar and sent flames thirty feet into the air, setting the shed and then the repair service office building on fire.

Well, Alexander, that was a dumb-butt move...so much for the element of surprise.

Startled by the blast and sudden burst of heat, Le Guin almost lost his grip on the metal ladder. The yard below him was a blazing inferno and the sky above him lit up with streaks of lightning. The bizarre scene could have come right out of an old Frankenstein movie. Then he spotted Alexander running toward the second gate.

My psychic pig...did the demons enter you? No matter... you can't stop Virion — but Virion will stop you shortly.

As he approached the second gate, Alexander had to hold up his hands to protect his face against the searing heat of the burning buildings. On the ground, he saw Le Guin's laser gun. Something told him to look up at the rig and when he did he saw Le Guin almost to the top looking down at him and smiling.

Alexander pointed the pistol at Le Guin. Then he had second thoughts. *Shit! I might hit the vials...but what are the odds of that? If I hit Le Guin, he might fall and the vials will probably burst on the deck down here. Shit! Oh well, what do I have to lose? That's a better scenario than letting him release the viruses up there where the wind will carry them to Hell and back...and right over Houston.*

Alexander braced himself against the aluminum gate post, took aim, and fired. The first round hit the frame of the rig to the right of Le Guin's head. There was a lot of metal bracing between him and Le Guin, especially looking up through the structure. To his frustration, the next two rounds seemed to hit nothing. If Le Guin was aware of Alexander shooting at him, he showed no concern.

Finally reaching the top, Le Guin crawled onto the high platform. Struggling against the relentless wind, he wedged himself into a corner of the railing and removed the utility belt from around his waist. He set the timer for thirty seconds and turned it on. Then he stood, holding the utility belt high above his head as if he were an Olympic champion celebrating the gold medal for the oil rig climbing competition.

Le Guin looked down at Alexander far below on the cat

walk and shouted, "Behold Dr. Alexander, you are about to witness history…a little homo sapien downsizing, if you will, as my little demons find their herd of swine. Then Legion will be saved again!"

Alexander couldn't make out what Le Guin was shouting over the storm. He braced himself again and fired two more shots. The second one scored, hitting Le Guin in the abdominal area. Le Guin dropped one arm and grabbed his stomach. He looked at the blood on his hand for a second, then stretched both arms out again, holding the bomb above his head. It might as well have been a mosquito bite. Alexander remembered his drill sergeant warning them not to carry a .32 into battle because if you shoot someone with it, it will only piss him off.

Feeling like he was running out of time, Alexander sprinted across the catwalk and onto the deck of the rig. He figured that if he climbed up toward Le Guin, he might get a better shot. He stuffed the little pistol in his belt, grabbed hold of the ladder, and started climbing up as fast as he could. When he looked up, he was blinded by constant flashes of lightning.

He took two more rungs up when suddenly a bright, glowing figure appeared in front of him. Alexander stopped climbing, shocked, mouth agape. It was a nude male figure with long, flowing, golden hair and large white wings spread from the back of his rib cage. He was holding a sword up high in his right hand as if poised to strike. His left hand was stretched out in front of him toward Alexander, palm out, as if to warn him. Alexander was mesmerized by the apparition's eyes because they looked like multi-colored kaleidoscopic patterns. Before Alexander could gain an ounce of composure, the figure rushed forward through the ladder and knocked him free of the rungs.

The fall to the deck of the rig was only about ten feet, but it seemed to take…well, time actually ceased functioning. He felt as if he was weightless in space—an astronaut floating backwards in the void. As he fell back, Alexander looked up and the glowing, sword yielding figure was gone. But he could clearly see Le Guin above him, standing on the platform, holding up the utility belt and laughing maniacally.

Then, in slow motion, a blue bolt of lightning emerged out of the stormy sky, striking the utility bag that Le Guin was holding above his head. The bag, the bomb, and the vials of virus exploded into flame and ash. The force of the bolt knocked Le Guin off of the drilling rig as if he had been hit by a Shinkansen train.

The next to the last thing Alexander saw before he passed out was the blue jumpsuit bursting into flames as Virion flew out over the ship channel and plummeted like a meteorite into the angry water. It wasn't the lake of fire...but it might as well have been.

The last thing Alexander saw lying recumbent on the deck of the rig was a ball of white light parting the clouds in the stormy skies above him. He closed his eyes and whispered, "Michael."

78

When Richard Alexander opened his eyes again, he still saw the white light; only this time it was shining first in one eye and then the other. The rough, cold drilling rig deck had somehow turned into a bed. It wasn't raining on him anymore. The wind wasn't roaring in his ears. Nothing was on fire. There was a pillow under his head and someone was sitting beside him.

He pushed the pen light away from his face and saw the blurry image of a blue jumpsuit. "Jesus!" he yelled and tried to sit up. Then someone whacked him on the back of his head with a nine-pound hammer.

"No, Mr. Alexander, no one hit you on the head with a 'fucking' hammer or anything else just then," the young doctor wearing blue scrubs answered him, matter-of-factly. "You fell off of something—they mentioned a drilling rig—and landed on your back, resulting in a mild concussion and various abrasions and contusions on your arms and legs...nothing serious. You also suffered burns on both hands and the soles of both feet, but thankfully they're not serious either...mild second degree burns. The EMS technicians couldn't find your left shoe and your right one had no sole...it was burned out. From all the signs, you were hit by lightning or were very close to a strike. You're a lucky man, Mr. Alexander."

"Every time I get the crap beat out of me, somebody tells me how lucky I am," Alexander quipped, studying his bandaged hands. *Odd, my hands and feet don't hurt...just my frigging head.* "Do you know how my wife is—Maggie Alexander? She came into the ER earlier today."

"Mr. Alexander, you were brought in yesterday. This is Sunday afternoon. I wasn't on duty yesterday, but I will certainly find out for you. Your son and a friend have been in a couple of times. By the way, to keep you informed, we ran a C.A.T. scan on you to assess the damage and there is no hemorrhaging. Everything was clear."

"Except for those bullet fragments, huh?"

"Bullet fragments? You know, that is odd. We saw a reference to that in your medical records, but we detected nothing of the kind. If anything metal at all was in your brain, it would have definitely showed up. There is a minimal amount of scar tissue associated with that wound to your forehead, but absolutely no fragments. I'm certain of that. To paraphrase Yogi Berra, we X-rayed your head and there's nothing in there," the doctor added with a broad smile.

"Anyway, you'll have a headache for a couple of days, but other than the minor burns and bruises you're in good shape. I'm going to recommend that you stay overnight for observation and cut you loose in the morning. I'll be in to see you later."

"Dizzy Dean," Alexander said glumly.

"Beg your pardon."

"Dizzy Dean said the thing about the head X-ray...not Yogi."

"Oh...well, I guess their similarities are different," the doc replied straight-faced as he walked out of the room.

As the doctor exited the room, Jeffery and Doc Melton walked in.

"I thought you had to have a college degree and go to medical school to be a doctor," Alexander said. "That guy looks like he's still in high school. What's the world coming to?"

"The world ain't coming to nothing any different," Doc

Melton replied, "it's just that you and I are getting older faster than these youngster are. How you feeling today, Thor?"

"Thor?"

"Yeah...Thor. Seems like you threw a lightning bolt at Le Guin and deep-fried him. In fact, that whole repair yard went up in flames. You're one lucky dude that they got you out of there when they did."

"So everyone keeps telling me that. Jeffery, how's Maggie?"

"She's better. She's home now. But she's still like being around a Velociraptor," Jeffery answered, looking down at the floor.

"Well, son, who can blame her after all she and you went through? I guess I'd better get over there and see how she is."

"I wouldn't do that, dad. She really...well...she...doesn't want to see you...at least not now."

Doc Melton looked embarrassed for Alexander and Alexander just stared out the window, nodding his head. Jeffery was still staring at the floor. The silence should have doubled the barometric pressure in the room.

"So, how's E.Z.?" Alexander asked, looking at Doc.

"They had to do surgery on his shoulder. He almost lost the use of his right arm. Another quarter of an inch toward the ball and socket joint and he would be shopping for a stainless steel shoulder. I think he's going to recover just fine. Right now he's floating around on Demerol and enjoying all of the attention from the cute, young nurses."

"I guess I'm also in trouble for starting that fire at the rig repair yard."

"What are you talking about? The lightning started all that," answered Doc.

"No, I distinctly remember the pistol going off and..."

"Richard, you don't need to distinctly remember a frigging thing. The authorities and the shipyard people are all satisfied that the lightning started the fire. There are even a couple of witnesses. They were going to charge you with criminal trespass, but when they found out that you were pursuing that deranged serial killer and trying to prevent him from letting deadly viruses out into the air, they dropped all charges."

Doc Melton went on to tell Alexander that two security guards over in the adjacent shipyard were watching the storm out of a third floor window. They were talking about the frequent lightning strikes when one of them happened to spot Le Guin climbing up the drilling rig. They both testified that lightning was striking all around the rig when suddenly they saw a fire-ball shoot up and the buildings catch on fire.

"Then a second bolt hit the rig and that's when they saw a flaming Le Guin do a full-gainer into the ship channel. They notified the fire department and police on two-way radios and ran over to the rig. They didn't even know you were there until the paramedics got there and saw you lying on the deck."

"So, didn't they hear the gun shots?"

"Evidently not. They probably only heard the storm and the thunder."

"Well, the police have probably confiscated the pistol and they'll discover that Le Guin has at least one bullet hole in him."

"They never saw a pistol...the paramedics or the police... or they would have reported it. My guess is that it sleeps with the fishes along with your left shoe and Le Guin's body."

"Le Guin's body? They didn't find it?"

"Nope. He's a crab buffet by now...and good riddance."

"Good riddance we hope. That's disturbing that they can't find him. I know I could really use some closure to this, not to mention the families of those people he murdered. Well, at least I have my little recorder that I will gladly turn over to the cops. Le Guin exposed a lot of things about himself and his dirty deeds on that recorder."

"That's one of the things mom is so upset about," Jeffery

volunteered. "She doesn't believe he's dead and she's afraid that he will keep coming after us...and if not him, then the next maniac."

"Well, I saw him get hit by lightning, burst into flame, and fall into the ship channel. I rather doubt that anyone could survive all that."

"Are you sure you saw that, Richard?" Doc asked. "It knocked you unconscious, you know. It seems implausible that you could have witnessed that whole scene."

"I saw it all...and much more."

Alexander proceeded to tell Doc and Jeffery about the glowing, sword-yielding apparition that caused him to fall off of the ladder and the timeless fall backwards during which he saw the slow-motion lightning bolt hit Le Guin and Le Guin's fiery descent into the water. He described how the utility bag-bomb with the vials of viruses disintegrated into ash and smoke.

"If it hadn't been so profoundly real, it would have been ludicrous—like a scene out of *The Big Lebowski*. Had I still been holding on to the rungs of that steel ladder when the lightning hit, I would be a pile of burnt bacon. That vision saved my life!"

"I know it seemed real, Richard," Doc Melton replied, "and I know you've had visions, but being a scientist, I would have to say it was an hallucination induced by the shock of the lightning. Obviously, the bulk of the current was directed down into the water through the steel structure instead of through the ladder...therefore, the mild burns and no electrocution. The apparition was in your imagination; it couldn't have knocked you off of the ladder. "

"Well, that's certainly the logical answer, Doc, and I have no plans of sharing my vision with anyone in this place...I don't want to be taken up to the loony ward. But I know it was real. And as crazy as it sounds, I know who it was."

79

Three weeks later, the cleanup after Hurricane Michael was mostly completed. The category-two hurricane had done minimal damage overall to Galveston Island. Some BOIs — Born on the Island — said it was a miracle. They had seen a lot worse from smaller storms. A number of homes and buildings had lost shingles, and a few, partial roofs. The Mexican restaurant in which Alexander had his vision of the storm damage lost part of its roof...right over the table where they were eating. A few trees blew down over power lines, leaving part of the Island without power for almost a week. Flooding had not been a serious problem except on the west end of the Island, where a tropical depression down in Mexico's Bay of Campeche or even a strong south wind could raise the waters of Galveston Bay over the bulkheads, flooding some of the streets and roads. There, some of the homes got water in the garages and bottom floors.

But now, everything was just about back to normal. The egrets and herons once again waded through the marsh grasses for frogs and minnows. Out on the beaches, spoonbills and sandpipers foraged along the waterline for spider crabs while seagulls circled overhead looking for anything that might quell their voracious appetites. Out over the bay and Gulf waters pelicans floated on the summer breeze, searching for shrimp boats and schools of mullet. The surf was green and sprinkled with surfers. All was copacetic again.

On Monday morning, September 29th, Alexander met Zapata and Doc Melton at the Postoffice Street Coffee House, beneath his studio. They really hadn't had a good chance to debrief, as Doc had put it. The three hadn't been together outside of the hospital until then because Zapata had developed an infection in his shoulder and had only recently been released.

The doctors had decided to keep Alexander in the hospital for two weeks longer after he passed out while trying to go to the bathroom and they discovered a high fever and flu-like symptoms. Everyone, including Alexander, was scared to death that one of Le Guin's viruses might have infected him. Whatever it was went away in a few days, but they insisted on keeping him on lockdown for observation—under guard even.

The trio sat at a table outside under the shade of an umbrella. Doc snipped the end off of three cigars and passed them around. Puffy cumulous clouds rolled overhead out of the Gulf causing purple shadows to trip across the storm stripped limbs of the crepe myrtle trees. It was hot and humid, but a mild breeze blew and the smells of breakfast from a nearby café wafted across their table and mixed with the rich aroma of coffee. A trolley clanked by and stopped at the corner to let tourists off and on. The horn of a cruise ship moored in the ship channel blew long and low, causing the windows of the coffee shop to vibrate ever so slightly in sync.

Alexander started the 'debriefing' by going over all of the details from the time Le Guin met him in Wagner's house to when Doc and Zapata entered the scene at the National Lab. He told them that Le Guin had admitted to killing Westwood, Antoine, Millsome, the two women found wrapped up in paintings, and evidently many more…and that he had it all on his digital recorded, which he had turned over to the sheriff. Then he resumed from the time he and Jeffery got in the Hummer to chase down Maggie and Le Guin to when he woke up in the hospital.

They all swapped their versions of what happened during the shootout in the National Lab and Doc complained that getting shot in the ass never drew much serious attention... mainly snickering and snide remarks.

"I was the butt of everybody's jokes," he quipped with a wry smile.

Zapata added intrigue to the bizarre story by telling them he had just seen a report from the Lafayette police about a Wesley Le Guin missing and presumed dead from an offshore drilling rig that collapsed off of the Louisiana coast during Hurricane Michael...next of kin, one Dr. Lee Le Guin, father, Galveston, Texas.

He also showed them a newspaper article about a part-time Galveston resident killed by Hurricane Michael when his condo in Providenciales collapsed...a businessman and suspected mobster named Franklin Buscanni. The Galveston Sheriff's Department had evidence that Buscanni had frequently contacted the late Detective Gene Vincent. The man known as Toothpick, who was in the jail cell with Alexander, copped a plea and told everything he knew about his dead partner Tyrone and Detective Vincent. He even said that Vincent told Tyrone that Buscanni would be very generous if they would finish the job on Alexander that the assassin botched.

Suddenly, everything came together for Alexander. He leaned back and clapped his hands once, laughed out loud and said, "Yes! Of course!"

A grackle scavenging for scraps in the gutter was spooked by the outburst and flew up into the nearest tree. Zapata and Doc looked at Alexander like he had just morphed into an orangutan.

"Ok guys, now this is going to be a fixed-concept suppository, so pay attention," Alexander said excitedly, rubbing his hands together. "Remember, Doc, I told you that I knew who the apparition was?"

"Yeah, but you wouldn't tell me who."

"Well, I'm telling you now. It was the Archangel Michael... God's hit man, if you will. There were numerous paintings of Michael from the Proto-Renaissance through the Baroque periods in Europe. Two of my favorites are by Luca Giordano and Guido Reni. Both depict Michael defeating Satan. I haven't thought about them for years, so why would I imagine an apparition that looked like those images? The iconology of an image is a powerful influence on an artist when painting a historical figure—but where did the image of Michael come from? It could have come from the Bible...or maybe certain artists were also visited by the same vision...I don't know.

"But I know what I saw and whether I physically saw him or I imagined him makes no difference...the vision came to me and saved my life because I fell off of that ladder a split second before that bolt hit. I saw the bolt hit! That ladder was attached to the platform that Le Guin was standing on. Contrary to your theory, Doc, I would have gotten fried had I stayed on that rung another millisecond...yea, I got a shock and some minor burns because that's how close it was."

Doc nodded slowly and Zapata's furrowed brow meant that either he was following Alexander's logic or he thought it was total bullshit.

Alexander continued. "You see, what puts me in the same group as the artists who painted the images of St. Michael is spirituality. In my opinion, there are three things that create a spiritual connection to God...or Satan...or the Pillsbury Dough-Boy...whoever you worship. The first two are faith and prayer; the third thing is assignment. When God picks you for an assignment like he did Noah, Moses, or Paul—and countless others—it really doesn't matter how well you practice the first two spiritual connections. You don't have a choice.

"The artists who painted those images of Michael were deeply religious. Faith and prayer were the staples of their lives and they knew that art is the happening and becoming of truth long before any philosopher came up with it. I'm not that strong a Christian, but I have been given an assignment—a special talent—and ergo, the spiritual connection. The same vision of Michael came to me that come to those artists…only for a different reason.

"And speaking of my so-called gift, it apparently has nothing to do with fragments of a bullet in my grey matter. The doctors did several scans of my head and assured me that there are no metal shards in my brain…so much for my physiological theory of brain cell excitation by a foreign object. It's not physical."

Alexander lit his cigar and took a long pull on it to give Doc and Zapata a little time to digest what he had told them. Then he leaned forward again and continued.

"Now, what was the name of the hurricane that just blew though?"

Zapata squirmed in his chair a second then spoke up. "I'll bite…it was Michael, of course."

"Exactly! I know you two skeptics. You think that was just a coincidence, but it wasn't. The truth dawned on me in the hospital but it didn't gel for me until five minutes ago. Michael came in the form of a hurricane first and an apparition second to protect me and to end the evil deeds of Le Guin—Virion. Look at the pattern. First, he took out Buscanni who had been trying to take me out. Then he killed Le Guin's only offspring— the son of Virion—to kill that lineage. Then he threw Le Guin himself into hell. He destroyed a pattern of evilness and protected the appointed servant so that I could continue to use my gift.

"I finally accepted, laying in that hospital bed, that we're all here for a purpose—a purpose that's much larger than we

300

are, larger than our careers and our everyday lives. Sometimes our purpose involves the supernatural. Yea, I know, that sounds corny as hell. But I also know that is what God has been trying to show me."

"I guess I didn't realize you were that religious, Richard," Doc replied.

"This doesn't have anything to do with religion, not in the orthodox sense. As my preacher friend, Pastor Kevin, over at The Fellowship in Texas City is fond of saying, it's not about religion...it's about relationship. He knows what he's talking about. He's the best preacher I've ever heard and he's taught me a lot."

Doc looked first at Zapata, then Alexander, and said, "A fixed-concept suppository? Tell me that didn't come from your spiritual connection...or Pastor Kevin."

They all had a good laugh. Zapata and Doc assured Alexander that they understood his reasoning, even if they didn't necessarily agree with all of it. Then Zapata looked at his watch.

"Holy cow...I've got to get to work, boys. It's Monday morning you know. Hey, I thought you were going to teach on Mondays this semester, R.A."

"Not anymore. They had to find a replacement for me because of the extra time in the hospital. Anyway, I think I'll hang it up now...toss in the towel...take the big bow and nice fat severance check."

"Retire?" Zapata and Doc asked at the same time.

"Yeah, I've been thinking about it for a while. Anyway, I'm tired of the teaching routine and they're tired of me. I can't continue to meet the demands of academia, do my artwork, and run around identifying bad guys...and I can't seem to stop doing the latter. So, I might as well concentrate on my artwork, which is selling pretty well, and renew my private detective license."

Zapata almost choked on his coffee and pushed his chair back dramatically. "My goodness, Dr. Alexander, that's a considerable change of heart. A few days ago all of this was more of a curse than a blessing. Chasing bad guys isn't going to get you and Maggie back together, you know. What does Jeffery think about it?"

"Maggie is so upset that both her and Jeffery's lives were almost ended because of my involvement with Le Guin that she still won't talk to me...except to tell me that she's going ahead with the divorce. God put this burden on us and He's going to have to help us straighten it out. It'll take time...lots of time. As far as Jeffery goes, he'll accept it...he won't like it, but he understands his old man. Well, even if he doesn't understand me completely, he accepts me for who I am."

"When do you start your retirement?" Zapata asked.

"Technically, I guess I already have. I've been on sick leave and I have about three weeks of vacation built up and they already have someone in my place. Actually, I sent in my letter last Thursday and my chairperson called me immediately. So it's settled."

"So, what do you plan on doing first, Richard?" Doc asked.

"I've got my eye on nice fifth wheel and an F-250 that one of my colleagues at the university wants to sell. I've always wanted to do some landscape painting down in the Louisiana swamp land. Maybe I'll roll down to Henderson or New Iberia and rent a little houseboat on the Atchafalaya Swamp...let things cool off here in Galveston for a while. I'm not going to give up my house or studio here...and I want to keep playing in the band ever so often."

"So, when did you make this decision, Richard?" Doc asked, firing up his cigar.

"I reckon I made it between the time I fell off of that drilling rig ladder and however long it took to land on the deck. When I saw Le Guin and his viruses go up in flames, I realized that if it hadn't been for my 'gift', Virion would have unleashed pure hell into the world. Evil—with a capital E— would have won a huge victory. People would have been sick and died from that shit for years. It could have traveled all around the world."

Alexander blew another plume of blue smoke out toward the street. "I know y'all think I'm nuts, but as I was laying on that rig in the storm, I asked the Archangel Michael what I was supposed to do with the psychic powers I have…he just looked at me with those kaleidoscope eyes, pointed his sword straight at my heart, and said, 'The answer, my friend, is blowing in the wind. The answer is blowing in the wind.'"

414 - 2016 -